The fireworms were gathering for the attack. This could mean only one thing. One or more "cursed" people were among those in the camp below.

Act now or hang up the hero medal, I thought. I wormed my way over the ridge, upsetting the nestled fireworm. He stopped purring. In the starlight, I saw that my move may have precipitated the attack. Dark blotches detached themselves from the surrounding rocks, sand, and scrub. Debating whether or not to shout a warning to those below so that Shadow would have a chance, I thought furiously as I wove my way between rocks and down draws.

The last thing I wanted to do was to alienate the fireworms. . . .

DAYSTAR AND SHADOW

JAMES B. JOHNSON

DAW BOOKS, INC.
DONALD A. WOLLHEIM, PUBLISHER
1633 Broadway, New York, N.Y. 10019

COVER ART BY KEN W. KELLY

DEDICATION

For Beverly, of course

FIRST PRINTING, MARCH 1981

1 2 3 4 5 6 7 8 9

CHAPTER ONE

I was remembering more every day. That is, I recalled small bits, when somebody wasn't trying to kill me and run me all over the deserts of southwest America. And, hell, I'd lost the girl to them, too. But one of these days, I'd remember the lost years. It had taken me years of concentrated effort to drag my given name from the quagmire of lost memory.

I had been called "artistic," why I don't know yet, "a traitor" by the New Christians, as I seemed to be the only human being alive that was immune to the fireworms, and "a savior" by the various desert dwellers when I found them water. The latter is where the name "Daystar" came from, apparently some reference from the Church or Born Again Era. I didn't usually go by the name Daystar, although many times I have been recognized in some areas and then everything changes. Ordinarily, I wander into a town, a desert rat, whom no one thinks well of, find the local Storyteller, and take up my Storyteller apprenticeship once again. A few days after my arrival, I generally find too many children and old people dying of thirst, sign a contract with the local authority, and revert to my special technical field: dowsing.

Once there were legions of dowsers, but as water became more scarce the divining guild declined, and now few remain in this arid portion of the country. Another reason for the lack of dowsers is the high mortality rate; fireworms account for half the desert rats' deaths. I am, fortunately, the only diviner who can still consistently find water, if it's there. Perhaps this follows from my long association with the fireworms. At times, I have a strange dream of sleeping with a Mother fireworm.

Normal fireworms range from three feet to twelve feet in length, and in diameter the thickness of an arm to a stout leg.

Take an average man, rip out his upper and lower intestines, put black bristles on them, flip them into the desert, and you've got a picture of what fireworms look like. The bristles are instantaneous killers. Nobody knows what kind of poison they produce, but it's obviously nonterrestrial. They apparently thrive in the desert sands and rocks. And they attack man; some types of man are pursued relentlessly, even into towns and city strongholds. These poor souls are called "cursed." Hordes of the slimy things crawl, wiggle, and glide. By now, most communities know they can't be stopped; so, after determining the quarry, they merely pitch out the unfortunate individual and he takes his chances. Other men, fireworms just seem to chase off their territory if they can't corner and kill them swiftly. None of the so-called biologists understands yet. They don't even know where the fireworms come from, how they procreate, how they live and function.

I have discussed this with many of the "experts" and they have no answers. Long ago I stopped trying to tell them what I knew. I was outcast whenever I strove to brief them on the Mother fireworms that I'd seen. Perhaps some of my earlier tales led to the myths and rumors of one hundred-foot-long Mothers, sunburnt red, great gaping jaws, slender feelers for seeing or sensing. These tales are whispered, but no one claims to have seen such, except me, that is. A dune had risen in my path, and kept lifting. A one hundred-foot monster rolled over, sand- and caliche-covered. Her belly split, and dozens of the flesh-colored fireworms emerged, snaking tentatively into the coarse sand, and away. They crawled from her in all directions, none ever returning. As usual, they ignored my presence. One of the little critters even crawled between my legs. The Mother, after eating the afterbirth, rose her front section some thirty feet high, looming over me, focused her feelers, seemed to shrug, and disappeared back under the dune. I continued my journey, not understanding any of it. I didn't discuss this with anybody at the time. Besides the fact that there was no one around, I was in my non-talking phase. And one of these days, I'd figure out my noncommunicative moods. Maybe further observation of Shadow . . .

But that was the problem. They had Shadow, whoever they

were. And here I was skulking around a ridge, waiting for their campfire to die down so that I could sneak in there and rescue Shadow.

That she was there I had no doubt. Although we didn't speak much, she less than I, there was an empathy between us, something almost tangible. I felt her presence, down there in the depression where her captors had made camp for the night. When I first saw her, she was a mere slip of a girl—undernourished, unkempt, and unwashed. And she was worse than I had been at that age. She didn't talk, she avoided all people, and she wouldn't meet my stare. Don't get me wrong, she wasn't shifty-eyed like some of those New Christians, and her eyes were an odd shade of violet, but she simply preferred not to look at anybody. In those days, not too long ago really, I was the only anybody around. Both of us remained aloof from the last vestiges of humanity in our corner of the world. When supplies were needed, I'd go into town and sell the location of small water holes. Shadow would disappear. But when my business was finished, I'd just head for wherever I was going in the first place, and pretty soon she'd be tramping along behind me. In retrospect, I think that my efforts to communicate with her broke down my own barriers somewhat. Before then, I wouldn't talk to anybody, save for grunted phrases necessary to acquire what few provisions I needed. Since I'd found her, Shadow had grown into a beautiful young woman, jet-black hair somewhat muted by the desert sun. The skinny kid I'd rescued had filled out her tallish figure well.

It was getting late and they put out their fire, a smart concession, as dried dung way out here is hard to come by. Additionally, fireworms have no healthy fear of fire. Speaking of which, one of the smaller fireworms crawled over my legs as I observed the now darkened camp. He snuggled up against my side and purred, just like a cat! Seldom had I an experience such as this. I felt the bristles rub my clothing but they didn't pierce it. My luck still held. This little fellow was longer than I was, but merely the width of my forearm, so I thought that perhaps he was a foundling, recently born from a Mother, and hungry for the womblike companionship he had just lost. At least temporarily, he'd keep the bad guys off my tail. Should someone approach, he'd get excited, curl and uncurl, and lash at them. Many times I had seen it.

That was one of the reasons I worried about Shadow. With

me she was safe. Alone she was nimble and quick-witted enough to avoid the fireworms, although they probably wouldn't harm her. There was sort of an armed unfriendly truce between her and the fireworms when I wasn't around, yet she never did take any chances. However, I wasn't sure how the fireworms would react to her among other human beings. Especially if one or more of them were the "cursed," those whom the fireworms relentlessly chase. Of course, most of the cursed didn't know they were cursed until it was too late. Those who did stayed away from the territory of the fireworms, sticking to the water enclaves or the coast. But lately I was developing a theory that the cursed did know they were marked by the fireworms and cleverly kept clear of the wrong places.

Soon it would be late enough to sneak into their camp and see what I could do about Shadow. I didn't know how they had captured her, but they had. It wasn't like her to be caught. The group was large enough to have put out a netlike search and come up with her. But why had they missed me? I knew that I was their target. Their intelligence must have been excellent to know that we, Daystar and Shadow, traveled hereabouts. Which led to the thought that there must be some kind of organization behind the search to kill me.

Shadow had become the bait.

I would not let them have her.

Obviously I had some allies. I detected under-earth movements all around me now. Fireworms are hard, if not impossible, to see at night. With a little experience, though, you know they're there. I concentrated on the ridge line on the other side of the depression. A couple of faint stars were lined up right on the crest. Then something came between one star and me, momentarily. So the rim around the camp was ringed. The fireworms were gathering for the attack.

This could only mean one thing. One or more "cursed" people were among those below. Fireworms won't ordinarily go too far out of their way to attack normal people, much less gather in hordes. Except in one case: when a cursed one was around.

Which all added to my problems now. Fireworms didn't bother me a bit and had in fact helped me by keeping people out of the desolate arid stretches. But now they were poised to flood the depression below and kill everybody there. And everybody included Shadow.

I didn't much mind the death of fifteen or twenty bad guys, since they were trying to kill me. I just didn't think that the fireworms, in their bloodlust, could discriminate Shadow from the rest.

Act now or hang up your hero medal, I thought. I wormed my way over the ridge, upsetting the nestled fireworm. He stopped purring. In the starlight, I saw that my move may have precipitated the attack. Dark blotches detached themselves from the surrounding rocks, sand, and scrub. Uncurling and emerging from beneath the sand, they looked like strings of spaghetti and bean sprouts individually climbing down into the bottom of a wok. Debating whether or not to shout a warning to those below so that Shadow would have a chance, I thought furiously as I wove my way between rocks and down draws. The last thing I wanted to do was to alienate the fireworms, if they were intelligent enough to note my behavior. I suspected they were, as they did seem to act either on their own or as a group. Perhaps there was some sort of lower-level communication between them.

I scurried faster, hands and knees torn from the rough ground. Overtaking the leaders on my side of the advancing and closing circle, I paused to locate Shadow. I could see the back of a nodding guard, hunched on top of a flat rock. A dark form snaked over the rock and wrapped around him, quick as the blink of an eye. When they were in a hurry, fireworms could virtually fly for short distances. There was a muffled noise and the writhing pair fell to the ground.

Then I sighted Shadow. Damn, I thought I'd broken her of that. She sat, wrists tied to ankles in an upright position. But she was rocking herself, backward and forward and side to side. I knew what she was feeling: totally withdrawn into herself, mind blazing, incomprehension of life and current circumstance; brain refusing to stay in gear, knowing something terrible was wrong. It had taken me many long, patient months and years to coax her away from that manifestation. Only our strong empathy held us together, two misfits, outcasts.

A shout from another guard aroused the camp. Yells and screams of pain and agony filled the bowl. It was an eerie experience, two sides of a battle, one silent and deadly, and one noisy and ineffective. A fuel lamp came on, casting a dim, yellow light about. Ineffective, I said? Hell no. A wide-angle laser lashed out. There was something deeper than met the eye here. No one I ever talked to knew from where these weapons came. Another laser swept the area, sizzling fireworms. The stench of burnt flesh filled the hollow and I gagged. Yet the fireworms continued to swarm down from the ridges, ignoring the deadly light. Some men ran about with solid metal spears, aside from lasers, the only sure tool with which to kill a fireworm. If you're lucky, you jam it through the fireworm into the ground, and they wrap about it, dissolve it and ingest the metal. Some type of self-perservation mechanism, I presume. But it stops them and eventually kills them. The two lasers continued to sweep the battleground, not pausing to miss friendlies. Several of the lackies with metal spears bit the dust along with the fireworms. But the fireworms kept coming.

Seeing my only chance, I rose and grasped one of the metal rods lying about from a recently live Shadownapper. I figured that I wouldn't look out of place, a human rushing around with his fireworm spear. I made a straight line for Shadow, seemed to trip and go down near her and rolled up against her thigh. She recoiled. Shadow didn't like to be touched at all. There had been very little physical contact between us previously, just when necessary, as when assisting each other up an unscalable cliff or something similar.

I dropped the spear, whipped out my knife and cut her bonds. By now, Shadow had recognized my aura or whatever it was that we did together, and cooperated. She spoke no word, but touched my hand. She actually touched my hand! Another hundred years and we might even kiss and say hello and good night aloud. I've got to have my dreams, don't I? Once, that was all I had: dreams.

She had known I was out there, just as I had known she was down here.

We crouched there together, waiting for our chance. Screams, curses, and laser cracks filled the night. The bad guys were holding their own, but just barely. Outside the circle of light, the ground was littered with the remains of fireworms. I felt sort of bad about that. I mean, they had befriended me and never harmed me. But I also understood the humans' point of view. The two men with lasers were now coordinating their efforts, back to back, slowly rotating around an invisible axis, fire covering the entire battlefront, keeping it almost clear. We couldn't sneak off into the night, unless we wanted to join our ancestors, whoever they were. I waited for an opportunity.

When that opportunity came, I didn't believe it myself. I thought that one of the weapons would overload, overheat, or run out of charge and then we could scramble out. No such luck this time, as the bad guys must have had new lasers with full charges. Those weapons would cost a lot of water to own, months' worth of water credits to a standard town.

Suddenly the ground directly in front of Shadow and me erupted. A ton of Mother fireworm boiled out of the sand. Now maybe people would believe my story, if any of these guys made it alive to tell theirs. This Mother charged straight at me and Shadow, veering off only when it got close enough to distinguish us from the other humans. Both lasers focused on the head and feelers. As the Mother died, she still had not come all the way out of the sand, but she managed to whip her body in a rolling motion, and smash into most of the men left in the group. Unfortunately, she missed the men with lasers. But this was our chance.

I grasped Shadow in my arms and rose. She squirmed to get loose. She knew she could run faster than I.

"Hold still, damn it! You'll step on the bodies out there." That made sense to her and she subsided. We didn't know if she was as immune as I was, but there wasn't reason enough yet to take chances.

I sprinted for cover, feet squashing over charred remains of fireworms. The carnage made me ill.

"It's him!" someone shouted. "He's got the girl!"

"Shoot the bastard."

"I can't, dammit."

Several crossbow quarrels clanged off nearby rocks. I folded Shadow in closer to my chest, shielding her from danger. I sensed that the urgency of the moment had overcome her revulsion of personal contact. What a helluva way to learn.

Then something ripped into my shoulder and I stumbled, Shadow's weight dragging me down. Oddly, the shaft in my shoulder saved our lives, as a beam seared through the space we'd just vacated. I rolled into the cover of a small group of rocks, still clutching Shadow to me. I felt unusual fear rise within her. Shadow wasn't afraid of anything. Her thick hair blinded me and a line of pain scorched across my thigh.

Shadow rolled free and I started crawling up a draw to the side.

I risked a glance back. One laser still searched us out and the other was cleaning up the remainder of the fireworms. My shoulder wouldn't function too well and my thigh was spreading the flame of agony throughout my body. Whatever else, I wasn't immune to pain.

"After them," came a faint shout.

Shadow took the lead and scrambled up the draw, trying to reach the ridge and escape. She looked back, eyes glinting in the starlight, concern written on her face. I bit my tongue and followed. She came back and crouched beside me. She wanted to say something, but long habits persevered. She merely tugged at my clothing, trying to urge me onward. I knew that if I could go no farther, she would be doomed as well as I. And, hell, she was a good kid—not real talkative, but a fine partner nonetheless. So with failing energy and leaving a trail of blood I preferred not to think about, I followed her up and over the ridge. My knees and palms were already bloody pulps, so I ignored the consequences and scrambled. I managed to snap the bolt and pull it free.

Out of habit, we headed deeper into the wasteland. We'd never been a pair to search for help, most of the time taking care of our own problems. If we found we couldn't handle whatever fate threw our way, we usually faded into the nearest desert. Only a few people on earth had the courage to strike out into the nameless wastes that covered much of the planet. More likely, only a few people could cope out there. I was the best. I could find water. And we had pockets sewn up with emergency rations: blocks of seaweed concentrates for vegetables and dried earthworm and insect blocks for protein. Shadow had learned amazing tricks to cooking these in various combinations. We carried the best quality, too. San Diego put out a great kelp concentrate that had more vitamins and minerals than any Chinese farmer in the north could grow on his plot in any number of vegetable products.

I had a feeling I wasn't going to make it through the night, so I made Shadow carry my jacket with the concentrates. I don't know whether or not she figured out my ploy, but I indicated that it was too heavy for me to carry.

We dodged into a ravine and followed it westward. You learn not to provide a profile to dangerous pursuit. It's an acquired habit, and a valuable one. We had been chased about some before and knew most of the tricks. Our strange appearance as a pair caused many eyebrows to be lifted in more conservative communities; they didn't like what they couldn't understand, so witch-hunts were common. In such places, the names Daystar and Shadow were a death sentence. However, angry townsfolk could be counted upon to give up the chase when their quarry struck out into the desert, or stood amid several fireworms. Even the hardiest gave up the chase after such sights. And the legend grew.

We stumbled onto a flat, open expanse. It was probably the rim around the deep desert, the lost spaces where no men went. There was a light a couple of miles behind us, swinging to and fro. I cursed. All they had to do was follow the blood. Since there was no use in concealing our tracks, we ignored such trail-wise tricks and concentrated on making distance. I aimed straight for the heart of the great dunes that appeared in the newly risen moonlight. As usual, there were no clouds. High, thin, wispy clouds could be seen on occasion, but never the lower, thick layers, although I had seen the latter a few times, once in a Chinese berg in Oregon territory and again in San Diego. But that was a long way from here. The waste that we fled into was known as the Alamo Aridity, somewhere north and west of San Antonio. Texans always claim the biggest and the toughest of everything, and looking out on the land, I could believe it. I'd seen coveted photos of the moonscape from ancient Librarians, and this looked much the same.

I could make it no farther. I had to rest. So I slumped to the ground, back resting against a cooperative rock. Shadow showed agitation at the delay; she kept glancing to our rear. Since our relationship was mostly nonvocal, we'd become expert body-language readers. Over the months and years growing up together, we'd learned each other like a traveler knows fireworm track on fresh sand. And there was something deeper, too. We could read emotions, not just physical wants and needs. True, we could each tell when the other was tired, hungry, thirsty, in need of bathing, upset, impatient, and so on. But somehow our empathy overlapped with the reading of movements. It was weird when you almost knew what the other person was thinking. But the gift did allow us to operate well as a team. I suspected that Shadow was much better at it than I was.

All this led me to comprehend her current worry. Her fidgeting indicated she was scared of our pursuers. Well, so was I. Although danger never bothered us, we knew when to fear for our lives. Neither one of us had any peers in the desert. We knew of no one who had ever gone as deeply into it as we did. Yet those who followed us doggedly still came. Why? Why were we so important? Shadow's concern was more practical. The lasers. I had seen one once. The Sheriff of San Diego had shown it to me, the only one on the coast. He'd found it on a dead man who had apparently drowned and washed ashore. I had caused a momentary sensation by locating a water source on the far side of the mountains from the sea. Thus, San Diego could expand and grow various crops, and these on land instead of in the Pacific. I got a thousand water credits for that find, and most of them were still good in any area that had reciprocal agreements with San Diego. What's more, I actually got to eat some real food. The Mayor of San Diego and the Town Council treated me to a real beef-steak dinner—corn, greens, bread, and a large swordfish steak. I ate until I could ingest no more; and paid for it the next day. My system wasn't accustomed to such rich foods and I was ill for a week. But it was worth it.

As for lasers. In all my travels, I had heard of no more than four or five. And those guaranteed absolute sovereignty to the communities that possessed them. They were well guarded from theft, and were worth hundreds of crossbows and machetes in battle. No one knew where they came from originally. There had been no contact with the Monitors in over a hundred years, other than the normal weirdos who claimed nighttime visits. Certainly the Monitors had them, but they, according to legend, did not interfere in our affairs. They'd shown up somewhere nearly a thousand years ago, and cleaned up as much as they could after the Holocaust. Now, rumor had it, they merely orbited the earth and waited. They must have great patience. Long-forgotten stories related that the Monitors were the sentinels of our solar system, preventing some other aliens from a takeover bid. I knew of many such tales, as I was an apprentice Storyteller. Ours was the task of maintaining history. But the years eroded the discipline into scattered bits, each Storyteller striving to keep his knowledge intact with an unbiased view. Only rumors and wild tales filtered through from other parts of the globe. And I have no doubt that much myth and many exaggerated tales found their way into Stories, as evidenced by the tales and legends about Daystar and Shadow.

However, these wanderings weren't bettering our situation, and Shadow was becoming terribly agitated, so I rose wearily and we continued our journey from fear.

It would help me to assess who was following us and why. Shadow had been their captive and could perhaps tell me something of them. Since she was in the lead finding the easiest way through the waste, she couldn't see me and I saw only her back. In the starlight I admired the way she had filled out her jeans. Our jeans had cost plenty, being imported from the east. Her back straightened as she must have intercepted my thought, or at least the concept. Perhaps she sensed a change in my attitude toward her as a girl. I don't think she could tell that my thoughts centered on her derrière and the womanly swells as something nice to behold, but probably she knew that I was thinking of her in a different role than that of partner. To hide my embarrassment, I sent out a warm glow that said I was glad I had her to rely on in my time of utmost troubles. Her strides seemed stronger.

The mental effort required to communicate that way was draining my strength. I couldn't do it other than to impart basic emotions now. She must have been cringing the whole time as my body was sending out signs and waves of pain. The warm glow must have seemed a cold beer on a hot day to her.

So I had to try verbally.

"Shadow. Who are they? Did you hear anything to indicate what they wanted?"

She hesitated in her steps, then continued walking. Her vibes told me, although I may have gotten them mixed up in my pain, that those men had been beneath her notice and that she'd turned off the outside world when they'd captured her. She could do that, withdraw from reality and into herself, just as I used to, although I hardly bothered anymore. When one of us did it, the other would have to watch closely in case we injured ourselves. The mind would burn, as if on fire, and race seemingly out of control. No external stimuli could break through the barriers our minds would erect. It was something natural, or so it seemed—a sort of catharsis.

"Shadow, you've got to try." Attempting to use a commanding voice, I suffered physical and mental weakness and I couldn't convey the urgency of my request.

An imperceptible shrug of her shoulders gave me her answer. No go, pardner, leeme alone and let's get the hell away from here.

So I shut up and concentrated on putting one foot in front of the other.

Dawn came and went, heat rose, dry heat, unlike that of San Diego where there is humidity. In San Diego you could actually feel that you were breathing. You knew something was going down your throat and into your lungs. It was a nice feeling.

We stopped for a rest on the far edge of a great sand dune. I could see our tracks through the deep sand, making almost a straight line across the waste. At least Shadow still retained her sense of direction and sanity. I had only been able to follow. Left on my own, I would've wandered in circles.

Below us was a small, rocky valley—just a level, hard place in the vast expanse. A scrawny mesquite grew from the middle of the rock. I looked back, eyes unaccountably blinded by the sun on the sand and rocks. Not far off I thought I saw movement. Shadow caught my welling fear and checked, too. Shock emanated from her and I catalogued three people from the look on her face. So, three after us. And her mind said we had only a few minutes. We'd never been afraid of danger; in fact we courted it. But common sense dictated that now we were in deep trouble. My fear was for Shadow's safety.

We scrambled down the hillside to the hardpan and ran across it, gaining valuable time while our pursuers labored through the deep sand. But they'd catch up to us when they hit the hard stretch, too.

As we passed the mesquite, I sensed water. Ordinarily, I use some sort of equipment to dowse—a forked branch or a metal rod. But that was just window dressing for the locals so that they wouldn't get excited over what some had called "supernatural" or "witchcraft." Paraphernalia lent an air of technology to the procedure, and was therefore acceptable.

"Shadow. There's water under that tree, should you ever need it."

She acknowledged my words and kept running.

I could run no farther. My thigh felt as if it were rotting off and the crossbow quarrel had pierced my shoulder cleanly: it hurt like hell and I thought it might already be infected. I fell to the ground.

Shadow came back. She glanced between me and the top of the dune we had just come over. I closed my eyes.

A shout from afar told me we had been sighted. Alarm spread from Shadow in red waves.

I managed to open my eyes and look back. Three figures raced down the side of the dune. We were only a few moments in front of them. I still didn't know what they wanted; but they must have been brave men, I gave them that.

Shadow grasped me gently by my good arm and pulled me up. I didn't have any strength, so I leaned against her. She jerked back momentarily and I started to fall again. Then she rushed to me and swung herself under my good arm and supported me that way. She made to go forward and stumbled under my weight, 190 plus. The only thing that gave me strength to assist her was that she sent out more waves of alarm, blue this time. That meant she feared for my safety. She had finally realized that this might be one situation we couldn't get out of by ourselves. The legend of Daystar and Shadow was soon to come to an end.

So I lurched ahead, supported by Shadow. We stumbled along like a three-legged dog pulling a heavy cart. Once I got into the rhythm of it, the going was easier. From somewhere within the automatic portion of my brain, I noted that I'd stopped bleeding. Somehow I didn't think that this was a good sign.

We came to the edge of the hardpan and plowed into the soft sand. Shadow steered us toward the juncture of two dunes, or sand ridges, knowing that I couldn't make it up another slope.

I heard feet pounding behind us, but couldn't waste the effort to look back. Things looked bleak. We struggled on through the sand. I couldn't breathe too well anymore; each lungful of air burned my throat and chest. I couldn't seem to get enough oxygen. I felt Shadow crying inwardly in frustration. I stumbled again and collapsed over her shoulder, no longer able to move my limbs.

She grabbed my bad arm and the pain almost knocked me unconscious. But she ignored my screams. Wrapping my arms around her shoulders, she took my weight on her back and shoulders and dragged me onward. Shadow was tall for her age and no longer a child. Her age could have been anywhere from seventeen to twenty, we didn't know for sure. She must have weighed about 120, but she was still small compared to me, six two and just shy of 200 pounds. A hard life had made me big and strong. But she managed the load with less effort than I thought possible.

My dark hair fell in front of my eyes, obscuring my vision. Her legs were sinking to her knees in the deep sand. I observed all of this as if from outside my body. Without direction, great waves of desperate determination shot out from her. Shadow was deathly worried about me; and my condition was nothing to brag about then. I don't know whether she cared for me out of loyalty to a long-time partner or something deeper, but I sensed concern in her mind over my immediate welfare.

A laugh came from close behind us, and I heard hoarse breathing. Sometimes I think Shadow can see behind her. She took four more steps, unceremoniously threw me down on the sand, and turned to face our pursuers.

I rolled a couple of times and came up on my belly, trying to see what the hell was going on. Shadow had her knife out and was calmly awaiting their arrival. I think I realized then that Shadow had more dignity in her little finger than most people ever hope to have.

Three men in nondescript clothing approached her. The one that impressed me had a great bear of a head. Shaggy hair hung all over his head and his face looked as if it had lost the battle with smallpox after incendiaries had had their try. He held a laser, pointed loosely at Shadow.

"Don't you worry none, girl," he said. "I ain't gonna waste any charge on you."

The other two spread out from his side and made a movement to encircle us.

One whispered, *"Muerto, ahora."*

The ruined face grinned evilly and advanced on Shadow. She held her ground. I sensed resignation as she decided to take as many of them with her as she could before they killed us.

She shot a parting wish at me; a warmth enveloped me, a second of happy togetherness, and something much deeper that I couldn't then fathom.

Then the ground erupted. Sand seemed to fly in the air from numerous explosions. The largest Mother fireworm I had ever seen rose in front of me, opened its mouth to full extension, and swallowed me.

As I tumbled into the gaping maw, I heard Shadow scream my name, "Robin!"

CHAPTER TWO

Déjà vu. Head over heels into the depths of the beast. Emotions burned out with loss of physical ability. Worry for Shadow penetrates, senses return somewhat. Still breathing, I think. But how? Feeling of esophageal muscles the size of great tree trunks from the mountains. I moved along, aided by the stirrings of the innards of the creature. Try to stay conscious. Remember Shadow . . . She's out there faced by three terrible men. Willpower, help Shadow, self-discipline deserting. Am I still breathing or is this death? Consciousness fading, memory titillating curiosity, the experience not new, as if I had gone through the same thing before . . .

A small child, swallowed by a gargantuan red monster . . . Before that, what? Similarity of experience opens memories suppressed . . . recall hazy, as if outside observer . . .

"He's flawed." An old argument. A beefy man once, but sparse and gaunt now. "You know, one of my brothers was the same."

"He's our child. We love him. Or at least I do." The mother grasped her child possessively. The child reacted, squalling, disapproval written on his features. He did not like to be picked up and held. Why must these large people talk so loud? He hissed at the woman. She sat him down on the floor.

He knew it was time for his brain to burn again. Every time someone said love, his brain revolted. Previously, his stomach would squeeze bile into his throat, but he conquered that problem in his subconscious life, where he spent most of his time.

The argument raged around him, seemingly from all sides.

"Damn you, woman . . . you know I don't want to do it any more than you do. But we have others to think of. Our clan would be blackballed if we didn't follow tradition. One child is a small price to pay. What of A, G, and L?"

"But, Davi, he's so cute. He doesn't even know what we're talking about. And look, you've upset him."

"Put his wool cap on him, woman, else he'll smash his small cranium on the adobe."

She did so, caressing her child. He cringed from her. "I refuse to cooperate."

"He's my son, too, you know. A father doesn't like to lose his son. We knew it was coming. He's over three years old now, and hasn't learned a damn thing. When the other children were three, they had learned to talk, to eat, to cooperate inter-socially. But not him, not R. At his rate, he'll keep the R until death. The other children will have full names. A is almost ready for the N to be added. Hell's bells, R doesn't even look at me anymore. And we had a horrible time training him to function biologically correct. Kid would crap anywhere. No, he's got to go, in accordance with town policy."

The small child wished the large people would go away and leave him alone. His burning brain was receding now, but he didn't want to share a new awakening with any others. His mother watched him, love shining through her features. The child hated her, or so he thought. With her eyes she implored him, but he immediately shifted his gaze. He debated whether to climb the trellis outside again. The words of the adults were there, but he ignored them. He'd heard it all before. He could not understand all of the words and phrases yet, but he was making good progress on his own. The older siblings around had long since given up trying to help him. He flapped his arms.

They had called him "artistic" again. At times it gave him a warm glow, but at other times it was used as an obscenity.

"Marg," his father continued, "I tell you that my water credit is already slipping. The whole burg knows what is happening in our home, and the whole burg knows what has to be done about it. The Policy. Out. Into the desert."

"No," she said simply.

Thwack. Meaty open hand contacts face of mother. Tears well. She cannot speak. Shakes her head, backs in front of R as if to protect him with her body.

Father storms out, door slams.

For the first time, R felt emotion, thick as smoke in the room. Had he cared at all, he would have reacted, and terrible things would not have come to pass. One gesture would have sufficed. But he retreated into his standoffish manner, which wasn't too difficult for a three-year-old. Almost against his will, he started to reach out to touch his mother's leg, to reassure her that she was on the right side at least. But a cockroach intervened and changed destiny. The thumb-sized insect scuttled from a shadow under the rough-hewn table. The child saw, retracted his arm, and scampered after the roach. With a flying pounce he was on it. Without so much as admiring his catch, he popped it into his mouth and swallowed it whole. The thing tickled his gullet as it went down.

Because the child could not express his affection to the mother, she must have been heartbroken. She had stood up for him before, and guarded him religiously during trying times. But month after month she received no appreciable response from him. Only the thin thread that was the essence of motherhood kept her adamant. The child knew this, but ignored her anyway. He could tell she was of failing health, all of her time devoted to her child, R. In his fever-wracked brain, he could sense that she was drifting away from him. Her resistance was practically gone. She had become an old woman in the time he could remember, not many months at all. She no longer bathed him quietly at night, using her own portion of valuable water. Yesterday he had knocked the mug of water from her hand and she had wept. These things and others fled through his mind, but he didn't care. He'd gotten his daily protein, and was happy, for his overactive body burned everything he could ingest.

She had collapsed now, sobbing openly on the staunch wooden bed. Soon the other siblings would complete their chores or daily education and return. They would studiously ignore the smallest child, other than the newborn L in the slatted crib, and go about their business somberly. Only when out of his presence would they behave like normal children. His mother and father had argued over that, too. He was affecting all of their lives. His abnormality was like a damper on family activity. He knew, but couldn't cope yet.

Suddenly, his mother rose and came at him. He scrambled farther under the table. She grasped him roughly by the left arm and dragged him out. She lifted his small body and forced him to look at her. He swung his head so as not to look in her eyes. With one hand, she held his head immobile. He shifted his eyes to and fro to avoid her gaze. He could not close his eyes, even though he wanted to. In their roving, his eyes, and perhaps his emotional reception center, read what he knew was behind her gaze. Surrender. He wanted to cry, but for a change, he couldn't.

L was the latest sibling, and she began to howl from her crib. The mother sobbed at R and clasped him to her breast.

Late that night, when R thought everyone was asleep, he rose and wandered outside. He liked the night and the shadows it provided. Bright objects protruded from the dark velvet above.

He sensed a movement behind him and turned quickly. Someone was at the door watching him. He heard his father's voice from inside, rough and callous from the necessity of a fateful decision, and his mother's form detached itself from the door frame. She caught him up before he could escape.

"I love you," she said.

She unfolded her rough cotton cloak and exposed her breast, heavy with milk for L. She forced his head against her nipple.

"Drink, R. Suckle as much as you can."

He didn't want any of the milk. Even he know how valuable it was for the newborn L, packed with protein and nutrition. She squeezed her breast and the thin milky stuff dribbled into his mouth, choking him. He had to swallow to breathe. She sat on a wooden bench and propped him in her lap, forcing him to suck on her breast. She continued to squeeze the life-giving fluid out until he could drink no more.

She sighed heavily. She did not refasten her cloak, and he knew this was the end. She forced his head to rest in the valley between her breasts. It was late and he was too tired to resist, drowsiness overcoming him from the gorging feeding. They sat that way for an hour, the child dozing fitfully, the mother crooning her love.

An oil lamp came on inside the adobe hut, and the mother tightened her grip on the child. L was crying softly, sounds floating through the open window on the night air.

She began talking to him, almost as if talking to herself so quiet were her words. "Your birthing was an ill omen. There were complications and, if you care, the delivery almost killed me. I was lucky to have conceived again. Then you wouldn't feed; you refused breast milk for many days until we thought you would die. And when you finally learned to drink my milk, you began screaming a great deal, refusing to be comforted, just as you do today. I know you will not respond to me, but I want you to understand." She clenched him tightly to herself. "It was doomed from the beginning, and now, I have not the strength to carry on longer. Three years of this and I cannot take more; I have sacrificed much, and the other children lack for a mother's hand. They, too, are jealous of you, of the attention you receive. But it has been ill-fated from the beginning, and I have no more fight left within me." She closed her eyes and rocked him, hurting him with the fierceness of her grip.

Finally, the mother pulled a cotton shirt over her child. The pockets bulged.

"I have seen intelligence burning inside your eyes," she whispered. "So I know you can understand me. In your pockets there is a gourd of goat yogurt and a block of insect protein. Use it if you get hungry." Her grip seemed to strangle the child.

"We can spare no more water. Forgive me for what I do. May the Lord clasp you to his bosom."

His father came out of the house. His mother didn't want to give him up, but a cuff from the large man loosened her hold, and he was torn from her breasts.

The father carried him loosely under one arm, and strode along the deserted street out into the wasteland. The child could hear her wailing long after they were out of earshot.

At dawn the father still walked strongly. He was known as the strongest man in the village. As the only blacksmith and metal worker within miles, he did a booming business. But he had many mouths to feed. Offspring, wife, a brother, and wife's parents. The child could feel regret from the man who was his father, but this was overshadowed by firm determination.

The sun was high in the sky as the father tired. The heat had baked all the moisture out of the small body. He could feel fear from his father now. He looked around, a captive spectator to what was happening. Many small movements came from the sand alongside the path. The boy had seen fireworms before and knew what they were. He'd gone to investigate a curled up fireworm once; his mother had screamed and raced to him, plucked him out of the sand just before he'd touched it. She shouted and ran. His father and some neighbors raced to the sandy pile and killed it. The boy felt sorrow on the occasion.

Then he saw flesh-colored specks rising and falling in the deep sand paralleling the trail, keeping up with the pace his father set.

Sweat from his father's armpit drenched him, but he was ignored. Finally fear welled up and out into the open from his father. He sprinted ahead, for a few minutes outdistancing the pursuing fireworms.

His father was breathing heavily now, grunting in exhaustion from each laden step. A lone mesquite loomed on the horizon and the father raced for that goal. Stumbling, he reached the tree and leaned wearily against it.

The child was unceremoniously dropped to the sand. He looked about and saw a few bones, what he would recognize later as rib cages from children. There was an ominous air about. The lone mesquite seemed to symbolize something and he felt twinges, but could not identify the feeling.

The father wore a pained expression. He glanced out into the desert warily. The whole area seemed to be alive. The sand writhed in places, caved in elsewhere, and spouts of the stuff leaped into the air.

His father knelt beside him.

"It's the Policy," the father said, weariness overcoming him. "You're artistic. Here, drink."

He held a water gourd to the son's lips. The boy swallowed greedily.

"I stole it for you." The father watched as the child finished off the water and licked the rim dry.

"Vaya con Dios," said the father. He took one last look at the child and turned abruptly. He trotted off along the trail, glancing from side to side. The ground alongside the path rumbled with movement.

CHAPTER THREE

I watched my father run off until he was out of sight. I didn't know if he'd make it back to the village or become another victim of the fireworms. They were all around now, boiling the surrounding area with their movement. I sat back, exhausted, and leaned against the tree. Small flesh-colored heads and medium-sized heads appeared out of the sand around my safe area. It was as if I sat in a sanctuary.

Presently the fireworms emerged from underneath the land. They ringed me on all sides, approaching slowly. I knew I should be scared, but oddly I wasn't. I was a mere three years old or thereabouts. My curiosity was insatiable.

They approached menacingly, slowly squirming across the ground. But I could no longer see them. My brain was on fire again. This was one of the worst rages I recalled. It shut everything out, sun, sand, heat, thirst, and danger. I beat my head against the trunk of the tree. Maybe I screamed, I don't know.

When I came out of it, the advancing hordes had stopped. All faced me, macabre situation. Things remained that way for a long time. The sun slowly crawled across the sky, voyage uninterrupted. I grew hungry and pulled out the goat yogurt. It had soured slightly in the heat, but I ate it anyway. Wiping my fingers clean on sand, I continued to watch the horde of fireworms watching me. At dusk, my thirst was overwhelming. With nothing else to do, I ate the block of insect protein and wished for a drink of cool water, *agua frío*.

Later, I fell into a restless sleep, awakening at times to see the crowd of fireworms growing in the moonlight. The whole desert was an unmoving scene of fireworms, broken only by small, open stretches of sand. My nose itched from the change in smell.

And I was terribly thirsty. Somehow, I knew there was a small amount of water underneath the mesquite, but after a few moments of scratching at the surface, I gave up the effort.

I was awake at dawn when the commotion came. A great mound of sand was rolling toward me like a wave in the desert. Fireworms slid out of the way or were tossed aside by the speed of passage.

Finally, the surface before me caved in and an enormous head lifted from the depths of the sand. For about fifteen of my body lengths behind the head, sand cascaded off the carcass of the Mother fireworm. She was bigger than the town meeting assembly room in the village, and I thought that much more of her remained buried beneath the sand.

Her head loomed over me, matching the height of the mesquite. She seemed to study me for the longest time. And, strangely, I could not move my eyes from her gaze. Her tremendous feelers held me an unwilling prisoner to their attention.

After long minutes of intense scrutiny, she lowered the front of her body to ground level and straightened out. Her head inched across the sand to me. Her mouth opened, as if the front of her head were split horizontally, and something flicked out to me. I felt it wrap around me and tug me gently into her head. Then I was bowling down a long, moist tube, sand and rocks accompanying me.

I didn't know if I was dreaming then or now. I didn't know if I was alive or dead, but I didn't want to lose the memory. I'd had flashes of this story in my brain throughout my life so far, but this was the clearest recollection yet. Was it real or a dream?

And what had happened to my father? And A, G, and L, my fellow siblings? A would have grown into Annette by now, as she was the oldest. G would probably be at the Gregor stage, wanting only the y ending. L, the youngest, would be Lorilard one day, but may have only reached Lori by now. If she lived without the milk. Perhaps Mother had saved some. In our town, as in a few other isolated communities, it was the custom to identify people at their growing stages by letters in their names. As a child started his education, he would add a letter. Reaching puberty, maturity, professional level at his chosen field, all required additional letters. For instance: R was my childhood name. Had I been normal, when I received my first schooling and was beginning to progress, I would have been called Ro. When I started into puberty, Rob would be allowed by the elders. Robi would be mine under a comprehensive and complicated formula, devolving from the factors of age, apprenticeship, or manly deeds accomplished.

And when I became a full man, depending on circumstances, that of contributing to the community in some serviceable way and being able to support a family, Robin would be my name. But more than a name. A status or title might be closer to the truth. It enabled the full-named person to be fully responsible, part of the governing body if that case applied, able to make contracts for services, and, among other things, a responsible citizen who could speak for his community to strangers and to other such groups which required our community acquiescence in some item or policy.

My mother had been called "Marg" when I was dumped in the desert. She was young at the time, and perhaps her allowing my father to abandon me would suffice for her to receive the last "e" and become "Marge." Would I ever know? Or more truthfully, did I ever want to know?

But the most exalted status of names came when the elders allowed you into the inner circle of themselves. Had I lived my entire life in that town, grown into adulthood, followed prescribed ways and worked hard, had a family and contributed to the community in some significant manner, and lived to a ripe old age, I would've been called "Robin of El Paso." But screw them and their goddamn names and closed societies. They had cast me out. Since that time I'd avoided the El Paso area, even though it meant going far out of my way occasionally. I wasn't yet ready to pursue my heritage.

CHAPTER FOUR

In one of his monologues, the Professor had told me how his monkeys had found me.

"I was resting alongside the trail, many days out of San Antone, and the monkeys had wandered off to investigate the area, probably to add much needed organic material to the earth, and I heard a tremendous screeching. I thought, damn, they'd run into a fireworm. What could I do, legs almost paralyzed and all? But all of my monkeys had gone around a rocky ridge. I couldn't get along without them, could I? They took good care of me and I owed them succor."

Here he paused for breath, decapitated a small, succulent barrel cactus, and sucked on the pulp. I hadn't been able to find any water hereabouts.

He continued. "So I sighed, patted my trusty fireworm spear and whipped the oxen into motion." He was a peddler, a freighter, a Storyteller, and a Newsbringer. Sometimes Newsbringers were Storytellers and vice versa, but not always. He was in a hurry then, he said, because he'd get a bounty on each farmer he could recruit for a place called Seattle.

"At the time, I was bringing a load of San Diego kelp for San Antonio, and some knickknacks, and didn't want the valuable cargo to be lost. But I would be lost without my monkeys to do the work, so I beat the oxen ahead. They're stupid beasts and were afraid of the fireworms, naturally, but they were more afraid of me. So I rounded the slope and there were all my monkeys, jumping up and down, raising general hell on the lip of a draw. I couldn't understand. The smell of water must have attracted the monkeys. That Abraham, the old boss monkey, could smell water, if it was open to the air, from a mile away. Not as good as you, boy, but good in his own way. At any rate, they were all looking into the draw when I pulled up beside them.

"There you sat. I could tell from the marks at the bottom of the draw that you'd dug three or four feet down with your hands and water had seeped to the surface. You were playing in it, splashing muddy water about. A couple of smallish fireworms wiggled around you and you were having the time of your life splashing them with mud. I tell you, boy, I'd never seen anything like it. The monkeys all scampered up on the wagon and old Abraham, he just climbed on the lead ox and sat. I couldn't believe that you hadn't been killed by contact with the fireworms."

He shook his head, still in disbelief of the sight. "The fireworms noticed us and I was prepared to whip the oxen the hell out of there. The two fireworms began to crawl out of the depression toward us and you put a restraining hand on them. Strangest thing I'd ever seen. Well, eventually they crawled off and left you simply sitting there. You were bareass naked as the day you were born, seemed ten or twelve years old, and were sunburnt to a crisp. I'd never seen anything so red. But the mud must've helped. I called to you and you ignored me. Boy, I want you to know that grated on me. I called and called and received no response. Well, I couldn't go down there myself on account of my inop legs, so I sent Abraham after you. Why, I don't know. He went down tentatively. You inspected him and then ignored him. Well, he couldn't cope with the situation, so he just had a drink and left. I sent him back with a pail to fetch water for me and the oxen. When we'd all drunk from your water, I called again and told you we were leaving. You didn't pay any attention. So we left."

More out of hunger than curiosity, I remembered following the old man. The wagon rolled along the trail with me behind. Occasionally, when the oxen made droppings, a monkey would jump off the wagon, scoop it up and toss it into a sling carried beneath the wagon. This interested me for a short time, long enough for darkness to fall and the Professor to stop and make camp.

A small fire was lighted and presently I could smell food. I realized I was ravenous. And I couldn't remember a damn thing. All I knew was that I had been wandering around in the desert and could eat one of those oxen.

I came closer to the camp and the monkeys twittered among themselves. I watched them unhitch the oxen and hobble them nearby. The old man had lowered himself to the ground and crawled to a mat that another monkey had laid out. They brought him some sort of foodstuff from the wagon. My mouth watered.

For some reason, I was reluctant to go in.

"Come on in, boy. I know you're out there."

I moved closer.

"Food, son."

I was in the circle of firelight.

The old man held out his hand with food in it.

Hesitantly, I walked up to him, hunger overcoming my revulsion at human contact. As I approached, all the monkeys ran from me, hiding under the canvas-covered wagon.

I leapt for his hand, snatched up the cake, and ran off. I couldn't remember eating anything so wonderful.

I slept in the desert that night, found a small spot of water, quenched my thirst, and made some more mud to soothe my burns. I had helped at the earlier wallow, and the cool slimy mess took some of the pain away.

It went on like that for two days. I'd come close to get food, and skulk back into the desert, only to follow his wagon at daybreak. That monkey, Abraham, kept a watch on me. When I found my water, he'd wait until I was finished, then with a half dozen of his fellows he would bail the seep dry and carry the water to the wagon.

On the second night I was so sore and sunburned I couldn't sleep. I must have passed out about dawn, but when I came to, I was in the wagon, underneath canvas, and lying on a soft pallet. I never found out how the old man had gotten me up there. My body was anointed with a foul-smelling grease, but the pain was ebbing away.

We fell into an easy routine, the old man talking and me listening. I hadn't yet said a word to him. He couldn't understand my not talking, but he made up for it by being overly garrulous himself. He didn't understand it, but he accepted it. He never was one to force his ways on anyone else. That was one of the reasons why he was a loner: community rules and regulations weren't for him. Perhaps I learned to be a free spirit from him, although I must admit that I was well on my way without him. But he did firm up my resolve and, though I didn't know it then, helped shape some of the precepts and principles by which I operate today.

He had a benign face; head ringed in white fluff, and thin, spindly legs that wouldn't hold him up. As a Storyteller and Newsbringer, he taught me to read and write, and many other things. I soon found pleasure in learning for the sake of knowledge alone, something I have never given up.

Men like him were few in those days. He had visions of a reunited human race, all working together for the expansion and reestablishment of a technical environment. He kept a log of all the land he traveled. He'd refer to it constantly, examining places he'd been before. Once, he was overjoyed.

"See that?" He pointed at a vacant expanse, with only some small scrub and lichens growing on rock outcroppings.

As usual, I didn't answer; I was becoming interested in life again, under his tutelage, but declined to speak.

"Eight years ago, there was no scrub, no lichens. Another proof that the earth is reclaiming herself."

When I'd become well enough to walk, I walked beside the wagon, needing the exercise. I helped out as much as I could. When I had eaten sufficiently for many days, I became strong enough to lift him in and out of the wagon. Many times he told me what a difference that made. I'd seen him crawling about while following the wagon, and could tell that I saved him much labor. He did have an old wooden wheelchair that he used in towns, where the surface was hard enough to support the wheels. And he could move around on crutches if he absolutely had to. The monkeys accomplished most of the mechanical details for him around the camp. They were well trained and picked up certain assigned duties easily.

The Professor gave me an old pair of pants to wear and a long-sleeved shirt. I wrapped a bandanna around my forehead. While traveling, if I felt a brain burner coming on, I'd simply take off running. This seemed to assuage the urge, and eventually the wagon and the Prof would catch up to me. Sometimes I'd run as far as ten or twelve miles and have to run back if he made camp at dusk without reaching my position. The wagon would roll up, Abraham sitting regally on the neck of the lead ox, and I'd fall in beside and continue walking. Sometimes the Professor would simply talk all day, and by virtue of that, I became an apprentice Storyteller. He told me tales of history and current events as much as he knew. He always had a new and witty story. It was from him that I first heard of the Monitors.

"What?" I said.

To his credit, he went blithely along, deigning not to notice my first word. "Yep, they're up there somewhere, circling the globe, waiting, ever patient, waiting. Waiting for what, I don't know, but there are tales . . ."

He was trying to sucker me into saying something else, but I didn't buy his gambit.

He smiled, acknowledging my silent victory. "Through generations the story has been handed down, and for lack of reinforcement, the stories have gradually died out. Nobody wants to believe them much anymore. But as I have heard, and it's documented by some Librarians, they came just after the Holocaust."

Librarians are the most revered of all people. They are fed and clothed and housed free by any community lucky enough to possess one. They hoard old books and tapes. Find a decent book, and name your price. The Librarians would sell their souls for a book they didn't own. The Prof had a few books himself, surprisingly, and from these I learned to read.

"As you may know, once, there was a great technical society on Earth. Then came the Holocaust and at the end of it, the Monitors showed up and helped keep the human race alive. But they were too late to prevent wholesale destruction. The atmosphere was affected, and the land. The middle of this continent has evolved into a great desert called Centralia, which we travel on the fringes of. Some say that they are protecting us from another alien race, one who would benefit from total arid conditions on this planet. But they simply circle us in the sky. There has been no contact for centuries."

"None?" I queried. I was caught up by the possibilities, more of the Prof's influence, no doubt. One thing he hammered away at constantly was learning. Knowledge was the best tool a man owned, he often said.

"Well, there is one undocumented episode. The hydrogen plant in San Diego that powers the desalination plant failed. The technicians could not repair it. It is said that one night a strange airborne craft landed. The technicians fled in terror, but soon the generators were turning and the craft departed. On returning, the technicians found that the hydrogen plant worked better than ever, with more efficiency and generated power. This caused a surplus of power, and new irrigation was possible. San Diego expanded, and I made a bunch by Newsbringing and recruiting new citizens."

When we finally arrived in San Antonio, the old man bought me an expensive pair of jeans and boots and a jacket to ward off the cold night.

I couldn't recall ever seeing so many people at one time. It upset me, and I withdrew into myself, generally staying in the wagon. The Prof sensed my distress, and soon we were on our way with a consignment of Star beer for New Orleans, apparently a gift for the Mayor for some past favor.

I think this was the happiest time of the old man's recent life. He never spoke of his past, but he spoke of history, told me about the land we crossed and great events he had witnessed.

He managed, with my help, to tap one of the beer kegs and we'd sit around the fire at night and he would talk. He was a grizzled old man, with large gnarled hands, burned almost walnut brown from the sun. He remarked frequently on the fireworms and told how they used to bother him before I came along. I couldn't answer his questions, though, so he finally gave up asking me about them. He attributed our good fortune to the same source that allowed me to find any water that was nearby.

He finished off one keg of beer before we reached the township of New Orleans and managed to doctor the invoice and accompanying letter to reflect that we were to deliver three kegs instead of four.

We journeyed together for five or six years, me getting an education, and the Professor and his monkeys getting fair return for the water I found them.

After the second year, the Prof hit upon a money-making proposition. We'd scout the edge of the desert around small towns and larger cities, find water, and sell it to the government or whatever agency dealt with such things. This relieved us of carrying cargo to strange and often unsafe places.

Outlaws were a problem in those days, within short distances of populated areas. No one but us was about at nights. When menaced by such gangs, we turned and raced the other way. Fortunately, the monkeys provided sufficient early warning.

Then Abraham was killed.

CHAPTER FIVE

We had approached a squalid village, loaded with several casks of water to sell for provisions. Dung hadn't been collected from the street and open sewage flowed through improperly dug channels. The people were a lowly lot. We pulled up in front of the largest building and a crowd gathered.

A great hunk of a man emerged from the doorway. The crowd quieted as he looked us over. His gaze lingered on me then went to the Professor.

"Good day, *señor,*" said the Professor.

The man didn't reply.

"We have water to trade for supplies," said the Prof.

The monkeys were nervous; all except Abraham climbed to the top of the canvas, tails twitching nervously.

"Water?"

"Yes. *Agua.* Good, sweet water."

The big man turned to some men. "Check it out."

Several detached from the growing crowd and rummaged around in the wagon.

"I must protest, sir. This is an invasion of my property," said the Professor.

"Shut up, old man. We like it, we'll take it."

An old hag had approached my side of the wagon. She stood bent and stared at me. Her face was wrinkled with age. She showed some Chinese blood in the shape of her features.

"Miguel," she said, "leave them alone. This young one appears to match the description of Daystar in the old legends."

"You are a fool, old woman; you and the Librarians you go to consort with."

She snorted and addressed the Professor. "Did the young man find the water alone, or did you stumble onto it?"

"He found it."

"Miguel, call off your dogs. Dire things will occur should you not heed my warning."

A crash interrupted this strange conversation. A splash followed; they'd broken into one of the caskets. "Miguel," a voice called, "what they say is true, there is much water back here."

"Well, bring it down then."

"Sir," said the Professor, now thoroughly irritated, "we have not yet struck our bargain."

"You shut up too, old man. We take what we want from you. Be quiet and we may let you walk from here with your lives."

The Professor shrugged helplessly. I felt unaccountably confident, but sad that our fortunes had brought us to this end. The Professor couldn't walk anywhere.

Miguel's arm snaked out and he snatched Abraham off the rump of a nearby ox. His iron grip held the ancient monkey immobile.

"These creatures may be edible," he said, "and we can use the oxen ourselves."

Abraham wasn't to give up so easily. With his sharp teeth, he bit a large chunk of meat off Miguel's wrist. He worked his head back and forth to worry the skin and break the body's bond to the muscles he had in his teeth.

Miguel cursed, and with his other ham of a hand, reached over and tore Abraham's head off. He tossed the body aside.

The Professor trembled uncontrollably in anger. He paled significantly. There had been a special relationship between him and Abraham.

Miguel was still spouting obscenities and holding his injured flesh.

"Take them!" he shouted.

I hadn't said a word until then. I knew the Professor could do nothing, for we had no weapons other than words. I think I was spurred to action more by the foul stench of the place than by the situation. And, as usual, the danger didn't affect me.

"Wait," I said. "I will find you more water than you can use, right here in your village." I'd never strung so many words together in my life, but adrenalin aided my efforts.

Everyone halted and you could hear mice scurry.

"I told you!" screeched the crone.

I felt the pressure rise within me, brain threatening to accelerate abnormally, ruining our only chance. I fought an inner battle.

"Explain yourself," said Miguel, interest aroused and momentarily forgetting his wound.

"Follow me." I jumped down from the wagon and shot a glance at the Professor. He nodded imperceptibly. He knew he was to whip the oxen out of there if I could get the crowd away.

The old hag was berating the crowd with promises of my prowess and this may have made them forget the wagon and the Prof.

I knew the Professor would be worried, because I usually indicated hidden water sources to him so that he could negotiate for their location. On the ride in I hadn't shown him this water possibility; therefore, the Prof knew I was lying to them all. But he also knew that I could outrun any person he'd ever met.

I walked toward the edge of the village more confident than I felt. Miguel and the crone led the noisy crowd behind me.

I went as far as I dared into the sand, until the crowd became too restless to stall any longer. I cast about for evidence of what I sought. Miguel was muttering unhappily now. I thought I sensed some. For dramatic effect, I raised my hands straight into the air, holding them somewhat apart. I closed my eyes and turned in circles. Then I knelt in the hot sand. Intentionally, I turned my back on the crowd so they could not see what I was doing and plunged my arms into the sand. I got a good grip on the slimy flesh and breathed deeply. I was still fighting my mind for control.

With a great effort, I suddenly stood and turned to face the crowd. Sand fell from the body and a nice-sized fireworm dangled from my hands.

I held it above my head and threatened the crowd with it.

A sudden unbelieving silence followed. Then there was panic, screaming, and a stampede to turn about and run for the village. As Miguel collided with those behind him, I flung the fireworm clear about him, ensuring his quick death. He screamed and fell to the sand, writhing in agony. The old hag slapped her thighs and laughed, a high, cackling whine. She was the last sight I saw as I took off running around the edge of the village and my brain burned.

My mind took over and I hardly noticed when I passed the wagon rolling on its way on the opposite side of the town. With long, ground-eating strides, I ran for hours until I could regain control. Contritely, I trotted into camp long after dark. The Professor clasped me on the shoulder and left me to myself.

In the morning all he said was, "Thanks, son."

Thus began the legend of Daystar.

We had a problem, though. Abraham had been the straw-boss of the other monkeys. He'd be hard to replace. Or so we thought.

One of the monkeys had retrieved Abraham's body. What was left of him was held in the embrace of his mate, Fidelia. She had shrieked over him the whole night through.

In the morning, the Professor was lamenting his loss and trying to figure out which monkey to appoint to Abraham's position. There were a couple of strong, young bulls, but the Prof didn't know if they were mature enough to carry the load. They could be trained, but it would take much work.

As he was discussing this with me in a one-sided conversation, all the monkeys gathered and Fidelia led them off into the sand. Under a scrub bush, they scooped a hole and placed Abraham's remains in the depression and covered him up. They all trooped back in a line and Fidelia began chattering. The morning chores hadn't been done and soon there was a flurry of activity. The oxen were harnessed to the yoke, camp was struck and we were ready to travel. Fidelia yammered a command and all the monkeys dutifully obeyed her, climbing to their accustomed places for the journey. Except Fidelia. She leaped nimbly to the lead ox and looked at us. I had to hurry to get the Prof on the wagon. Fidelia slapped the shoulder and we were off.

Fidelia was every bit as good as Abraham if not better. She ran the camp with an iron hand. She didn't hesitate to cuff a recalcitrant worker, and things went along fine for five or six years, as I said.

Until Sacramento.

Some day, if I don't mature by then and learn any better, I will return to Sacramento and burn it to the ground.

For they killed the Professor.

CHAPTER SIX

We rolled into Sacramento with Jubal as strawboss. Fidelia had died a natural death and was replaced in the hierarchy by her and Abraham's eldest son, Jubal. He was large for his size, maybe five pounds. It was surprising that the Prof had instigated a self-regenerating society of monkeys. Before I'd come along, he had a ragtag band of hybrid Capuchin monkeys. He'd trained Abraham and that worthy had founded a dynasty, a simple society dedicated to the welfare of the Professor. New generations had learned their tasks within their own ranks without the Prof, or me, aiding them.

By this time, I was an avid knowledge seeker; that is, I was curious. I'd gotten over most of my self-centered philosophy of life and had begun to take part in the activities of the Prof. He no longer did all the bargaining and communicating for us. I helped when I could and felt like it. My natural reluctance was fading.

At the time, I didn't know why we were going to Sacramento. We'd brought some mail from San Diego to Bakerstown and there wasn't one reason to travel all the way up to Sacramento. Sacramento was not on our regular route. Some of the things the Prof had done were strange, but I hadn't paid much attention. In some cities he'd disappear for a few hours. Other times, we'd wander aimlessly, ignoring possible economic gains, just so that he could visit a place. But he never explained. Occasionally, he'd select an excess monkey or two and turn them loose in some wild, uninhabited area. And the monkeys were breeding swiftly. We had more of them than we needed. But he never sold one or gave one to any human.

On the trip into Sacramento, it occurred to me that there was some method to the Prof's seemingly mindless wanderings about the country. The purpose had not emerged, but there was an unidentifiable pattern to it.

Sacramento was the stronghold of the New Christian faith. Some said that it was not a faith, but a growing empire. The Prof had previous ties here, I learned, and wanted to check out these stories, from an anthropological standpoint, or so he said.

Sacramento wasn't as big a city as San Antone or New Orleans, but it was fair sized. Streets were crowded and vendors clogged each corner. The Prof said that the reason Sacramento was prosperous was that the New Christian Church ran almost everything and there was enough water to support small industries. This provided growth and the ancillary people to maintain a thriving population. But he was doubtful when he spoke of the New Christians.

I took an unusual interest in the sights and sounds. There were a great many red-robed priests about, and for some reason, the Prof didn't like what that portended. He was a staunch individualist, claiming that the church subjugated the people and that they were not masters of their own future. All was decided by the church and its representatives.

We rode into the Chinese section to stay with friends of the Prof. He must preferred the Chinese, as they would have nothing to do with the church, it interfering with free enterprise and all. And the Chinese were businessmen here, first, last, and always. On the outskirts of the honeycombed Chinese marketplace, we stopped at the compound of Sun Yen Chang.

Sun Yen Chang didn't have the mythical pigtails. In fact his hair was shorter than mine. I guess it was the Chinese farmers migrating from the north that gave the false concept of pigtails.

The little man didn't reach to my chest. But there was a bright intelligence behind his eyes. I had the wheelchair down and was lifting the Professor into it when he came running out of his shop.

"Professor!" he shouted, clapping his hands in anticipation.

"Sun Yen Chang, *nĭ hǎo ma?*" said the Prof. How are

you. The Chinese did not use the small-town name sequence that relayed status. They had their own concept of "face."

"*Pùhăo. Nĭ?*" said Sun. Not well, and you? My Chinese was only rudimentary, and I was having a hard time keeping up.

"*Hĕn hăo,*" said the Prof. Very well. I could get the easy ones.

The Prof said something I couldn't translate.

"*Pùmáng,*" said the Chinese. Not busy.

Formalities over, the Prof introduced me as his "*érhtzu,*" or son. I beamed.

We went inside and had tea. Jubal would take care of the oxen.

There followed a long conversation in which Yen Chang lamented business losses due, I gathered, to the New Christian Church tightening its grip on the populace. Edicts from the priesthood made it increasingly difficult to operate in Sacramento. Free enterprise was on its way out. And Sun Yen Chang ran a Chinese conglomerate, his own store plus a variety of other businesses. He headed sort of a family empire.

I met his son, Sun Tsu Liu, who was his first assistant and ran the day-to-day details and mechanics of the business.

The Prof and Sun Yen Chang talked of current events and philosophy for several days. Most of this was carried on in esoteric Chinese that I couldn't follow. So I wondered about the town, snooping and seeing the sights.

The Chinese marketplace was the most interesting—a combination of city blocks jammed with stalls and stores, accessible by winding through alleys, and convoluted passageways wound through it. Anything you could name was for sale, including food delicacies I'd never heard of, like eels, sea slugs, and a panacea made from snake bile laced with wine. Clothing was cheap because of the labor conditions. For instance, Sun Yen Chang ran a group of cottage industries and clothing marked with his brand, and "Made in Sacramento" was highly sought after. Mah-jongg parlors abounded, contrary to the New Christian ethic against gambling. I sensed that this would be a sore spot in Chinese/New Christian relations soon.

One of the booths, with Sun Yen Chang's hash mark above it, sold *Sui* oil. Now, I have pointed out that much of the land was arid, but some was arable and in use. Still, the amount of trees grown and harvested was not enough to make all the necessary wood products. Consequently, items like wooden furniture, structures, and tools had to last years, even lifetimes. Sometime before the Chinese began emigrating across the northern bridge and down this continent a Chinese chemist had invented *Sui* oil, meaning something like "Years Old." This wonderful substance preserved wood almost indefinitely. The only problem was that it caused the wood to be more flammable, but that was ignored generally. Some paints claimed to do the same, but the ravages of time showed that *Sui* oil was by far the better preservative. An old legend had it that the chemist got his formula from the Monitors. Of course, nobody believed it.

Strange sights, sounds, and smells assaulted me.

Sun had suggested that I go to a palmist. His son, Sun Tsu Liu, accompanied me to an old man, the premier palmist around. I thought he would simply read my hand and spew forth a few platitudes, like maybe a number seventy-eight would fit a young Caucasian.

How wrong I was.

The old man sat in a corner of the marketplace, didn't even have his own stall. His hair was almost gone and I guessed he was blind in one eye. Yet the surging crowds gave him a wide berth as they passed. A tin bowl of rice rested between his legs.

Sun Tsu Liu bowed to him formally and squatted in front of him. He spoke with him softly, so that I could not hear. Then Tsu Liu passed him several watermarks and motioned me to sit in front of the old man. Sun withdrew.

The old man grasped my hand and stared at it. Wrist, palm, and knuckles were scrutinized. Then he dropped the hand and stared at my face. Tsu Liu had told me that not only does a palmist read hands, but the customer's destiny is read in his face. Eyes, nose, jawline, all had their own significance.

"Daystar," muttered the old man. His face chilled and his good eye rolled.

I nodded.

He gazed at me and said not another word. Finally, he motioned Sun Tsu Liu back over. He handed the watermarks back to Sun and turned away.

Sun made some query and was answered quickly.

Sun grasped my arm and dragged me away.

"What was that all about?" I asked, somewhat miffed by the apparent rejection.

"He refused to say. He cannot trust himself to foretell properly, but he *was* scared by what he saw. He was much troubled."

I shrugged this off as an old man's whim. But when I glanced back, he had rolled up his mat and was leaving.

Sun Tsu Liu told his father about it and Sun Yen Chang and the Prof discussed this strange occurrence.

On other unaccompanied walks, I noted that the Sacramento River water supply from the mountains was drying up. It was so messy that it was hardly usable anyway. Of the many ground water sources I scouted, most I found were not of sufficient productivity to support the city for much longer. I estimated that in a very few years Sacramento would face catastrophe if new sources were not identified and brought into operation.

I told the Professor about this and it settled him.

"Sacramento is doomed anyway," he replied. "The New Christians have a stranglehold here and will drive the city to ruins before their water dries up." He paused and looked at the Oriental gardens around us. Sun's store was the front portion of an old Mexican-style hacienda, with a center court and apartments around it, all built of adobe and some lumber. The center of the court had its own well, spouting water through figurines in the middle of a pool. They consumed their own water here and were not dependent on the city system.

"Yet," he continued, "there are good people here and I'd hate to see them suffer from the lack of foresight that the New Christian leaders seem to have. Do you think you could find an alternate source for them?"

"Sure. If it's there."

"Please do so."

I nodded, put a pack together, and left. Jubal was restless, so I took him along, riding on my shoulder. I arranged the pack so that it would counterbalance his scant weight.

For several days I scouted the area in a twenty-mile radius around Sacramento. Near a place called Folsom my senses told me there was a vast underground supply. I wandered around this area trying to teach Jubal how to find water and verifying my search. Jubal didn't learn well but he tried.

Satisfied with the results, I returned late one night. I found the Prof and Sun Yen Chang arguing heatedly. They fell silent when I came up.

Respectfully, they greeted me. I nodded to the Prof. He turned to Yen Chang.

"As I said, it is getting dangerous here for me and we will soon take our leave. But I wish to make a proposition to you."

"Certainly, my friend. I have done business with you before and am reminded that when I do so, my profits are reduced. But there most certainly are profits."

The Prof smiled at the compliment. He seemed to be saying that Sun had paid him an honor. "Are you aware of Sacramento's water policy and how long the quantity is supposed to last?"

"Surely. As we discussed, the government is withholding much bad news. The population would not be so happy with the Church were it known that the New Christians were lying about the water supply. In my business, it pays to have such information."

"How much is there?" the Prof asked me.

"Enough. If used right. Years' worth."

Sun perked up at the conversation even though he didn't know what we were talking about.

"Suppose," started the Professor slowly, "that we could show you a new, long-term source?"

"It would be worth many water credits and perhaps make rich men of those who controlled it."

"And powerful men," the Prof amended.

I knew the way his mind operated now. He saw the possibility of a wedge driven right through the heart of the New Christian Church.

Sun agreed with a spate of Chinese too fast for me to follow, but I did hear the words "New Christian" several times.

"Fifty percent finder's fee, after costs have been met," said the Prof.

Sun reflected shock. "But it is not done this way."

"I am thinking of the future."

"The common procedure is to pay the finder's fee, a flat sum, upon verification," Sun shouted.

"Tell Jubal to pack the wagon, son. We're leaving. There's an old Chinese proverb to the effect that it is unwise to do business with a friend."

Sun protested some more, but a bargain was struck. Thirty

percent after the plant was in operation for two years. Thirty percent of the profits was a great amount of money.

Sun smiled. "I have your word?"

The Prof nodded.

"It will take many years to develop. I cannot foresee a profit for at least five years, depending on the location."

"That's fine," said the Prof. "Have the documents ready first thing tomorrow, for I do not know how long it will be safe for us to remain. And also, put them in the name of my son."

I was surprised at this.

But he said, "Son, you found it. And somehow I don't think I will be alive to see it through. Humor me."

In the morning, I traded the location for the water to Sun's son, Tsu Liu, for an impressive document written in Chinese script. The Professor verified that all the terms were met and we all shook hands.

"It's Sunday," said the Prof. "And I would like to attend a New Christian Church service. Then we will take our leave on the morrow."

"Do you think it's safe for you to do so?" Sun asked, worry etching into his face.

"It's broad daylight and I don't think they'd try anything. Besides, they don't know I'm here."

"Don't be too sure. There are spies everywhere. Your wagon is conspicuous. And you who almost cannot walk are well known to the priesthood. They knew you are here." Sun shook his head in obvious disagreement.

"Nonetheless, I wish it. My son will take me." His mind was made up, and when the Prof had made up his mind, it couldn't be changed.

So I put him in a borrowed rickshaw and towed him to the cathedral, some five miles distant from the Chinese section.

The seat of the New Christian Church was in an immense building, of block construction. Inside, the mammoth open space was visually interrupted by scaffolding built here and there, long rows of wooden pews, and someone in time past had constructed wooden interior walls. Oil lamps and candles were copiously placed about to provide sufficient lighting.

Carrying the Professor inside, I was struck by his lightness. Either he'd been losing weight recently or I had grown stronger. Perhaps it was a combination of both.

Acolytes directed us to a seat near one of the walls. Other

people were filing in, and when the services started, I estimated there must have been a thousand people inside. I began to get claustrophobia and had to command my mind to relax.

Red-robed priests conducted the initial ceremonies, opening with prayers and chanting. I noted most of the New Christians were Caucasian. Very few were Chinese or Hispanic. Then the priests went on to routine matters such as announcements, calendar of events, and so on. Black-robed individuals came and went, these being upper-echelon staff members, a cut above priests.

Everyone was asked to bow his head and remain in silent prayer for the entry of the High Priest. The congregation complied, but neither the Prof nor I did. We watched avidly. Acolytes raised velvet curtains covering alcoves set back in the walls to reveal glass cages. Wriggling fireworms filled the cages.

A hidden choir chanted, "Comes the tamer of the fireworms, comes the tamer."

A man of average height emerged from behind some curtains on the pulpit and approached the speaking platform. He had exceptionally long hair and a beard. I didn't know his name, but I would have cause later to know it and remember his face.

Assistants pushed trolleys behind him, each with a glass cage containing more fireworms and oil lamps, coming to rest encircling the High Priest from the rear. His robing was a combination of red and black, with a wide blue sash.

He spoke softly at first, so that I almost couldn't make out his words. But his voice rose in pitch as he went along—a fantastic speaker. He exhorted his followers to damn the ungodly, to ignore attempts to return to technical life. Was not God angry with the pinnacle of technical achievement reached ages before, so angry that He caused the Holocaust? And more of the same.

Then he got off on blasphemers. "And there is one among us who has spread dissension and lies about us over the countryside."

I didn't hear any more as rough hands grasped the Prof from my side and lifted him over the back of the pew. How had I missed their presence? I must have been mesmerized by the High Priest's speaking ability.

They carried him down the aisle, jeers coming from the

worshipers, who were just now figuring out that the Prof was the blasphemer. I made to rise and a knife poked its way into my side. I was urged up and along the aisle behind those carrying the Professor.

"And another, too!" screamed the High Priest.

Hisses and catcalls followed my unwilling progress. We were halted in front of the semicircle of fireworms.

A thousand people were on their feet shouting for our deaths. Hell, I'd never been exposed to such goings on before and was overwhelmed. My brain started to race and I fought to control it. If ever there was need for a clear head, now was the time.

"What shall we do with them?" the High Priest screeched. We were both held firmly by many men, red- and black-robed. I couldn't move.

"Feed the fireworms, feed the fireworms." The chant of the crowd was automatic, as if this ritual had been accomplished numerous times before.

The Prof shouted at me over the din. I could barely make out his words. "Don't bother with me, son. Escape if you can." He didn't seem worried.

I wasn't ready for what followed.

"See how he bleeds," said the High Priest, and one of the black-robed men whipped out a long knife, jammed it into the Prof's midsection, and ripped it upward. The Professor's eyes bulged and blood leapt from his mouth. He was dead before I comprehended the extent of danger we were in.

They pitched his body into a tank of fireworms as large as our wagon. The top was quickly pulled back over it. The fireworms boiled inside and covered his body.

I was stunned, too stunned to move or speak.

Before I went berserk, I said my last sane statement for many months. "Throw me in live, Priest, and I will put on a great show."

"Live, he says! We have more mercy than that." He faced the crowd. "This one wishes to disregard our courtesy, and face the fireworms alive. Shall we grant his last wish?"

"Yes!" the crowd roared, as if one. The bloodlust was on them all, including those of the priesthood. I could sense a mass orgiastic pleasure pervading the atmosphere.

At the time, I didn't care to live or to die, but I wanted revenge for the Prof.

"Throw him in," said the High Priest to his assistants. I

took a long look at him; in case I got out of this, I wanted to remember him.

Roughly handled, I was lifted, the top was pulled aside, and I flew into the cage. I smiled grimly.

I landed on a mass of slimy bodies, poisonous bristles retracted, and I squirmed beneath them to give the appearance of a boiling mass.

Silence had fallen over the congregation and they watched as the fireworms covered me. It was as if all present held their breath simultaneously. I found a rock, almost a boulder, on the bottom of the cage, crouched, and smashed the glass. For a moment, no more; the whole place was more silent than before.

I stood and stepped out, fireworms wrapped around and over me. I held my arms straight up and then out from my shoulders to allow the fireworms on me to slither around my body.

"The wrath of Daystar will be upon you!"

Then I went berserk. I sent fireworms flying into the crowd in the front pews and at the gathered New Christian priests around me. I grasped a wooden bench and smashed open other glass cages nearby. Fireworms were literally boiling all over the place. Most of them attacked the priests and staff members of the New Christian Church as if they were cursed ones. Totally mad, I raged at them.

Not happy yet with the results of my handiwork, I picked up some of the oil lamps and smashed them against the wooden walls of the church. I flung into the crowd, which was now one panic-stricken, screaming mass of people. I knew, in my burning brain, that I had to do something to atone for the Prof's death.

So I burned their goddamn church down.

People were jammed at exits, screaming with fright, and fighting each other for a chance to live. The fireworms were making quick work of the priests up front. Most were down, and fireworms were striking at the rear fringes of the crowd. Flames started to crawl up the front walls, burning frescoes, religious paintings, furniture, and leaping from various curtains hung about the great hall. It would soon be an inferno, impossible to escape.

I saw one child trampled in the human stampede. Then, even while out of my mind, I felt some regret for what I had done. I could rationalize to myself that the New Christian

Church was a diabolical agency, but I knew that would do no good later when I recovered my senses and realized what I had done. Doubtless, many women and children, and even some men, were not at fault here. They were merely malleable clay with which the priesthood worked.

A small group of priests had gathered around the High Priest and hustled him off the stage to a side door covered by a velvet curtain. I still held a couple of smaller fireworms in my hands and lashed into them with full force. Bristles came out and I felt stings in my hands and arms. Fortunately, the poison did not affect me. Priests were falling like flies.

The High Priest scuttled through the doorway and I made to follow. But a burning tapestry fell and barred my way.

The whole place was now in flames. The crackle of the ever-expanding fire drowned out the screams of those left inside. A massive pile of people at the doors prevented those behind them from escaping.

I ran to the nearest exit, flailing my fireworms like a pair of ten-foot whips, and cleared a path. A small female child was being stomped by adults, so I roughly kicked her before me, rolling her out the doorway. I left a path of destruction and dead in my wake. Smoke fumes stung my eyes and it was difficult to see until I reached a few yards out into the street. People were milling around, wailing. Crowds had drawn from nearby, perhaps some awaiting the next services. They drew back when I emerged from the smoke wielding my fireworms. I must have looked like a devil from hell, killing indiscriminately. They backed away, clearing a space for me. I stopped and panted, facing them defiantly.

Fortunately, conditions dictated that water was worth more than churches and other buildings, so no one attempted to put out the fire. That's one of the hazards of a dry ecology.

Some escaped priests pointed at me and shouted to the crowd. I caught the words, "Daystar," "devil," "blasphemer," and "murderer."

Though some were still in a state of panic and could not control themselves, others, priests included, still retained their sanity. They swelled toward me, a mass of humanity, all of one mind: to kill me.

I still didn't care about my final fate. Thus, I lit into them with my bloody fireworms. Windmilling my arms, I cut through the mass and found myself on the main thoroughfare. People were streaming from all over, gathering to watch the death of a great edifice.

A knife slashed my hip from behind, and I turned and dealt with that priest; a quick flip of the wrist sufficed.

The angry mob surged toward me again and I flung the two fireworms into their faces. I turned and raced off down the road, knocking aside people as I ran. Others stared at me with no comprehension. I had blood all over me; my shirt was singed and smoldering. There must have been the look of death on my face, for people leaped aside to be out of my way.

Soon, I was running unencumbered freely on the cobblestones. Glancing over my shoulder, I saw that I had company. A large group had taken out after me and gathered other volunteers as they ran. Soon the street behind me was full of the chasing mob. A great pall of smoke overhung the scene.

Still in the berserker rage, I turned on the speed. My normal running rate was about nine miles an hour, in a ground-eating lope. When I wanted to go faster, I could maintain a twelve-mile-per-hour pace, as measured by the Prof. Now I estimated subconsciously that I might be traveling a pace that would carry me some fifteen miles in an hour.

Another glance shot over my shoulder showed me that the mob had fallen far behind. I slowed so as not to waste all my energy. To further discourage immediate pursuit, I dodged through side roads and through several alleyways. I hoped that this would give me enough time. I came out upon another thoroughfare and slowed to a walk so as to not catch anyone's attention. But with the blood, soot, and wild look about me, this tactic failed, although those passersby did not know what I had done. I trotted off again, working my way toward the only sanctuary I knew: Sun Yen Chang's home and business.

Shortly, I reached it. Barging through the doorway, I found Sun being briefed by an out-of-breath Chinese. He shouted a spate of orders at some of his helpers and turned to me. Several of the others ran out.

"Quickly. You must leave. They know you came from here. You have no time to dally."

"But the Professor . . ." I stammered.

"He's dead, and you cannot help him now. Your life is in danger of the utmost, and you are endangering us, too." He gestured. "Out back, my son is filling your backpack with food. I will keep your oxen and other goods and put them in your account, collectible later. You must go now."

I didn't know what to do. My whole world had gone up in smoke. I was hunted. My mind still raced, but I could understand what was going on.

The noise of the approaching mob echoed in the confines of the street outside.

"But what about you?" I asked. "Will you not have to pay?"

"No. I am powerful. See?" He indicated a growing crowd of Chinese gathering outside. "They will not dare challenge me now. But I will have to allow them to search. They cannot harm me if you are gone. You must hurry!"

He turned and scurried out a back door. His son, Tsu Liu, was stuffing my backpack with provisions from the wagon. I hastily threw in a change of clothes. The monkeys were about, jumping around with excitement. They knew something was amiss. Jubal clutched at my pants leg in sympathetic fear. Sun and I ran out of the compound, followed by an unlikely conglomeration of Chinese, children, and monkeys.

Sun pointed in a southerly direction. "There's your best way to elude them. It leads directly into the wilderness south of the city." He grasped my hand and pumped it.

Jubal had climbed my shoulder and I was of a mind to take him with me, a reminder of days and times past.

I nodded to Sun and ran off. Other Chinese were coming out of the woodwork, it seemed, and the small street was packed full of them behind me. They were jamming the local area with their bodies. Pursuers would be hard pressed to move, much less follow. A screech came from behind and Jubal twisted my ear. I looked back to see a monkey running after us, falling behind from my swiftness. It was Jubal's mate, Henrietta.

I stopped and waited for her. More Chinese flowed past me and as Henrietta climbed on my other shoulder, I reflected that the New Christians had better step softly, else they'd be overwhelmed by Chinese. Perhaps I started something. From the passing faces, I saw that there was an ethnic solidarity about the Chinese, and a determination. Hell, anything was better than New Christian rule. I threaded through them, a bloody, burned Caucasian, with a monkey astride each shoulder. My hip still bled through the rent in my clothing.

As the way cleared, I ran again, having to adjust my stride

to counterbalance the strange weight of two monkeys on my shoulders. We must have made quite a sight.

Running past startled bystanders, I eventually emerged from the Chinese section. Following Sun's suggestion, I headed south. Presently, habitation thinned out and we were on a major north-south thoroughfare. I knew there would still be pursuit so I kept up a fast pace. We would not be hard to recognize, and tales of the strange man with two monkeys would be rampant through that part of town.

I settled into a step that would cover eight miles in an hour and ran for the sheer pleasure. The more I ran, the less my brain raced, and soon I was back in complete control of myself.

But I had not run fast enough. For behind me appeared several riders, each goading his horse or camel to its utmost. On a short-distance run I could not lose them. But I could maintain a faster pace than riding animals for longer distances. Thus ensued a great race: two monkeys and I speeding along ahead of a mob on horse and camelback.

I had a sufficient headstart to overcome their initial spurt of speed and the race settled down into a battle of endurance. They loped along behind me, hurrying too much, not knowing of my long-distance running abilities. I kept pace with the leaders, maybe a half mile in front. They whipped their mounts to catch me and I increased my speed a little. The pumping blood through my head cooled me down and aided in returning me from the madness. I virtually flew along the roadway. Soon, their shouts diminished, and they fell behind, mounts laboring from the long race. They were riding their horses to death. Camels were smart enough to quit on their own despite the whipping sticks.

Presently, I, too, slowed down, afraid that I'd burn myself out, though I continued to run at a good pace, leaving pursuit well behind me. Eventually, I lost them or they gave up, fearing the wilderness. I kept running, glorying in the mental dampening effect of it.

I vowed to return one day and assure the instant demise of the New Christian High Priest. I realized I did not even know his name. But I'd find him.

I told Jubal and Henrietta that the Professor was dead and that we were on our own. They seemed to understand. My mood went black with sorrow. The Prof had returned me, from what I knew not, but he had made a human of me. The

Prof's death seemed to offset the other deaths I'd caused, and I cast those worries aside. Except for Miguel, I'd never taken a human life, and hadn't intended to do so. But it seemed probable that I'd accounted for a couple of hundred at least.

Damn! I'd told them my name, too. The legend of Daystar would take a new turn, and not a good one. Once the priests got the word out to the rest of the country, my name wouldn't be worth a dead fireworm. At the time, I didn't know that I would polarize populations for and against that church. It would cause me much anguish in years to come.

As soon as I judged I was far enough away from Sacramento, I took an easterly trail and headed for the mountains.

I had some idea of becoming a hermit. I'd done without human contact before and could damn well do without it now. I'd joined the human race, albeit on my own terms, for awhile, and found it lacking. Now I was forsaking my heritage again.

CHAPTER SEVEN

I headed for the mountains and for weeks worked my way south. I made a poultice of herbs and moss for my hip wound and soon it healed.

Perhaps I have given a wrong impression. Most of what happened to me occurred in arid zones, where life was eked out from the dry land and water was scarce. These locations lay mainly on the circumference of the great wasteland that was the center of the continent. And some dry areas lay outside what we desert rats called Centralia, too. Of necessity, population grew around abundant water sources, the most precious resource, and consequently water became a medium of exchange. I had water credits issued to me by several political strongholds. These were transferable only to those places that reciprocated. Yet, nearly all towns honored water credits from major cities, such as San Diego.

In the wilds, there was some greenery, too, unencumbered by people. There had to be to maintain the carbon-dioxide-oxygen cycle. At any rate, some of these areas were unpopulated because of distance from commerce routes, inaccessibility due to terrain, and nonproductivity of the soil. It was in such an area that I now traveled, swinging south, following a series of mountain ranges, which sometimes enveloped cultivated valleys. I stayed clear of habitation, wishing to be alone.

In the months that followed, I infrequently came down from the chilled mountains to isolated villages to trade for food. I told no one my name, but I couldn't be mistaken, for a wild-eyed young man with two monkeys perched on his shoulders is not unremarkable. Yet, I found no problem dealing with the people.

I eventually came to a place with great sequoia trees and wandered through the magnificent forest for days on end. I had to make camp for a week or more as Henrietta gave birth to a young son. And the monkeys found this place acceptable, too, as there were plenty of nuts and grubs in the undergrowth to satisfy their hunger. A tongue-moistened stick plunged in a mound brought out termites and larvae, prime food for the monkeys.

Months had passed, and even though I was never one for social contact, loneliness had settled heavily on me. I determined to move on.

But the monkeys, Jubal, Henrietta, and son refused to join me. I stormed off against their constant yammering. Two days later I returned and set up camp in the same location. I waited for them to find me. I saw them flitting through the trees, but they never came close again. Finally, I gave up and started out again, feeling lonelier than ever.

I skirted the ruins of the Angels area, swinging wide into the wasteland, avoiding contact with the bands of cutthroats that thrived there. A minor water find sold to a drying-up village gave me a bunch of San Diego water credits, so I decided to go to San Diego and spend my money.

I came into San Diego from the east, following the trail. To stop that night I had to find water, so I wandered a few miles along the east ridge, noting that foliage seemed to be unsupported by visible water. It couldn't rain, could it? Not much anyway, on this side of the mountains. Eventually, I located the source, an underground river, springing from somewhere deep inside the mountains. I found a place where I could dig and the sand filled with the water. I drank well that night. Perhaps I would be able to bargain this water to the officials in San Diego, much the same as the Professor had done in Sacramento.

The first thing I did when I reached the city was to hire a barber, bath included. I didn't shave much yet, but he scraped the incipient bristles off without any fanfare.

Then I looked up the Major. He worked in a great building, and his minions wouldn't allow me in to see him. Finally, I had to confide in an aide. I asked him if he'd heard of water dowsers, and he allowed as how he had. I told him that I'd found some water, but wouldn't deal with anyone but

Hizzoner. There were no Chinese here then, and I felt that I'd better do business with the officials, since San Diego enjoyed a spotless reputation with its hydrogen plant and seawater desalinization project. Additionally, San Diego was a well-managed city, that I could see from simply walking through it. I knew that the government needed to expand the arable land to maintain the population. So it was a simple matter of negotiating with the Mayor. I'd heard that San Diego was not in bed with the New Christians, as were many other parts of the country, so that added to my confidence in its elders.

The aide said that they'd been propositioned by desert rats before, and it wasn't worth their time,

Finally, I asked, "Have you heard from Newsbringers of a diviner called Daystar?"

I had his attention immediately.

"Yes, but we heard that he was dead."

"Wrong."

The Mayor threatened that I'd better not be misrepresenting myself, since one so young couldn't be Daystar. Quite frankly, he didn't believe me.

So I struck a deal, his signature for a great amount of water credit with the San Diego authority if the find proved to be as vast as I claimed. He dispatched a team and I settled down to investigate San Diego. Later, the find was verified and I was wealthy and much feted.

I'd only seen the ocean briefly before and it fascinated me. Soon I was spending all day on the rocks at the edge of the sea. I learned to swim, taking to it naturally. Days passed and I swam more and more. I think I liked it because it was wet. Off a point overhung with cliffs, I met my first dolphin. A pack of them swarmed around me, squeaking eerily. I knew they were friendly, as I felt their auras. My emotional reading ability was increasing in leaps and bounds, perhaps because of exposure to the dolphins. I never could communicate with them, but we got along. My old revulsion to contact didn't seem to bother me here; the dolphins' graceful motions were definitely nonhuman, and I related to them.

One day, I was paddling around with a group of dolphins about a half mile out from the cliffs, our normal meeting place. I sensed that the dolphins were becoming upset. I searched for the answer. I'd heard of sharks, but had never seen one, and didn't see one now. A movement caught the corner of my eye, and I spied a group of figures at the lip of the cliff. Then two of them tossed something like a bundle into the air. It fell into the sea below them with a splash. They turned and left.

The dolphins were quite agitated now. They raced to the foot of the cliff leaving me all alone. More out of curiosity, I followed. One dolphin braved the waves smashing against the cliff face and retrieved the bundle. It turned out to be a human girl. The dolphin dragged the pitiful thing to me. She spewed water and coughed. Obviously, she couldn't swim, so I towed her ashore.

I dragged her up on the sand and watched her vomit seawater. The dolphins watched from the shallows and soon left.

There was something about this girl. She appeared to be five or six years younger than I was. When she had recovered, I tried to ask her what had happened.

Then she drew up within herself and rocked back and forth. I had gone through the same thing, and was still prone to do it occasionally. I felt electric waves emanate from her, telling me that her brain raced and she'd shut out reality.

I had found Shadow.

CHAPTER EIGHT

There was no doubt that Shadow had been cast out. Society had thrown her to the seas much as I had been abandoned in the desert.

My problem now was what to do with her. That she would be recalcitrant was an understatement. If she was in the same shape that I was, then she would be a bundle of trouble, anxiety omnipresent in every action.

During the time I had waited for the water source to be verified, I had snooped around, visiting local Storytellers and Librarians. The former had nothing to add to my store of knowledge concerning my different mental conditions. Nor did the Librarians—artistic meant simply creative skill in some form of endeavor. Of course, I didn't just walk in and tell them my history and problems. I approached them in an oblique fashion. I wasn't yet ready to confide in anyone. My resolve to chase down my heritage was hardening. El Paso loomed large in my hazy preplanning. Maybe not soon, but eventually, I'd have to go there.

There I sat, naked and shivering on the beach, watching this kid rock back and forth, totally ignoring me. I realized that I wasn't anywhere near as capable as the Prof. He had had a lifetime of experience, learning, and knowledge. Besides, he had had more than his quota of patience. I doubted that I had the ability to care for and bring up a homeless waif. Was I not a wanderer? Hell, I'd not even followed up on my Storytelling apprenticeship, and my memory of the long, convoluted histories was atrophying by disuse.

With no thought of what to do next, I quickly dressed and sat next to her, careful not to touch her.

Eventually, she came out of her trauma and looked at me. Violet sparkles peered from underneath dark brows. Her gaze was vacant, unconcerned for the world around her. It came to me that since she was many years older than I when she had been cast out, she might not have the depth of the problem that I'd had. But those eyes. They committed me to salvage her. I was in the neighborhood of sixteen or seventeen years old, and she might have been ten, although her emaciated condition could have misguided my guess. Additionally, because of my blotted memory, I knew not how old I was, either. I'd not yet begun looking at girls in the light of amour. But her eyes bonded me to her, as if we were the only two people left on earth.

What the hell. I acknowledged that I was lonely. The Prof had provided more company than I wanted to admit. Maybe, just maybe, I could bring her back to human. She'd already made it ten or eleven years, so perhaps she wouldn't be as difficult as I was. Maybe even an easier case.

I offered her a food cake from my pocket and she drew back. Evidently, curiosity, such as I'd encountered, accounted for her initial interest. After being tossed off a cliff, one expects to wake up dead, so to speak, and when fate is thwarted, it merits investigation.

She was naked as a monkey, wet, and shaking from the chilling evening sea breeze. Disheveled, miserable, and depressed would describe Shadow then.

I took off my heavy shirt and draped it over her shoulders. She didn't flinch, nor did she acknowledge the gesture. Oh, well, I knew it wouldn't be easy.

Since this isolated beach was some miles from my habitation, driftwood hadn't been scavenged recently. I gathered some and built a fire. Knowing she wouldn't move to it, I constructed it close to her position.

I yearned for some snake soup, which the Chinese claim warms your blood in the winter.

Then came decision time. Should I leave her and depart for supplies and clothing? Or should I remain and watch over her? I didn't want her gone when I returned. I sat and thought it out. She hadn't moved, hadn't touched food. I retrieved my pack, drank some water from a bladder, and set it next to her. She didn't touch that either.

"It wouldn't hurt if you drank some water."

No response. Only eyes.

"Look, you've got to sustain yourself."

Eyes losing vitality.

"I know how you feel."

Eyes said get lost, buster, nobody knows how I feel.

At least I got a rise out of her that time. Try again, strike while the iron is hot, whatever that means.

"I was the same as you, once." Don't admit you're still that way.

Eyes had gone from curious to vital; now they were merely alive.

"Truly, I didn't say a word for years."

Eyes totally uninterested now.

I was desperate, patience, which I never had, dying like the fire.

"You can't deny you feel I'm like you. I can sense your emotions."

Eyes closing.

"Shit." I quit.

Rummaging around in the pack, I came up with my tattered blanket. I was getting cold myself, but I threw it over her in disgust. She shrugged it off.

Mad now, I picked it up and wrapped it around me. She was staring into the fire, totally ignoring me, fascinated by the twinkle of flames.

What a saint the Professor was, I realized.

We stayed that way for a couple of hours. Presently, I realized she was asleep, dozing in the upright position. The events of the day must have been too much for her. I took the blanket and laid it at her side, gently pushed her over on it, and rolled the flap about her. She didn't react, but her eyes opened and she remained frozen with her knees tucked into her chest. Eventually, the warmth got to her and she dropped off again.

I built the fire up, enough to last several hours. Then I took off out of there. I could feel something boring into my back but refused to look.

I ran like hell, hoping that I could find a shop open at this hour. A half-hour's running got me into town and the market district. I must have been a sight on the road into the city, half-naked and running as if for my life.

My pockets held a voucher for a large amount of water

credit drawn on the San Diego water authority, so I had sufficient funds for whatever I wanted.

A few shops and stalls were still doing business. I bought another backpack rather than waste time making one. Two new blankets would help, too. I didn't know any of her sizes, so I bought traveling clothes, a heavy shirt and jeans, describing her to the shopkeeper. Finally, we came up with what seemed to be a close fit. I added a pair of moccasins much like mine. I'd found them easier to run in than the heavy boots I started with. And journeying toughens your feet, too. They were laced with thongs so they could be modified to fit different sizes. Underclothing was difficult, as I never had occasion to bother with such until now. On a whim, I also purchased a bright scarf and a few ribbons for her hair.

At another store, I bought an additional water bladder and more rations, enough to last us a couple of months. It was a heavy load, and we'd have to split it eventually. For an arm and a leg, I bought some real beef jerky, something to entice her with, if she chose not to cooperate.

When I arrived back at the beach, the fire was down considerably, and she had apparently not moved. But the food cake was gone and the bladder was lighter. This small encouragement made me think that I'd made the right decision.

I didn't know it at the time, but this was almost my first self-initiated attempt at being human. I'd never done anything for anybody else in my life, unless it benefitted me directly. Except for the Prof, of course; he was different. Maybe this was some sort of subconscious therapy. It certainly took my mind off my problems and gave me something to focus on.

We stayed on the beach for a week. I swam a lot with the dolphins, but she wouldn't come in the ocean. She'd simply walk the beach, withdrawn. But she did come to eat regularly. The sun browned her, and she began to fill out. She didn't approach my sunburned walnut color, but I could tell that regular high-protein and vitamin food, sunshine, and freedom were filling her out. Her eyes didn't have that totally wild look all the time now. She never uttered a word.

I'd wanted to leave immediately, concerned lest someone come by who knew her and took objection to her current status: alive. But I thought it better to remain as long as we could to cement her reliance on me. Actually, I was afraid that she wouldn't come with me.

She wore the scarf all the time. It was probably the only nonfunctional thing she'd ever had. She didn't help around the camp, but there was little work and I could handle it all. She did keep meticulously clean, that is, after I tossed her in the ocean and scrubbed her with expensive tallow soap. And to keep up my appearance, too, I started shaving. My beard didn't grow at any great rate in those days, and once or twice a week was sufficient. Anyway, I had to buy a razor. I couldn't keep my knife sharp enough to shave with, so I splurged and bought a straight razor. The shopkeeper, whom I'd done business with, liked me. He recognized me as the one who'd sold the city the water rights a few weeks earlier and was of a mind that I was a celebrity. He threw in a small pouch on a leather thong and showed me how to hang it around my neck, pouch hanging just below the back of my neck with the razor inside. It would serve as a hidden weapon, he assured me. Little did I know how valuable it would turn out to be.

I made her a necklace out of bright seashells we found on the beach, running a thong through them. She paraded around for quite awhile, showing off the necklace, poor though the effort was, to herself. She'd sit and fondle it for hours.

She never went into the city with me, but seemed content to stay on the beach forever. From my own experience, I knew that a change in routine would upset her; so I determined to remain as long as possible.

One day I had gone a few miles north to gather wood, as we'd used up all the driftwood within easy distance of our camp. An ominous feeling overcame me: in my mind I felt something was wrong. I ran back to camp.

When I ran up, three men had her pinned down on the beach and were trying to rape her. They'd ripped up her shirt and were tearing off her jeans. And she was only ten years old. God, what perversion.

I was so goddamn mad, I didn't even notice what they looked like. As usual, I had no fear of them. I even liked the danger.

Unfortunately for me, there were no fireworms to save us here on the beach. So I merely charged into them silently, fury burning at my insides. She had withdrawn into herself at their onslaught and was curled up, stiff as a fossil.

I bowled two of them over and scrambled up. This took

their attention from her, and they came for me. I grasped a good length of wood from the scattered firewood I'd dropped and faced them.

"It's just another kid," said one.

"Kill him," said another.

They advanced on me. I wanted to shout to the girl to run, but I couldn't. The tension was causing me to retreat into my mind, just as she had. I fought to maintain consciousness. Action would help clear the fog.

One thing I learned in the Sacramento mess was that there is no substitute for offense. Defense doesn't win any battles, although you do live to fight another day. So I laid about me with the log and one went down. The other tackled me with a leap. He outweighed me enormously and his fetid breath made me gag.

This one held me down and I had only one free arm.

Number three came up to help. "This kid looks like the one they call Daystar," he observed.

"I don't care. Kill him."

Number three jumped for my face with both boots and I managed to roll aside, causing all three of us to end up in a tangle of arms and legs on the sand. Surprisingly, I came up with the razor in my hand, slashing right and left. After a little practice, I got the hang of it and stopped swinging indiscriminately. There was blood all over; the two were screaming, great ribbons of red over their bodies. So I cut their throats to end all the noise. In the heat of action, life meant little to me.

The one I'd swatted with the driftwood watched in horror, leaped up, and ran off down the beach.

I started to run after him, knowing that I'd overtake him easily, when the carnage and the gore caught up with me. I had to stop and vomit, over and over, until nothing but green bile dribbled down my chin. I fell to the beach on my hands and knees and blacked out, hands over my head, trying to burrow into the sand.

When I came to, I was quite weak, mad at humanity. All I wanted was to be left alone, but people kept interfering.

I looked around and there was the girl, sitting next to me, watching, playing with her necklace. It was the first time I'd withdrawn in her presence, and perhaps the first time she'd witnessed anyone else in her predicament. Maybe this was what sealed our relationship.

Trying to compose myself, I was rough on her, ignoring her at the time of our first understanding. I plunged into the ocean to remove the blood from my body and clothes.

When I came out, she'd made as much repair to her clothing as possible, and was standing, staring at the bodies. Flies had gathered, and the smell was grotesque, but not as bad as that of the burning bodies in the New Christian Church.

I thought about dumping them in the ocean, but decided not to. The hell with it. Then the thought struck me that one of them had gotten away. He might have friends and bring them back.

Quickly, I started packing. She watched me curiously.

"We've got to get out of here, girl, whatever your name is. He might bring reinforcements."

I made two packs, gave myself most of the weight, tossed her the light one, and stepped out. She didn't follow.

"Look, damn it, it ain't safe to stay here." I knew the change in routine would result in acute anxiety for her, but we had to leave.

I started out again. She still didn't seem of a mind to accompany me. I shrugged, remembering what trouble I gave the Professor. "And don't forget your pack," I said savagely over my shoulder. I swore bitterly at myself, seeing the hurt in her eyes.

I didn't check for a mile, but I felt her behind me, somewhere not too close. I was the only familiar thing she had now, and I was pretty sure she'd cling to me.

When I judged we were far enough from the city, I turned east, no goal in mind, just to get away from there.

After several hours, it became apparent that the girl wasn't as fast as I was, and I had to slow my pace. She still walked behind me, lugging her pack. I was mad at the world then, so I didn't worry about her feelings. We made decent time anyway. There was over an hour of traveling time left in the day, but the girl was limping now, unaccustomed to the trail. So I stopped and made camp.

I worried some then. We were in fireworm country, and I feared for her safety. Since she was a city girl, I hoped someone had taught her to have a healthy respect for fireworms.

She slumped to the ground when she reached the hollow. I was busy setting up camp. She barely ate that night and fell asleep with a block of kelp and seaweed concentrate in her hand.

The next day was more of the same. I thought about heading north to visit Jubal and Henrietta, but discarded that idea. I needed to make a clean break from the past.

We continued eastward, skirting the desert. After a week she conquered blisters, chafing, and the sun, and swung along at my side. When she went catatonic or whatever, I stopped and waited. Then we'd take up the trail again. Water wasn't plentiful, but I found enough to keep us going.

I started talking to her as the Professor had to me. I told her of him, bragging of my acquaintance. She seemed most interested when I told a story about the monkeys and how they'd fouled something up or played in their spare time. It was hard for me to admit, but I told her of growing up with the Prof, and of how, when the urge to withdraw came over me, I'd run to burn myself out.

That must have impressed her, for the next day, she just started running, right in the middle of one of my stories. Not wanting her to forge the trail alone, I ran with her, keeping up easily. But she ran harder, and then I knew that she had to be alone, so I dropped back a hundred yards or so and followed her. The first time, she didn't run very far, but in a few years, she got to where she could outrun me. I cautioned her to stay within sight.

The exercise and right diet was immediately effective, because it seemed that she ate more, was no longer thin to excessiveness, and so help me, I could almost watch her grow. I had to remind myself that she was still very young, five or six years younger than I, but it was difficult. Since she didn't talk, she couldn't exhibit many childlike mannerisms. Oh, she pouted when she was unhappy and refused to do her share of the work, but I happily ignored her.

I found myself talking more and more, almost emulating the Professor too much, relating his stories, using his inflections, taking on some of his traits. I'd never talked so much in my whole life. I tried to explain this to the girl, but she didn't react. At least it might have given her some hope for her own future.

We found that we were mentally linked one day while skirting Fenix. I'd caught glimmerings of emotions from her when they were strong, but I couldn't decipher them. I'd guessed that she read me, too, but we hadn't then tried to communicate that way. I'd brushed off the San Diego incident as coincidence.

The girl had run ahead, trying to stave off another withdrawal attack, and since she had learned to handle herself well, I didn't worry about it. I stopped to relieve myself, certain that I could catch her anytime.

I'd just readjusted my pack when I felt a blinding pain in my head. It was like a wordless scream, but my ears weren't the receptors. I didn't understand, but I knew something was wrong.

I dropped my pack and sprinted ahead. Rounding a great rock outcropping, I skidded to a stop. The girl was standing, petrified, in the center of the trail, and a couple of medium-sized fireworms were advancing on her from two sides. Other heads popped up around her. The emotion she broadcast jarred me right out of my moccasins. My brain ached with the immediacy of her terror. I jumped to her and she grabbed me as if she were drowning.

The fireworms stopped at my appearance. I lifted her and ran out of there. But I had noticed a curious indecision about the fireworms. There had not been the killing fury that I'd seen previously. I hoped that the girl would be as immune as I was, but somehow I didn't think she was.

She regained her senses and struggled to get me to let her loose.

We continued our journey across the land, heading south into Old Mexico. Conditions were better there, outside the desert areas. Mexican technology hadn't caused the pollution and degradation of the water supply as had that of the land to the north. Even so, vast overpopulation and the Holocaust of ages past had pretty well trimmed the fat off the land and it hadn't quite recovered yet. I improved my Spanish and the girl and I saw many new places.

We worked our way back up north after a couple of years, my eventual goal being El Paso. But the girl's presence softened some of the drive in me and I didn't think finding my heritage so important then. I was a young man, not particularly fond of people, with no responsibilities.

Yet I found a growing urge, almost as if destiny were calling.

I taught the girl how to find water, but she didn't have the knack for it that I did. She learned the tricks of the game, like what terrain formations, flora and fauna, insect life, and so on would be harbingers of water. That put her even with the other desert rats, but only I had the internal mechanism for locating the source precisely and estimating the flow, quantity, and quality.

We generally traded in small towns, getting more provisions, renewing our clothing, and me Newsbringing. With that and selling water, we made out all right. Sometimes we carried mail between places, after we'd established a good reputation.

Then we came to Hermosillo.

After completing our business, we wandered about this particular town, eating tortillas with jalapeño sauce. Beat the hell out of our normal fare of concentrates. The girl came into this town with me. Sometimes she waited outside the larger towns, afraid of people.

We stopped at a fruit vendor's for some watermelon, an excruciating delicacy when you could find it. But I forked over the payment, splurging, since the girl was with me. She ate hesitantly at first, then with great bites, juice running down her chin, spitting seeds in a nearby bucket. She gorged herself.

The vendor, a cute young thing that I would have spent more time getting to know had not the girl been present, smiled at me.

"She eats like she has never tasted watermelon before, no?"

"I don't think she has," I said.

The girl looked up as we spoke, then went back to eating.

"I have seen you walk about the square this afternoon. She is like a *sombra,* that girl, to you."

I nodded. *Sombra,* the way she used it, could have meant shadow or spirit. I thought the latter more appropriate, but the señorita said, "*Sombra,* yes, like your shadow."

Well, the girl had yet to say the first word to me, so I didn't even know her name. With our relationship, it hadn't been necessary to use names.

After that, I called her Sombra, which she didn't like. But when I called her Shadow, she sort of glowed lukewarm, so that's how she came to be Shadow.

CHAPTER NINE

We'd roamed thousands of miles since, covering territory and years. Shadow seemed to grow like a weed, slowly overcoming her handicaps. The legend of Daystar and Shadow grew to where we were well known. Perhaps that fact led to our undoing.

We were on the water contract search for San Antonio in the Alamo Aridity when they captured Shadow.

The Mother fireworm ate me and the next thing I knew, after hearing Shadow call my name, was that I was sitting naked in the desert. Again.

But this time I remembered. I knew what had happened before the Professor had found me. My wounds were healed and I felt in the peak of physical and mental condition, although I still didn't know what had happened to me subsequent to ingestion by the Mother fireworms.

Then I was down again, realizing Shadow was gone. My fingers scratched my face and encountered a few months' growth of beard. Damn!

The last time a Mother ate me, it lasted six, seven, maybe eight years. But my memory of the years the first time, and the months the second time, refused to come. What had occurred to me during those absences?

Off in the distance, I spied the lone mesquite. I made my way there, hoping against hope to find evidence of Shadow. Three men, at least one with a laser, had cornered us. I'd been wounded, severely, and Shadow had attacked them with only her knife. What had become of her? Of them? Had the fireworms gotten them all? One thing was certain. I had a lot more questions than answers. Trudging barefoot through the sand, I experimentally cast out, mentally searching for some sign of her. Whatever wavelength we communicated on was vacant.

On the sand just before the hardpan and the tree, I found bones. Two large skulls and a rib cage lay bleached and half buried in the sand. Tufts of hair stuck to the skulls. Neither was the build of Shadow. I dug frantically about, praying that I wouldn't find her.

I didn't.

A buckle or two and a knife were all that I could turn up. No indication of who the men were, nothing. I went to the tree. A hole had been dug a short distance from the base; someone had used a knife to dig for water. With my bleeding hands, I redug the hole and water seeped into it. So whoever it was had found water. I'd be willing to bet that it was Shadow, for I'd told her of that water.

I drank my fill and sat, slowly being baked in the heat of the desert.

What was my next move? Worry for Shadow hindered my thinking processes, and I had to strangle the thoughts of her to think coherently. Naked and alone in the desert might sound bad to some, but it wasn't much of a problem to me. I had a knife and water, and fireworms wouldn't bother me. Take stock, Robin.

Okay, what's next?

Establish a goal.

That's easy: find Shadow.

How?

Track her.

The wind's blown all the tracks away over the months. Impossible.

Then search the area, check the towns, talk to people. Maybe somebody's seen her. If she got away, she had to have supplies. Make a thorough search.

If that search is negative?

Find whoever's been trying to kill you. Maybe they have her. And destroy them.

The afternoon sun was racing for the horizon, and I didn't want to travel at night. So I ran in concentric circles around the mesquite, expanding the radius of the search for evidence on each pass. Nothing.

I slept the night, shivering, under the tree.

In the morning, I set out upon our back trail, naked, with a knife in my hand.

Shadow would have waited. If there were one chance in a thousand that I was alive, and Shadow were free, she would have camped right there and waited. She knew that I was immune to fireworms, therefore she would've stayed as long as possible. There weren't any evidences of anyone's staying at the mesquite.

In haste, I started running, seeking hard ground to speed my progress. Eventually, I found a trail to the south and east, took it and ran some more. My feet were blistering from the scorched earth and my body wasn't used to the physical exertion, but I kept on.

After many miles, the country changed slowly: scrub sprang up, and there were hills and rocks rather than sand only.

The Mexican sat on a rock beside the trail. I slowed to a walk. He glanced up from under a huge sombrero, weathered face sporting a bushy mustache.

"*Hola, señor.*"

"Hello, yourself."

"You make a strange sight, my friend, running naked in the desert, wielding a knife fiercely. Some people would think that you were a lost spirit."

"Not lost. Just looking for some clothes."

"I, too, am searching, but not for clothing. Would you like a drink?"

In the desert, someone only offers you water if he likes you or wants to specify that his intentions are innocent. I accepted. There was something decent and trusting in his eyes.

Time to try out my first inquiry. "I am looking for a girl, a young girl, perhaps seventeen years of age."

"She is gringo, like you?"

"Yes."

"I have seen no such woman. Where did you lose her?"

"Twenty or thirty miles into the desert, and maybe two months ago."

"*Señor,* no one goes that far into the desert, save perhaps . . ."

"I do. She was my partner. She was called Shadow."

"Ah, so I thought. You are the one they call Daystar?"

I nodded.

"No, I have not seen her. I would have known something strange about her had I encountered her. No, I am sorry."

"Where do you come from, *amigo*?"

"From Mejico. But recently, I have stayed in the small village some miles south of here and north of San Antonio de la Bexar."

I eyed the crossbow and fireworm rod at his side.

"Can you actually find water?" he asked. "Even in the desert?"

"If it's there, I'll find it. Who are you going to kill?" I indicated his arsenal.

"Only reasonable precautions. You see, I also seek a woman. My sister. Men with lasers kidnapped her. I do not think the crossbow will stand against them, but I must do what I must do."

Lasers! I tried to hide my enthusiasm. "When did this unfortunate event occur?"

"Some six weeks ago. They came in the night to the cantina, saw her, and took her. When people attempted to prevent them, they were menaced with a laser. It is very peculiar, no?"

"Hell, yes." Six weeks. I had no way of telling whether I'd been gone for six weeks or more or less, but it was close. "And you have no idea where they took her?"

"Would I be out here without *Díos,* searching, if I did?"

"No." Stupid question. Think. "Why would they take your sister? Is she a valuable personage?"

"No. She was living with friends, shall we say dodging an arranged marriage, one that I thought, as eldest in the family, would benefit our entire family."

"I was under the impression that only Chinese selected spouses for their siblings."

"One does what one determines best for his family. But that is past now."

"Where have you searched?"

"It seems to me, *señor,*" he paused for effect, shoulders straightening, "that you ask many questions of things that are not primarily your affair." His handsome face reflected a strong will, just underneath the surface.

"*Por favor,* forgive the intrusion upon your privacy. It's possible that the same men who kidnapped your sister also took my partner. You must understand my concern." I was trying desperately to be diplomatic. But if that tact didn't work, I was ready to try something else, something stronger.

"They had lasers, too? The ones that took the *señorita Sombra*?"

"Yes."

"When?"

"I don't know. I'm not even certain they took her, but if so, it would have been approximately at the same time frame that your sister was taken, maybe a week on either side."

"And you have been running naked in the desert ever since?"

"It's a long story."

"It's true then, what they say about Daystar and Shadow? That you are like the wind in the night? That you never need carry water?" His curiosity was showing.

"Sometimes people exaggerate." I felt odd. Our desert, almost hermitlike existence was something I couldn't explain easily. We'd avoided most human contact, and this was definitely not normal. But here was a lead and I couldn't afford to lose it. To change the subject, I asked, "These men who took your sister, what did they look like?"

"I have only reports of those who were present." He described them. Caucasian and Hispanic. Could have been the same group, but then again, may not have been. "I have searched all around San Antone and this was my last trail to follow. I will go somewhere next."

"Where?"

"I do not know. But I have dedicated my life to relentless pursuit."

"You do not have to search farther out this trail, as I have covered the entire area. There is no one." I was getting sunburned standing there talking to this man.

"I believe you. But Diego Garcia does not give up easily. I have heard rumors of other kidnappings to the west, and I will pursue those clues. Perhaps they are related, no?" His shoulders had stooped, lowering in discouragement. Then he perked up. "But where are my manners? I am convinced that you are Daystar. Who else would be alone in the desert with no fear of the fireworms? I must return to the village and obtain provisions. Perhaps you would accompany me and we could find clothing for you. Or do you prefer to go as you are?"

"I would appreciate your assistance."

We walked the trail together and talked.

"Was your sister, uh, I can't put it delicately, Diego, ever ill?"

"Ill, *señor*?"

"I mean, perhaps something wrong with her mind? No offense intended, Diego, but I must know."

"*Sí*. Then, she always has been standoffish. It was thought that she ate peyote when a child, and it scarred her brain. But she was a good woman, *señor*, although she did seem not to take interest much in things until she reached adulthood."

We talked more along the way, but I didn't learn anything else.

Garcia's friends loaned me some clothes. They were a poor lot, residing in a village some miles from San Antonio. For their kindness, I found them a seep that would elevate their standing in the community and provide them with a salable commodity. This cemented my relationship with Diego. We decided to travel together until our paths should part.

We went on into San Antonio, where I found a respectable Newsbringer. He confirmed what Diego had said about more recent kidnappings. I hoped that if they had Shadow, they'd keep her as bait for me. I was willing to take their hook and jam it and the line and the sinker down their throats.

I also purchased a new razor and used it.

We traveled west with no further clues. The only thing left for us was to go into El Paso. In large cities one can usually find information gathered in a more methodical manner than in the villages, where rumors were rampant. Facts were what we needed. I dreaded the day when we arrived, but there was nothing to do with it. I chafed at the delay that Diego caused. Alone, I could have gone at least twice as fast. But it was pleasant to have a companion. I found Diego an intelligent observer of humanity, somewhat cynical, nevertheless a man of thought.

We headed south, giving a wide berth to the Carlsbad Taboo, which was said to be radioactive still.

As we neared the city, I wondered about my parents, my heritage. Would I be thrown out again?

We came to El Paso.

CHAPTER TEN

We'd followed the Rio Grande bed to avoid the Carlsbad Taboo on the southern rim of Centralia and came upon the city from the southeast. Mountains sprang up to the north and west.

I swung east to the small hamlet that had been our home. Diego came with me, and I was forced to cover my trepidation. We treaded through the village, and surprisingly I remembered the location of the family dwelling.

As we neared the place, I became more anxious. What would I say? They had cast me out because of some silly town policy, although since then I'd learned that the policy was an offshoot of the New Christian ethic: one of their basic tenets was to kill mentally defective children. Something to do with devils. I'd never paid much attention. Interworkings of society had passed me by while I scoured the uninhabited wastelands.

Diego Garcia was quiet, sensing that I needed companionship without conversation.

The adobe hut was the same as I remembered it, but much smaller. It hadn't changed in over twenty years.

Hesitantly, I knocked at the entrance frame and stepped back. Presently a black man emerged.

"Yes?"

I didn't know what to say, but I plunged in. "Once, perhaps twenty years or so ago, a family lived here. I am looking for them. The father was a blacksmith named David and the wife was called Marg or Marge. Do you know them?"

"No. I've been here only a few years."

"Please forgive the intrusion." He nodded and I signaled Diego and we walked away.

"I sense you are troubled, *amigo.*" Diego seemed genuinely concerned.

"I used to live there and was lost as a child," I said, debating whether to tell him more of the story. "I would like to find my family to see what has become of them."

"I think I understand."

"Now, I'll never know."

"Let us ask some people who live here."

I headed for the Newsbringer and Diego went elsewhere; we agreed to meet later.

The Newsbringer didn't know my family, and I went looking for the Mayor. Not many records were kept in those days, so that option was out. Larger cities tried to keep records, but seldom did a small village bother.

Diego caught up with me before I found the Mayor. "*Señor,* I have learned something."

"What is it?" I didn't know if I wanted to know.

"I do not like to bring bad news, but the parents and children are gone from here. This I learned from an ancient cantina owner nearby. He thinks that some of them died before the rest left, but he doesn't remember which ones. I am sorry."

"Oh." I didn't know what to feel.

"But there is one thing," he continued.

"What thing?"

"Was one of them called 'Annette'?"

"Yes. A sister."

"Ah. She has made good. She is now the chief Librarian for the main city of El Paso, an exalted position."

"I'll be damned. Let's go."

We left the outlying village and went into the main city, some miles to the west. When we arrived, Diego begged off, saying that he would pursue his investigations in the Mexican barrio of El Paso, just south of there. We agreed to meet the next day by the public watering fountain in the suburb of Ciudad de Juárez.

Libraries are the most valued possessions of a city. They are worth their weight in water. Occupying the best buildings, they are constantly utilized. Information and knowledge was a commercial property and the libraries traded on these ideas. You could go into a library in search of some bit of information. A Librarian or an assistant would help you find it if it was there. Then you paid the necessary water credits for the help. Seldom would you be allowed to touch a book or tape. But you could watch the Librarian do so.

I mounted the wide steps of the El Paso Library. It was located in the city administration block, solidly ensconced in the center of the city and safe from raids.

A large foyer was occupied by several desks, those of Librarians and assistants helping customers. I could smell the musty reek of old leather and paper. El Paso was famous for its library, as the dry climate preserved books well.

I approached a counter where a young man was repairing an ancient tome.

"May I help you?" he asked.

"I am looking for Annette. I understand she works here."

From the look on his face, I gathered that I spoke with less than civility, referring to Annette in a discourteous manner. But what the hell, I was a desert rat and not accustomed to civilization and its strange formalities.

"Yes," he replied haughtily, wrinkling his nose in disapproval. "Annette works here. But you will have to deal with one of the lesser Librarians or assistants. She is too busy to be bothered with routine business."

My mind was beginning to wander and I felt the gears of my brain go out of synch. A minor withdrawal was coming on. I didn't have time to fool with the young man. I fought to control myself.

"If she's here, tell her Robin wishes to see her." I folded my arms as if to say, that's it, buddy, get a move on. The commanding manner of Daystar worked its magic and he scurried down a hall.

He came back with a guard. "The guard will escort you. Annette thinks you are a hoax and she must be protected."

I walked ahead of the guard along a corridor. A door stood open at the end and he motioned me inside.

It was gloomy here, but a breeze indicated good ventilation. A strikingly beautiful woman sat behind a desk. Books and papers were haphazardly scattered around. The guard stood at my shoulder.

She reminded me of mother, she who fought so well for me, but finally lost the battle. It was Annette.

I was too shocked at the resemblance to speak. I'd forgotten my withdrawal symptoms and the urge receded.

She spoke, her voice authoritative. "What is it? You claim to be Robin. Who are you?"

"You do look like mother," I said.

She stared at me for a moment. Then, to the guard, she said, "You may go. And see that I am undisturbed." He bowed and departed.

"Can you indeed be little Robin?"

"I am."

"Your countenance is familiar, bearing some resemblance to the family. But you were carried into the desert, as was dictated, and left. You're supposed to be dead."

She was up and in front of me, looking at my face.

"Well, I'm not."

"Can it really be you? I see mother's eyes, but when you frown like that, a streak of utter cruelty transforms your face. You have had a rugged life."

"Yes." I was supposed to be doing the talking. Ask my questions and be on my way. But it wasn't turning out that way.

"Yes, I believe you are Robin," she said. "Why do you come to see me?"

Right then, I wasn't sure myself.

"Wait a moment," she said. She went to a shelf on the wall, dug through some papers, and came up with several.

"You match the descriptions, all right." She was shuffling through the papers. "But you are older than they say. Have you ever been in Sacramento and San Diego?"

"Yes."

"Did you, by some coincidence, happen to burn down the New Christian Temple, slay a thousand priests and followers, and eat fireworms?"

"New Christians like to exaggerate." I had lost control of the interview. I should have denied it, but I saw no reason to forsake my alter identity.

"You are Daystar?"

"Yes, some call me that."

"There is a reward on your head, preferably severed from your body. You and a girl named Shadow. Who is she?"

"A friend, a partner. Pay no attention to the rantings of the New Christians. I have come to ask you what happened to our family."

"Sit down, Robin. It's a long story."

After I had been taken to the desert, mother withered up

and died; she said that life had no interest for her. Father had worked himself to death in sorrow for the loss of his wife and the loss of his two sons, one me, and two, Gregory, killed by a fireworm. Annette had been the oldest and smartest; she became an assistant at this library and eventually the chief Librarian. The other daughter, Lorilard, had disappeared.

"You have done well, Annette. Our parents would be proud of you."

"Thank you. But what strange things have made you this Daystar?"

"I don't truthfully know, Annette. It just happened."

"How did you escape, alone and three years old, from the midst of a killer desert thronged with fireworms?"

"This, too, I do not know. It has something to do with my affinity for those same fireworms. I cannot say more now."

We conversed at length. Evening came and refreshments were brought in.

"Annette," I took the plunge, "why did they call me 'artistic' and then cast me alone into the desert?"

"I have been marshalling my thoughts for over an hour in anticipation of that question," she replied. "It is involved with medicine, physiology, and theology. Because it happened to you, I have done much research on the matter. Can you read?" she asked unexpectedly.

"Am I not an apprentice Storyteller and Newsbringer? Besides, Shadow and I carried mail in Mexico for a year or two." We'd made a bundle. We also had a perfect record, one that still stands: no non-deliveries. I'd taught Shadow how to read, pointing out words and saying them aloud for her. When she paid attention, she learned rapidly. But it was hard on me, as her proclivity for not talking didn't give me sufficient feedback to judge her progress.

"Good. Later I will show you the medical books, but for now I will summarize. You are not, or were not, artistic."

"What? But . . ."

"Wrong word. *Autistic* is the correct word. Doubtless, as a child you misunderstood."

"What the hell is autistic then?"

"Autism is an obscure mental disease, or so the old books state, hyperactivity of the mind and withdrawal from reality are both the symptoms and the disease. It is sometimes called

Kannerism, named after one of the early pioneers investigating it."

"You mean that I am mentally deficient? Hah!" I shook my head. "That's hard to believe. Daystar a psycho case? A schizo?" I laughed to cover my real feelings. If I was mentally aberrant, then so was Shadow, and I didn't like that thought one damn bit. "No, I don't believe it, Annette. I have too many accomplishments."

"Burned down any temples lately?"

I shrugged, avoiding my thoughts. Annette was trying to make this easier for me, that I could tell.

"You live in the desert, ignoring danger?" I nodded. "Another symptom," she said. "Let me list some of the peculiar behaviors." She held up one finger. "Do you play deaf sometimes?"

I nodded. I used to and Shadow still does.

"Do you lack fear about realistic dangers?"

"I guess." Shadow wasn't afraid of anything either.

"Do you resist changes in your routine?"

"Used to." Why had Shadow and I wandered alone for all those years? We could have done something useful.

"Have you communicated by gestures, preferring not to speak?"

I looked down at my hands. She was describing my relationship with Shadow perfectly.

"Avoid familiar touch with other people?"

I nodded again. Shadow had it a lot worse than I did. But I'd gotten over most of those things she was listing, and so could Shadow. I avoided Annette's eyes.

"No eye contact?" She bored on relentlessly.

I looked sheepishly at her. The great Daystar was being humbled.

"Marked physical overactivity?"

I nodded once more. We only walked about a million miles, always on the go. And, shit, we ran a helluva lot, too.

"Unusual attachment to a physical object, one or more?"

I thought of my razor and Shadow's seashell necklace I'd made for her in San Diego. I was also attached to Shadow, how I didn't know.

"Standoffish manner?"

I squirmed in my seat. I didn't want to hear any more.

"I'm sorry, Robin. I didn't like doing that. But I had to. I've studied it for a long time now, thinking of you."

"What do I have to look forward to?" I managed to ask, feeling strangled and a withdrawal coming on. I tightened my mental screws. Now wasn't the time to curl up or run.

"Remember that I prefaced my remarks that medicine, physiology, and theology were involved?"

I nodded, getting tired of nodding.

"First, medicine. Historically, autism was recognized as a significant mental-type disease, affecting primarily young children. At times, children with it were treated as being schizophrenic or mentally disturbed. When the symptoms were isolated, it was finally defined as a whole new medical problem. Some had it more than others, the degree of abnormal behavior higher. Others went through life with it knowing only that they were different somehow. A treatment was never devised for the problem. Concern, understanding, and love helped, but this was a long and unrewarding process. So the state of the medical art never increased. Then came the Holocaust and humanity has had other worries.

"Second: physiologically, autistic people *are* different. Not many of them lead normal lives, although little is known about the long-term effects. Most of the autistic children in the past have been shunted off. They were not properly helped, if the case was that they needed help. So autistic people were ignored, and left out of the mainstream of society. You are different, as you know from the symptoms I listed. One theory says that autism is an organic disorder affecting the brain. The pineal gland controlling the brain's electrical impulses has been thought to misfunction, as has the pituitary gland. But no one knows.

"And thirdly, theology. For the last few hundred years, people have been scratching to stay alive. Defective children are a burden. So they got rid of their burdens. Several religions adopted a similar tenet. Brutally, they advocate death to autistic children. Why? I don't know, since they do not particularly stress death for other mental deficients. Perhaps they are afraid of the autistic children. The only thing I can surmise is that people do not have the time or the resources to support those who are not capable of contributing significantly to their society."

"Shit," I fired at her, hiding my hurt. "I and Shadow have contributed to many societies. We've found enough water to support many cities. San Diego has thousands more green acres because of me."

"So you have a special talent. I don't argue this point. I'm only relating what I've found out through my research. I don't say it's right. I merely state what *is*." She hesitated. "I never have understood why the New Christian Church has so frantically called for death to autistic children. The practice has seeped throughout the country in the last century or two, and has become common even in those non-NC enclaves. I don't understand."

Well, neither did I. For the first time in my life, I was scared. Scared for Shadow. I'd been afraid for her before, during my search with Diego, but now I was chilled to the heart with fright for her. I was terribly upset at what I'd learned, but now I must find Shadow, and soon.

The legend of Daystar and Shadow founded on a couple of mental cripples. I was bitter. But then my so-called "diseased" mind took off on a tangent. "You said you had a wanted circular on me from the New Christian Church?"

"Yes, and several follow-ups." She held up the papers.

Several items fell into place. I thought aloud. "One. Autistic children are killed, in one way or the other. Two. The NCs had and a lot of other people want me dead. Three. There's been a recent wave of kidnappings, some of which we've traced. These cases were mostly adults who acted strangely, perhaps who had some of the symptoms you named. It is possible that these kidnap victims were autistic and escaped somehow the killing stage as children, or maybe developed the disease later in life." I paused for effect. "Does this not suggest something to you, sister?"

This time I held eye contact and watched her add it up. When her brows were raised high enough, I continued.

"I've heard reports of lasers, too, involved in the kidnappings. And the men who chased me and Shadow, and probably got her, had lasers. Life is taking a strange turn."

She said nothing, still calculating. I'd come here to find my heritage. To find why I'd been abandoned. And now I knew with a sudden clarity of my mind that my destiny was not yet fulfilled. Somewhere, there was a rational reason for my presence and my special abilities. This abated somewhat the blows that had just been dealt me. By the same token, I knew that Shadow was alive. I think I would have shriveled up inside somehow had she been dead.

"What does it mean, Robin?" she asked. For some odd reason, I liked being called Robin. Only a few people knew me as that, primarily Shadow. And she'd only used the name once.

"I don't know, Annette, but by all that ain't holy, I'm going to find out."

CHAPTER ELEVEN

Annette and I talked long into the night, until dawn, in fact. She urged me to stay, so that she could have professionals study me. I declined. I had to be after Shadow.

As I left, I asked her, "Are you making a good living here, sister? If not, I can find some water to provide for your future." I'd told her of my ability to locate water.

"No need, thank you, Robin. In El Paso, only a handful are my peers. I lack for no conveniences."

"I'll go then. If you don't hear from me for a year or so, I'll be dead." I scribbled a note on a piece of parchment. "Send this to Sun Yen Chang or his son, Sun Tsu Liu, in Sacramento. I suspect that they own the city by now. You're my heir, save for Shadow. Should she turn up somewhere and not me, I charge you with her welfare, although I don't think she would accept your assistance. The Suns should have a great amount of water credit gathering interest for me."

She glanced at the paper. "You write Chinese script well, Robin."

We shook hands. Then she kissed me impulsively.

It took me a couple of hours to find the fountain in Juárez. It wasn't time to meet Diego Garcia yet, so I made for the nearest cantina for tortillas and *cerveza.* El Paso makes good beer. I've been told it's because there are so many jackrabbits in the nearby desert, they have no trouble getting enough hops.

Diego slid into a seat at the table.

"Find your family?"

I briefed him quickly.

"There have been two or three kidnappings in the recent past, but none lately. And all are still unaccounted for. Those kidnapped were not necessarily affluent, and no ransom was demanded."

"We seem to be at a dead end, Diego." I finished a beer unhappily. I had to find Shadow. It was becoming more of an obsession with me than I would've expected.

"Almost, *señor*. I find rumors that Santa Fe is beginning to experience the same thing."

"Are you ready for travel?"

"Señor Daystar, if you're waiting on me, you're backing up. But let me obtain a bladder of this fine *cerveza* for our journey."

"It won't keep in the sun."

"I do not intend to let it sit around."

We swung north, still following the dry Rio Grande, drinking warm beer.

In ten days we skirted Albuquerque, striking out northeast for Sante Fe. A couple of more days and we made our way into town. Sante Fe, San Antonio, and San Diego all claim to be the oldest inhabited cities in the western hemisphere. I don't know about that, but Santa Fe would have my vote. It was ancient, reminding me of an old woman, her face pockmarked with age streaks. Cobblestone roadways, threaded through adobe shack towns. The main city was smaller than El Paso, but just as alive. Because of runoff from nearby mountains, water was not hard to come by.

Diego faded into the Hispanic barriors, searching for information. I wandered through the main city and spoke to the local police. They were cooperative but refused to talk about the problem.

Garcia turned up more information. "It seems that the kidnapping epidemic has beaten us northward now. There is word that one kidnapping took place in Taos two days ago."

Word travels fast, but then so did we.

We came into Taos at night, still undecided as to what course to take.

"You've got to try to find someone with the symptoms that the kidnappers seek. Then we'll stake him or her out. What to do after that, I don't know." That was the only plan I could come up with.

I waited while Diego filtered through the town. Along the street I saw a red-robed NC priest and followed him.

He finally came to an old church with the New Christian logo emblazoned around a cross. I watched surreptitiously for awhile, but could discern nothing unusual. If we turned up nothing here, I was determined to catch one of those priests and take him out into the wilderness for a question-and-answer session.

When it was time to meet Diego, I gave up the convert spying. He had found nothing.

"In fact," he said, "this town is strangely close-mouthed. It is as if there is a pall hanging over the city of Taos right now."

I had a feeling. "This may be our chance, Diego." I thought rapidly. We needed bait. I explained as much to Garcia.

He concurred. "You, *amigo,* are too conspicuous. You do not fit in here. I will do it. Loan me your razor, and I will shave this ornery mustache off, to make me look younger."

I didn't want to do it that way, but I was almost out of my mind with worry for Shadow. If they had her, they had held her for months. No telling what condition she was in by now.

We laid low the next day and I briefed Diego on how to act. He practiced a little, under my expert tutelege.

Doubting that nothing untoward would happen in daylight, we didn't go into our act until late afternoon. We selected a small out-of-the-way public square on the outskirts of Taos. Some merchant stalls and three small cantinas were the main attraction. I stayed out of sight.

Diego went there and acted crazy, in an autistic sort of way. He was hyperactive for awhile, then beat his head upon an adobe wall for a few minutes. After that, he curled up into a ball and lay in the warm sun. We knew it would take some time, so we were prepared to go about it all night if necessary.

After dusk, Diego went into a cantina to eat. He would stay there for as long as he could, acting strangely.

Nothing happened. The evening crowd of shoppers was thin and only a few locals frequented the cantinas. By nine, according to the stars, I was tired, hungry, and thirsty. I ate some concentrates and sipped water, cursing Diego for his luck of being in the cantina. He certainly wouldn't want for food and drink.

Presently I spied a red-robed priest making his way home or to the temple. An inspiration grabbed me.

Quickly, I judged his route and rate of progress. Then I ran ahead of him, around the back of the square, and raced up an alleyway to intercept him. I peeked around the corner and saw him coming.

Waiting until he was directly in front of the alley, I grabbed him from behind and held him immobile.

"Señor," I whispered in thick Spanish, "don't turn around, for I would not wish to be recognized. In the third cantina there is one who should not be. He acts strange, as if he escaped the will of the church in his childhood."

In my fashion, I faded back into the shadow, crouching to take advantage of the cover. The priest did turn and search, but like most city dwellers, his night vision was exceedingly poor and he did not see me.

Soon I was back at my position. I'd sneaked a look inside the cantina and Diego was still at it. I hoped he wouldn't ham it up too much and get thrown out. From the look of things, he was playing drunk right now, spending credits freely. That should keep him in the good graces of the proprietor.

By midnight, I was ready to quit, but I didn't. Diego and I'd agreed on several signals, whistles. I could have called it off, but was determined to wait longer. Lights had gone off all over the plaza by now, and only the three cantinas showed any signs of occupancy.

Suddenly, a half-dozen men emerged from the shadows on the far side of the square. They must have come in from the other side, keeping away from the major thoroughfares.

They wore wide sombreros, eclipsing their features. Straight for the cantina they walked, looking this way and that. I had a sinking feeling that I'd set up Diego too well. It might prove fatal to him. But it was too late to back out now. I waited.

Two of the men were posted outside and the other four went inside. Next I heard a commotion and they came out, dragging an obviously drunk Diego Garcia. I hoped that he was simply faking it, but couldn't be sure.

I was wide awake now, all senses open and receiving.

They dragged him down the nearest alley, which led them right past my position. I melted into the darkness.

The group skirted the town and, to my surprise, reentered Taos on a vacant street, almost silent. I drifted along behind them, flitting from shadow to shadow, never seen.

Not surprisingly, they came to the New Christian Temple and passed on inside. It was shortly after midnight. What was I supposed to do? The plan had worked perfectly, and I'd hoped to learn something, anything, as to the whereabouts of Shadow. But it was beginning to appear that the plan was ill conceived. What would they do to Diego? Did not my debt of friendship obligate me to get him out of there? Hell, I flat didn't know.

Squatting behind a stone wall and observing the church, I pulled out my sharpening stone and honed my razor and knife to a fine edge. In my mind the possibility of violence had increased to the probability stage. On further reflection, I determined that the church was but a small, local establishment, and could not hold many kidnap victims secretly. This may be a staging location only. On the other hand, suppose the kidnappers aimed to kill their victims? I could see that they wouldn't want a rash of murders to their credit, so they might hide their nefarious intentions by kidnapping, on the theory that no one would miss mentally deficient people, life being as difficult as it was. If such were the case, then why didn't they take them into the desert immediately and slay them?

I searched the emotional spectrum and found no hint of Shadow. She wasn't there. There had to be some other explanation.

Just one way to find out: I'd have to get inside. Taking my time while thinking my movements out ahead, I ate a hasty meal and drank a quantity of water. Settling my pack firmly on my back, I moved through the night, scouting the temple on all sides.

Fortunate that I did. While scanning the back of the building, a shaft of light struck out through a rear door. Fearing discovery, I hid in an adjacent pigpen. Silent as I was, I did not disturb the occupants.

Twenty-five or thirty people emerged from the doorway. Curious, I thought, and settled back to watch.

The group headed straight for the trail north. As they filed into the night, I took up vigilance from the rear of their procession. All was quiet, only muffled sounds escaping them.

I had to get closer to determine whether Diego Garcia was among the group. If he wasn't present, then I had real problems.

Running on firm ground, I circled the slow-moving group

and wound up on the trail some one mile in advance of it. They had to come this way.

Selecting a suitable hiding place, I covered myself, all but my eyes, with sand at the edge of a boulder, not many feet from the trail. An uprooted shrub hid my face. I remained motionless.

In a little while, I sensed movement and turned only my eyes to observe. Two men, difficult to distinguish in the dark, led the procession. One was armed with a laser. There followed some fifteen people, roped together by the neck, gagged with cloth, hands tied behind them. Guards with crossbows marched at either side of them.

Diego Garcia was at the end of the chain, stumbling a little as if drunk. Two more guards, again one armed with a laser, brought up the rear of the procession.

I was relieved that Diego had become part of the group. At least they hadn't seen through his act yet. This led to the thought that perhaps these men were only a pick-up and delivery crew. Where were they going?

I had to show Diego that I was there, if he needed me. Although our plan had been hastily conceived and was indeed vague after his supposed capture, we'd worked out a general procedure. I was to follow to where they went, whether it be in Taos or elsewhere. As they faded out of sight, I gave a low night-bird whistle, hoping fervently that there were night-birds in this part of the country. Diego stumbled again, worse than before, and I knew that he was now aware of my presence.

Rising and shaking the sand from me, I took my time. I didn't want to follow too closely, fearing discovery. No humans could elude Daystar in the wilds at night—or for that matter, in the daytime either.

I sat back to consider. Where were they going? There was no major habitation to the north that I knew of, just mountains that lay in Centralia. Perhaps they headed toward some minor village or community, but scavenging autistic people from these villages would prove unprofitable and take much time, with the possibility of exposure. There were more mountains ahead, and they were moving into Centralia, the great mid-American wilderness. These were wild lands, of hostile terrain, little water, and no habitation. What was their purpose?

And why kidnap autistic adults?

And what was the role of the New Christian Church?

Simple logic dictated that the NCs had made sure that all autistic children within their scope of operations were killed. And those that weren't killed were kidnapped. There had to be a correlation.

Were the New Christians at the bottom of the mystery or were they merely tools? I had no evidence for the latter surmise, and only circumstantial for the former.

There was one way to find out, though, and that was to follow. I had to rescue Shadow, and I was obligated to protect Diego Garcia. A disturbing thought came into my mind. I'd never really been concerned with human life before, save to protect or seek revenge for my friends, as in Sacramento. I'd now found out about autism. And all autistic children were killed and recently autistic adults were kidnapped. Did I not care? Why hadn't I become concerned with mass murder? And here I was worrying only about Shadow and Diego.

To avoid these painful thoughts, I rose and followed the procession of captives.

Throughout the night I followed, closing up at times to be sure of their location, and falling back. When and if they stopped for rest, I'd scout ahead, checking the lay of the land. I always try to know the local terrain. This makes it easier to move around. We were already at a higher altitude, and gradually climbing.

At dawn, they pulled off into a dead-end canyon, off the trail and out of sight. I didn't see much sense in it, as the trail hadn't been used recently. This was truly desolate country. But it was their show, and they probably figured that they weren't much more than fifteen or twenty miles from Taos and should play it safe.

I wanted to sneak up close to the camp and listen for any information I could hear. But the close confines of the canyon prohibited this. So I scouted the trail north, found a good place to sleep, and dozed off.

When I awoke, I was refreshed and drank the last dregs of water in the bladder. It was afternoon, so I checked the trail to see if they'd passed yet. I didn't think so, as I would have awakened at any strange sounds. The trail was still clear, so perhaps they traveled only at night.

I searched out water and found a small spring, frequented by animals and birds, and refilled the water container.

Thirst slaked, I returned to the trail and waited.

Shortly after dark I heard them coming. The moon was up

in quarter now, so visibility was better than it had been late last night.

I sensed them coming before I saw them. I caught fleeting emotions of fear, anger, and disappointment. It was a new sensation. I didn't think Shadow was with them; in fact, the thoughts I received did not reflect her aura. And these glimpses of emotions were not as well defined as those Shadow and I used. But it surprised me that I could pick them up. I tried to respond with a comforting glow, and found that it did alter their mental transmissions. They weren't aware of any outside influence, just knew something calming was about. I had to infer that the captives were not able to communicate with each other as Shadow and I did.

I hid in a rocky ridge as they came, some hundred yards away and overlooking the trail they must take. Seeing better, I observed that the captives carried various-sized packs, most probably containing water and provisions. Again, I chanced discovery and voiced a low whistle to encourage Diego. In answer, his shoulders straightened and his stride lengthened.

I now saw that several women were among the prisoners.

They stopped for sleep and food early that night and were up shortly after dawn, moving again. It seemed that they had passed the necessity of hiding during the day and traveling at night. This would make it easier for me to sneak into their camp for the chance of overhearing something useful.

That night I was able to come close, but all I could discern was that they didn't talk much. The guards went about their duties in a businesslike way, fed and watered the captives, made them lie down, and went to sleep themselves. They posted sentries, two at a time, with a tour lasting only two hours before they were relieved. The sentries always held the lasers. I couldn't get close enough to Diego to talk so I faded back and found a safe sleeping place myself.

Day after day we traveled north, treading through mountain passes, across plateaus, and through great canyons. I could understand why no one inhabited this land. Surprisingly, they were able to find water when needed. It could be that they were accustomed to this trail and knew of the water locations. I also noted that the farther north we went, the fewer fireworms were about. This I didn't understand.

Some of the prisoners were weakening from the dreadful trek into the upper wilderness. They had to be assisted by other captives or were prodded by the guards. There wasn't much mistreatment or abuse of the prisoners, just a general lack of interest on the part of the armed escort.

Then we came to a ghost city.

CHAPTER TWELVE

I ranged far ahead now, confident that I could find the party when I needed to. I was scouting the trail, winding through mountains and vast, sloping hills, when I came upon the ghost city.

I stopped and stared from far away. Piles of rubble, stone, some metal evidenced that this had once been a medium-sized city. Many such were known, and Storytellers knew of numerous others which had been abandoned in times past. From some of these stories, I guessed this could be either Pueblo or Colorado Springs, most probably the former.

An occasional pine tree showed that the land wasn't completely barren, but there were no people. I wandered through some of the dead city for awhile and then had to get back, not wanting to lose those I followed. They wound their way into the city, no interest showing on their faces other than strange looks by the prisoners. I guessed that the guards had been along this route before.

They made camp among the ruins. I found that I could come fairly close and hear them talking.

One soldier said, "We're getting close, you know?"

"Reckon we'll be there, maybe by tomorrow night," replied another. "I'll be glad to get to the citadel."

The kidnappers were apparently happy that their journey was almost over.

Suddenly, there was quiet and I heard the approach of someone from the other side of the ruins.

A sentry shouted a warning and all were instantly alert, lasers and crossbows held at ready.

An answering shout came back and they relaxed slightly. Soon eight more people filed into the ruins. Three apparent kidnappers and five prisoners. I would have to think this through.

All got settled and I heard wisps of conversation indicating that the later arrivals had come from Fenix.

The next morning they were off early, but one of the female prisoners had to be carried. The arduous trip had claimed her strength. They were forced to go more slowly that day as a result. That night they grumbled about the delay.

During my watching phase that night one of the younger prisoners went into convulsions. He gave a quick cry and fell to the ground. Others gathered around him and tried to comfort him during his attack. At first the soldiers were concerned that it might be a ruse, but it became obvious that he was in trouble. Some of the prisoners convinced the guards to let them handle it and they backed off. One prisoner even indicated that he'd had the same problem in the past. Annette had asked me about this. Apparently, some autistics were afflicted with mental disorders or other diseases such as epilepsy, encephalitis, or meningitis, to name a few. Fortunately, neither Shadow nor I had any of these. But it was more prevalent among autistics than normal people. My guess would be that these days only the strongest survive, and that those with additional medical deficiencies were weeded out at early ages. However, certainly some autistics could have grown into adulthood with these problems. This occurrence sobered me and gave me a new track upon which to think. Maybe we weren't all brain-burners only. Perhaps there were distinctions even within our ranks.

Already I was thinking of "us," the autistics, as a group.

We'd taken a different trail out of the ghost city, angling away from due north. We crossed a great plain between mountains and ahead I could see the range grow, probably the same group of mountains, but separated by the plain.

The combined two groups wound their way into the foot of these mountains and soon they went over the lip of a ridge.

I hurried to catch up and peered over the edge. A small plateau unfolded. The group of kidnappers and prisoners was halfway across it. Huge mountains towered above, the air definitely chilly.

A great, gaping hole was at the foot of the mountain. The

group headed for this. I stayed where I was and watched. Was this the citadel?

The entrance to the mountains must have been thirty feet high and at least fifty wide. I could see that there was ice on the mountains way above, so water was not a problem here.

A challenge rang out from the mouth of the cave. The approaching group halted as two sentries separated from the darkness of the tunnel. Both held lasers loosely pointed at the group I'd been following. The sentries recognized them and they were allowed to pass. The tunnel swallowed them.

What the hell was I to do?

I scouted the area in the daylight as much as possible while keeping out of sight of the mouth of the tunnel. On coming closer, I saw carved out of the base rock at the top of the tunnel, in weatherbeaten relief, "Cheyenne Mountain." This meant nothing to me. To each side of the opening was a great metal door, blast doors from times past, warped and rusting slightly. The place reeked of antiquity.

I had to get inside. Shadow might be in there. Was this my goal or was it merely a tunnel through the mountains? I didn't know, but the presence of sentries lent credence to the assumption that this was their final destination. Hadn't they indicated that they were close in the ghost city?

Fine. So how was I going to gain entry?

This one was closely guarded with lasers, so the obvious answer was to find another entrance—and be aware that there was probably a most sizable force within the mountain. I watched the opening for several hours, having exhausted all possibilities of entrance nearby. Random movements in the shadows told me that guards were still present.

I tired of waiting, anxiety eating at my gizzard, and set out into the mountains. Circling the base of the mountain that housed the tunnel, I searched for small doors, ventilator shafts, anything. Results negative. The project was doubly difficult as the mountain was not a lone mountain: it seemed to be the beginning of the continuation of the mountain range. It fed into others, not distinguished by itself. Nevertheless, I climbed through the rocks searching for ingress. Nightfall came and I continued my search, hoping that an incautious lamp might reveal other entry points.

I slept high in the crags that night, shaking with cold from the bitter strong wind.

Waking early, I scurried over hundreds of rock faces,

like a spider on a wall, hurrying from one possible site to another.

Somewhere above the tunnel entrance, perhaps a thousand feet higher, I encountered a ventilator shaft. The opening was large enough to take my body, but a metal grillwork crisscrossed the dark hole. Rods set deep in rock prevented any entry. I tested the crossbars with my arms and legs pulling simultaneously. Even with my considerable strength, they wouldn't budge. I tried to scrape the cement away from the anchor points, but my knife was inadequate for the task.

Feeling defeated, I was once more drawn to the tunnel opening. I found a comfortable roost and observed it during the day. Occasionally I could see a sentry moving within.

One entrance only then, and guarded with lasers. I was not yet ready to gain access by the obvious method: walk up to the opening and surrender. There had to be a way.

Perhaps if another party arrived I could check their routine, and find a way to sneak past the guards. But throughout the day, no one else approached the tunnel.

I was sick of waiting. All day I'd tried to reach out mentally and contact anyone who would receive me. But I didn't even get the faint transmissions from the prisoners that had accompanied me across the land. Maybe the rock was too thick.

Toward sunset, shadows from surrounding peaks laced over the plateau. I saw one opportunity.

If I could climb the face of the mountain near the tunnel entrance, I could perch on top of one of the massive metal doors on either side of the opening, and thereby await an opportunity.

I ate a quick meal and then got into my spider mode—it felt like it anyway—and mounted the side of the mountain out of sight of the opening. I climbed higher than necessary, sensing that caution would be the best defense. I wished that there had been fireworms around and I could toss a couple in the tunnel for a diversion, but no such luck. Presently, I descended directly above the entrance, clutching minuscule cracks and protuberances for support. Soon I was crouched atop one of the great doors. I leaned back into the shadows and remained immobile in case someone should chance to come out and look around. I studied the situation.

In a couple of hours of watching, I discerned only small movements within. Night had long since fallen. I was ready to try a flank attack when I heard a small noise outside. Apparently, the sentries heard it also, and one of them edged outside into the moonlight. He had some sort of apparatus on his head. It was hard to see, but it seemed that he had on goggles and a helmet, with a box, small and compact, perched atop the helmet. This gave me pause to think. When the earlier party had entered the tunnel, the guards' heads were unadorned. So they wore the helmets and goggles only at night. Only one conclusion could be drawn: the device aided night vision. And I'd been prepared to sneak inside, trusting darkness as an ally.

The noise did not repeat itself, and the sentry returned to his hidden position. I scanned the area to locate the source of the sound; maybe it had been some animal or rattlesnake. Never can tell in strange country what you might find in the way of local life.

I saw nothing then, until a minor movement caught the corner of my eye. Isolating the area took a little while. Eventually, I could see odd shadows against the mountain. They were cast from atop the opposite blast door on the other side of the tunnel entrance.

I froze.

Whatever it was over there was not very large. Soon I made out two shapes; no, three. They were immobile, perched on the lip of the metal door, just as I was. They hadn't seemed to notice me.

In a while, one of the shadows detached itself from its position and silently flitted to the ground, barely seeming to touch handholds. Two other shapes followed and they gathered at the base of the door, right next to the entrance.

I went about halfway down the inside edge of my door to see better. The three crouched figures were monkeys! The last time I'd even seen any monkeys . . .

But what the hell were they doing? A rustle of movement came and two of them crawled into the opening.

A minute passed. And another. Then came a shout and a brilliant flash of light, a laser, shot out. Two sentries appeared and stopped by something on the ground. Then the third monkey quietly stepped into the tunnel and I lost sight of him.

Afraid of missing my opportunity and still not understanding anything, I silently came to the ground and melted into the shadows, circumventing the two guards. They kicked at the floor of the tunnel. I smelled burnt flesh. They were bending over the remains of the first two monkeys.

Cautiously, I stole down the darkened tunnel, praying that they wouldn't look my way. I couldn't detect the third monkey by sight or sound. Had he seen me? I kept to the far wall, running my left hand along the surface, to be as far away from the guards as possible. Soon, I was able to move faster. The floor beneath seemed to be paved, and the going was easy. No obstructions hampered my forward motion. The tunnel gradually curved, and in a few minutes I could see light ahead.

I was finally in the citadel.

Remaining cautious, I increased my pace. Another curve in the tunnel, and light was available from some overhead source. It wasn't natural light but some artificial means; there was power here. To either side of the main tunnel various doors, large and small, opened. Some were closed, others were simple openings in the rock wall. They led into places I did not know, nor did I follow, as they seemed deserted.

Presently, I realized I was in a maze inside the bowels of the mountain. But I did not see any sign of the third monkey.

After what seemed hours, but was probably only twenty or thirty minutes of careful investigation, I came upon a great cavern. The glow above had shown all the rooms I'd encountered to be unoccupied. But the cavern held signs of activity. Few people were distinguishable from my vantage point just inside the tunnel. The space was vast, and machinery hid much from my view. There was an upper level within the cavern. I could discern openings off a ledge that surrounded the inner cavern, and cut stone steps led upward. A railing enclosed the ledge.

Not knowing what to do next or which way to go, I opened my mind for some sort of signal. Perhaps I could track the autistic people that way. I received nothing. So I transmitted. A ghost of a response answered me. Not much, just a hint.

Then two red-robed priests came toward my position and I had to run back down the tunnel to a vacant room and hide in the dark. They passed and disappeared in another room close by. But the fireworm was in the village now, to use a common cliché. New Christian priests! The significance of this rolled over me, although I'd expected something of the kind.

I came back to the entrance to the large cavern unsure of what to do next. A couple of men, garbed in ordinary clothing, were working on a piece of machinery nearby. At least all in the maze were not New Christian priests. These two barred my way across the chamber. Noise of movement behind me caused me to turn. The two priests were returning, cutting me off from escape. In moments they would notice me.

I was trapped.

CHAPTER THIRTEEN

The two men in front of me were working with a large piece of machinery and looking within. I guessed them to be technicians of some sort. I didn't have many seconds left. The priests were talking between themselves and advancing on my position rapidly.

I took a deep breath and walked into the cavern confidently. Once over the threshold, I could see better. There was a flight of stone stairs leading to the upper gallery. With my heart pounding, I strode for the stairs and climbed them trying to watch everything out of the corners of my eyes. The technicians didn't see me. At the top of the stairs, I kept going, clinging to the wall to give as little profile up there as possible. The gallery seemed to run completely around the cavern some twenty-five or thirty feet above the chamber floor. Doorways and passageways led off the landing.

Risking a casual glance behind me, I saw that the priests had followed me up the stairs, still talking. Perhaps they had not yet seen me.

Another whisper touched my mind and I took the first cross passageway I came to. This, too, was well lighted with some overhead filament. I lengthened my stride. A dark doorway provided momentary safety and I slipped into it. Checking my rear, I found that the priests were not coming my way.

Using the free moment to think ahead, I sipped from the water bladder. I searched out with my mind and the ghost of a thought, unintelligible, replied. At least I was on the right track. Continuing down the passageway, I was wary of discovery. The place was honeycombed with tunnels, doors to various rooms, and apparently numerous different levels. The area would have to be large, but according to my investigations so far the population was thin.

The passageway ended upon another cavern, smaller, this time. Abruptly, the tunnel spilled out onto the upper landing of this cavern and I carefully looked around. No one appeared to be on the gallery with me, so I looked below. The walls were packed with electronic consoles of the like I'd never seen. I thought that the hydrogen power plant in San Diego was complex, but this made that setup look like a Sunday-school picnic. Many people bustled about the floor of the cavern, some working about the consoles, others simply standing about. Red-robed priests were in the majority. There were also two or three men dressed in the red and black of New Christian staff. Several hovered around a chair of sorts where someone was sitting. The sitting person had a metal helmet upon his head, with wires leading to another console. Lights flashed about. New Christian staff members seemed to be questioning this individual and recording, apparently, responses or brain waves from him.

Surreptitiously, I watched for awhile, straining my eyes and ears to make sure I wouldn't be discovered. I had to guess that the one being interrogated was a prisoner. I tuned my mind toward him, and when he was asked a question or told something, I noted increased mental activity. But it would blur as someone else turned another piece of electronics gear simultaneously with his responses. It was all very mysterious.

I broadened my range and searched for a familiar thought pattern.

A hint of response came into my mind, though I couldn't identify it as specifically belonging to Shadow. It certainly wasn't from within this cavern.

Presently, the interrogated one passed out in his chair. Then it was that I saw he had been manacled to the chair. Assistants to the questioners unstrapped him, removed the helmet, and dragged him off. They went down a side passage on the opposite side of the cavern. If he was truly an autistic prisoner, then perhaps they were taking him back to the other captives. I could only follow in this upper level and hope there was a matching upper passage. Quickly, I walked around the gallery, again staying close to the wall to avoid discovery. There was a passage similar to the one below.

I followed it.

Several hundred feet through this tunnel I found that the entire mountain must be honeycombed with caverns and passages. This opened on another cavern, smaller than the one with the electronic consoles.

But this time the gallery was occupied. I had been walking silently through the tunnel with my mind open. As I approached the cavern, I felt a warning strike my mind. The thought was all hazy, like smoke drifting on a dark night. But it was a warning.

And it felt like Shadow!

If, indeed, she was in the cavern, she must have caught my presence and broadcast to me. The transmission was much stronger than the previous whisper, so I must be getting close. Myriad benumbed thoughts assaulted my mind. Not knowing what I was doing, I mentally threw up a filter, and held these other unwanted thoughts at bay. They had been overwhelming for a few seconds.

Aside, I thought that there was much to this autism and mind-talk business, and I would have to seek out some answers once I had the opportunity. But first I must find Shadow and get the hell out of there. An unwelcome thought sliced into this plan: what was I going to do about Diego Garcia and his sister? With all the stray thoughts that had just slammed into me I knew there must be many kidnapped people below. Did I owe them any allegiance?

I sent out a blanket reassurance on a wide spectrum to quiet the prisoners and gave me a chance to think. Cautiously, I approached the end of the corridor. Peeking out, I saw two sentries patrolling the upper landing. They were preoccupied with the scene below, obviously where the prisoners were located. Timing their movements, I watched for both of them to have their backs to me.

When the moment came, I stepped out and risked a quick glance from the gallery. Almost a hundred people sat or stood below, male and female. Some rested, and some moved around. Obviously, this was their cage. A few barred doors led from the floor below; the prisoners were held effectively, and well guarded. I searched frantically for Shadow or Diego, shouting with my mind.

Suddenly, I heard an exclamation from behind me. While my attention was below, two uniformed soldiers had approached silently through the same passage I had traveled. I turned quickly, drawing my knife. I should have thought of the changing of the guard up here. Cursing myself would do no good now, so I faced them.

By this time, each had a laser in his hand and was pointing it at me.

"Who are you and what are you doing here?" said the older one. He advanced, raising his laser.

I had no good answer, especially with a drawn knife in my hand. But I tried anyway. "The high priest sent me to check on the prisoners."

"Get him," said the other.

My arm raised to fling my knife, but commotion behind me indicated that the other two guards had seen and were approaching. What can one knife do against four lasers? Carefully, I lowered my arm and placed the knife in its sheath. My death would do no one any good.

I was grasped roughly, and my hands bound. I answered no questions. My knife was removed, but they didn't search me well, for my razor remained snuggled below my collar on my back.

During this, I searched below for a familiar face. All the prisoners were watching, silent spectators to the scene above them. I caught a well-known worried thought and as they dragged me away, I saw a beautiful, familiar ashen face peering up from within the crowd below. Violet eyes locked on mine, and my heart soared only to be dashed as I was spun around.

They dragged me along the gallery and into a room which held a series of stairs. Down we went through another corridor. They did not speak. We came out into the cavern with all the electronic equipment, followed a wall, and went into a side room.

This room was larger than I would have thought, like a small working chamber.

A voice I'd heard before said, "Well, what is it?"

"We caught him sneaking around the gallery of the prisoners, sir."

Red-and-black-robed, with a blue sash, the high priest rose and came forward. He was as I remembered, average height, long dark hair and beard, nondescript features; but what I thought of then as fanaticism burned behind his eyes.

"It's you!"

"Yep," I replied sagely.

"Where did he come from?" the high priest demanded of the guards.

"I don't know," said the one doing the talking.

The high priest squinted at him and then at me again. "Bind him to that chair, and have the captain of the guard report to me immediately."

"Yes, your Excellency."

I was tied to a chair and the guard left. One remained with me. The high priest strode about the room. It was well decorated, almost plush. The floor was of wooden construction, covered with rugs, and Chinese rugs at that. A desk sat against the far wall, and comfortable couches and chairs were scattered throughout the room. The New Christian logo was etched into one stone wall.

The high priest halted his pacing and faced me.

"How did you get in past the guards?"

"I walked."

He didn't like that so he struck my face.

"What are you doing here?"

"Fuck you."

That merited a severe beating. But his hands were softer than my face, so I fared all right.

Fortunately, before he was exhausted, we were interrupted.

A large man in a guard uniform entered.

"Lord Evan, you sent for me?"

"Captain, you see before you an infiltrator. He may be from the Monitors. I want you to find out how he came to be here. Your defenses seem to be weak."

"Sire, there is only one entry, through the main tunnel. And we have guards there twenty-four hours a day, with infrared vision for nighttime."

"How do you explain his presence then?" Lord Evan was becoming angry.

"I don't presume to yet, Sire. But I will find out. A while ago, two more of those pesky monkeys were intercepted at the entrance to the tunnel. Perhaps . . . no, we got them, we'd have gotten him, too. I don't know, Sire." He finished this last lamely.

"Well, find out. If you cannot identify how he broached your security, then I want all sentries for the last three shifts disciplined, and fiercely at that. This man," he indicated me, "is responsible for the deaths of hundreds of faithful followers already, and I won't have a recurrence."

"Who is he, my Lord?"

"The one we have sought for so long, need I tell you? I thought you were in charge of intelligence?"

"Daystar?" The captain wore a look of astonishment.

"Yes. It's been years since the Sacramento debacle, but his features are burned into my brain; although older, it is he definitely."

The captain shook his head.

I was an interested witness, using the time to regain my breath and command my mind to ignore the pain of the recent beating. My blood slowed appreciably and the hurt seeped out of me. That was another trick I hadn't known I could do, but at the time it seemed logical, so I'd done it automatically. If I ever got out of this, I'd have much to ponder.

"See to your defenses, Captain."

"Yes, Sire." He left in a military manner.

Evan turned to me again. "Are you going to talk?"

"Sure, what do you want to talk about?" Anything to buy time. But he didn't take my flippancy serious and struck me again.

"What is your purpose here, blasphemer?"

"Quite frankly," I replied, tired of the mistreatment, "I came to burn down your mountain just like I burned down your cathedral."

Evan turned to the remaining soldier. "Beat him until I return." He stepped from the room.

The sentry shrugged and started hammering away. He ignored my already battered face and went to work on my midsection. I rocked to and fro in the chair to avoid the blows, but couldn't do much other than try to roll with the punches, evading as much of the power behind them as I could. I tried mentally to prepare my body to accept the pain and that helped only a little. I didn't have full control of my thoughts then. He tired of body blows and started in on my head and face.

Gathering all my willpower, I mentally commanded him to lighten up. In a few moments he was merely slapping me with little enthusiasm. These blows stung but were not physically damaging. I concentrated further on the process, narrowing my mental field until he and I were the only ones left in the universe. Presently, the raining blows ceased and he stood there breathing hard.

I didn't think I could keep this up much longer. But I was saved by the arrival of the high priest.

"Got him in the right frame of mind yet?"

"Yes, Sire," growled the guard, voice thick and slow.

"Good. Take him to the inquisition hot seat." He pointed at the door.

I was groggy from the beating, trying my best to ignore the pain and simultaneously observe what was happening to me. My arms had swollen from the tight bonds, and the guard had to cut them loose.

I was dragged into the outer cavern. I smelled ozone in the air, like after a lightning storm. They slammed me into the chair I'd seen previously.

The guard stood back, and technicians snapped metal and leather manacles about my arms and legs. The gleaming metal helmet was placed over my head. Contacts applied to the back of my neck were cold and sticky.

"Is it ready?" Lord Evan asked a technician.

"Almost, Sire, they weren't expecting another so soon, so we have to reestablish contact before we start." Bald-headed, slim, he seemed to be in charge.

"Get on with it. They'll understand. Transmit that this is the one we have been waiting for, Daystar." He said "Daystar" distastefully.

Other technicians flipped switches and twisted dials on different consoles. So there was another agency at work here. It made sense. Our world didn't have much technology, certainly not this much anyway. And what little technology remained was dedicated to supporting life and labor on man's behalf. But this stuff had a different purpose.

Baldy acted in a supervisory capacity, directing other technicians and assistants. The electrical hum of many machines filled the air. Finally, Baldy came back.

"Ready, Sire." He pulled out a notebook. "Ask the routine questions?"

"I don't know what they want with this one," replied Evan. "Let me use the earphones and conduct this myself. There may be special instructions."

Baldy handed Evan a set of earphones, and he propped one side up so he could hear freelv out of one ear and listen to whoever was on the other end with his covered ear.

"You are Daystar?" he said to me.

I said nothing.

He nodded to himself or to the other voice on the earphone set.

"Turn up Gain Beta," he said.

Then I felt a probe into my mind.

CHAPTER FOURTEEN

I had been beaten and was sorely tired. So I didn't notice the probe as quickly as I should have. The initial outward manifestations were a splitting headache and nausea. Swiftly, I got a grip on my mind and forced it back.

Then began the mind war.

I didn't know what they were after, but I knew that I must fight it.

Out of the corner of my eye, I saw a type of scanner, lines regular, beeping across the green glass. Another probe hit me; my brain jumped and so did the pip on the readout machine.

"Was Professor Rosmanov a Monitor spy?" asked Lord Evan, grinning evilly.

So that's what the Prof's name was.

The line blipped a little and Evan scowled. I'd suspected something odd about the Prof, but certainly not this. I didn't answer.

Evan snapped, "What did the readout say?"

"Slight upsurge but insufficient movement to project accurately or verify." Baldy ran a hand over his now sweating head.

The foreign probe continued to work at my brain. I was sweating now, trying to find a barrier to erect. Finally, although unsure of myself, I was able to prop something in front of the probe. It fell back.

Baldy hustled over to a console I couldn't see, then came back. "Lord, he is fighting the probe. You must ask the routine questions so *they* can evaluate him and find an appropriate channel into his mind."

"I'm listening to them," said Evan. He turned to me. "Were you different from other children?"

I didn't answer, but the blip on the green glass did, and it jumped perceptively.

"First time we've got proper correlation with the other subjects, Sire," said Baldy.

Evan nodded. He asked me a few questions about my childhood and earlier years.

"Following the pattern, but stronger, much stronger," intoned Baldy.

Evan took a deep breath, caught my battered chin in his hand, and looked directly into my eyes. "In Sacramento you touched and threw fireworms without harm to yourself. Are you immune to their venom?"

Pressure built up within me, but I didn't answer.

"Holy water!" Baldy almost shouted. "It went off the matrix."

My head felt as if it would like to explode, but some outside force held it together and prevented this form of escape.

There was a higher pitch in the room now. Other technicians not directly involved had come over to watch. Just what the hell I needed: an audience. The blip had settled and so, too, had the accompanying singsong noise of a "beep" that indicated high points on the recorder. I was breathing harshly now.

I felt something grab my brain as if in a claw-hold on the living matter. I fought. My strength was draining, but finally it withdrew, though not as far as its former position. It had gained ground.

Evan was smiling with success and Baldy was sweating with anxiety.

Evan slapped me hard. The noise of the blip jumped again, and I thought that I would like to pull out my razor and slice him up a little. This distraction lowered the defenses of my mental barrier and something sneaked in, gaining a foothold. I didn't need to tell them about my hidden weapon, so I concentrated on anything but the razor. But my barrier had been broached. I erected a holding pattern around the incursion area, and fought to weave a stronger defense.

This was a strange confrontation. I was in a battle, a mind war if you will, marshaling forces I wasn't familiar with and fighting other unknown forces. Suppose I gave up and allowed the alien probe into my mind? Would it make any difference?

I didn't know, but somehow I did know that I didn't want to find out.

"Instructions," said Evan. "Go directly into the 'analytical phase.' "

I didn't know what that was but I didn't think it would be any more fun than the first phase. Dials were turned, more switches flipped, and the probe seemed to ignite. I felt burning phosphorus bore into my brain. I threw up another barrier just as the first crumbled. The damn thing was nearing the part of my brain that was *me.* I ran for a cave in there somewhere and built a wall in the mouth of it. As quickly as I mortared an adobc brick into place it melted and drained away. But I was holding it. Something tried to sneak out of the depths of the cave and I held it off with a mental back foot.

I was tiring quickly and the top of the cave started to compress, squeezing the life out of me. I grew a monkey tail and jammed it in as a stanchion, and the ceiling of the cave slowed to a crawl in its descent.

I groped for anything, any help I could find. Unfamiliar this was, and I was like a babe cast into the desert. An apt simile, as I dug below me and found water naturally, and this gave me strength. Another adobe brick went into place without melting. I was gaining, but only in defense. I was constricted, could only consolidate my position. The other side gathered forces and charged with renewed vigor. The attack was strong and I lost sense of external reality. The last thing I remembered seeing visually was Lord Evan and the others gathered around watching. Some showed amazement on their faces. Evan was sweating now, too.

Somewhere in the battle, I lost control over my bladder and could feel wetness draining off the chair and down my legs. But this gave me one sense that I'd lost already, a fingerhold on the real world, and I clung to it as long as I could.

With this idea cemented in my mind, I tried to fight physically the alien probe along with the mental battle. I rocked the chair, but it was bolted down. I tried to tear my arms and legs free, but they were locked fast. I couldn't see or hear what was going on in the room and could only try to fight physically by rote. It didn't work.

The adobe wall was crumbling in many places now. Lances

of pain were coming from all directions and the monkey tail was vanishing. I watched in horror as blood seeped from my body, pooled on the floor of the cave, and flowed into the adobe brickwork, stopping up chinks in the wall. I was draining fast. Soon I'd have no more blood to help and then I'd be dead.

I cast out in mental anguish as tentacles of flame came over the wall. A spark of a warm glow showed far back in the cave and mated itself to my soul. Shadow!

She was trying to help. Maybe she'd gone through the same thing. Her mind had reached me and together we valiantly fought unseen things and horrors of the nether world. The spark grew and grew. I felt I could breathe again. My monkey tail strengthened and held the roof of the cave once more. And Shadow was in there, draining blood from herself as a mother nurses her newborn, shoring up the brick wall. She had her knife out and cut off a probing tentacle of flame. She spit fire over the wall and the thing withdrew farther.

Then she was there, making her own bricks, slinging them up as fast as I could mortar them in position.

But the probes attacked again, with more force this time, as if someone had thrown brush on a fire. Still without knowing what I was doing, I shot back. Bolts from some unknown reserve leaped from me through firing ports in the adobe, killing and ravaging. But the more I killed, the more came at us. Shadow was shooting now, too; only this offensive drain caused our defenses to falter. A pool of fire seeped under the wall and another dripped from the roof of the cave. The adobe blackened and charred in the battle. Shadow seemed to fall beside me. She grew a tail also, but hers became a wide web of skin and shielded us from the heat. The web immediately started to smolder and blister from the heat. She had to withdraw it.

I was losing strength and determination now, draining even faster; I had no more blood to give to the cause.

Mortar flowed like liquid and adobe crumbled as if it were stale bread. Shadow threw herself in front of me to protect me, but she was being flattened by the attack. She cried out and a horde of tiny sparks came from the depths of the cave to help. The other prisoners!

These tiny sparks were being extinguished one by one. We were losing. A great volcano frog kicked the rest of the wall down and sat on his haunches and his long, snaking tongue darted out and snatched at the sparks like flies. They disappeared. Soon the remaining few retreated into the bowels of the cave.

However, I had rested, and from somewhere I summoned courage or something else to help. The frog had finished off the sparks and was eyeing Shadow. Like a dragon of old, a flame leapt from his mouth right toward Shadow's prostrate form. I sent out a herd of fireproof monkeys and they inserted themselves in the path of the flames. They disappeared, but Shadow was untouched. I reached out with an unused and unknown portion of my mind and pulled her behind me. I forced her to drink of the life-giving water I'd found and she recovered while I battled the frog. Great warts grew on my hands and I made the frog eat them. They choked him and he died. My strength had gathered and I followed relentlessly, lashing out with a blanket wall of my own. I chanted Storyteller mystic incantations and flames fell around us in puddles and extinguished themselves. Some flared back up, but a horde of little monkeys doused them with the water from my pool.

Then Shadow was back at my side and we walked through a wall of fire into the open in front of the cave. We were at the base of a mountain range. I called down an avalanche of ice, and it passed over us, bounding into the rolling hills below. The enemy died and retreated. Shadow grasped my mental hand and we waded into their last outposts. Matching our timing, we swept the area clean of the unseen enemy.

They made a last-ditch effort. Lightning came from the heavens and struck all around us. The very ground was aflame and shaking as if by some fantastic earth spasm. Their forces had gathered and they were throwing everything at us. Together we caused masses of fireworms to eat the lightning bolts, and when the standoff was unbearable a huge rain came from over the range and poured. The fireworms disappeared and the flames went out. Great rents in the earth from the upheaval were filled with cool water and they molded back into the earth we knew.

While we had the upper hand, we prepared my mental cave, that special part of me, into a fortress. Working feverishly, we built. But in that building, half of the structure was constructed by Shadow. We were forever tied together there, inside me, sharing the fortress. There was a significance to that concept that I didn't have time or energy to grasp, but some atavistic reflex made me accept the sharing. And she was in turn protected from the forces as well as I was.

We stood before the fortress at the base of the mountain range and challenged all devils in the lowlands. They retreated farther and farther until they were completely gone.

Shadow smiled at me and disappeared.

I put my hands on my hips and pouted. We had a good thing going and she had left. The rains had turned the land green, and I foresaw a new world; a gentle stream meandered through the rolling hills; sunshine was like food to growth which was everywhere . . .

CHAPTER FIFTEEN

". . . and with the new specifications, it will take days to repair . . ." Baldy was saying.

I came to, drenched in sweat and totally unsure of my world anymore. Remembering clearly, I had been as if two different people, one present in the cavern here and another in some odd dimension fighting a mind war that neither of us understood.

There was a different smell in the room now, one of burned wiring and exploded electronic components. Not that I was an expert in such matters, but I only had to look around to make my surmise.

Evan was obviously perturbed, storming about, berating technicians and priests alike.

Limply, I sat there, wondering what the hell was going on, what the hell had gone on, and what the hell was going to go on. I had no answers. Breathing raggedly, I tried to marshal my strength to face whatever might come next. Somebody had obviously burned out a machine or two. I hoped it had been my fault. The trauma of the great battle was already fading, edged out by concern for my present well-being.

Evan spoke into a microphone and took his earpiece off. "Good thing we didn't kill him like we tried for so long. *They* wanted to study him, and it is becoming more important to them, this crazy-people roundup. But our duty is to follow."

Whoever *they* were, they didn't have their signals together with the New Christians.

I felt weak, which I was, but not defeated. I didn't know

what was happening or where I fit in, but I'd find out sooner or later. A wave of nausea was my immediate reaction. I vomited.

I didn't feel very good at all, now that I noticed. Baldy hastily removed the helmet and loosened the straps and bindings on me. I slumped in the chair, totally exhausted, too tired to move or speak.

I promptly passed out.

When I awoke, it was slowly. There was a warm glow around me and my head was nestled into something soft. My eyes opened and there was Shadow, looming over me, concern written on her face, violet eyes boring into me.

I smiled weakly and she grinned, splitting her face with the most beautiful sight I'd seen in a long time.

"Robin," she said, in contralto, making me feel warm and wanted. She cradled my head in her arms. "I knew you'd find me."

Her word output had increased. I looked about. I found that I was manacled with strong steel at wrists and ankles. Chains stretched between them hindering my movements. Lights still shone in the prison cave, but it must have been the sleeping cycle, as most of the prisoners lay on the ground and slept. Four guards now patrolled the upper gallery. Entrances to the cavern floor were barricaded with crosshatched metal rods.

Shadow held water to my lips and I drank thirstily. I tried to talk, but could only croak, "Thanks for being with me, Shadow."

She beamed.

"What is going on here? Did you have to endure the mind torture on your own?"

"Yes," she said. "But when I went through, I was one of the first, and their machines and techniques were not perfected. It was easy." Her voice showed a haughty disdain for Evan and his wonder machines.

"Do you know what they plan to do with us after they finish examining our brains?"

"Kill us all."

It figured.

"Why are they doing this, Shadow?"

"I do not know, Robin, but they seem to be experimenting in our minds. There is something there that threatens them."

"Who are *they*? Whom are we threatening?"

She shook her head.

Whatever experiences Shadow had gone through, they had served to metamorphose her to a certain extent. She was no longer reluctant to talk. By no means was she gregarious, but compared to how she was before, she was one hundred and eighty degrees different. She'd been captured after the fireworm ate me, after killing one of her attackers and the fireworms killing another. Lasers had made the difference. She told me that the Mother fireworm that ate me had disappeared into the sand. From then on, it was one New Christian Church after the other, until they finally ended up here at the citadel. Little groups of kidnapped autistics kept filtering in for the past month or so, and here we sat. None of them knew why they'd been kidnapped until Diego Garcia had showed up, and in a hazy way had explained what I'd surmised for him.

I told Shadow of my sister and her investigations. She was much interested in this data, some that I hadn't told Diego, and agreed with me that there was indeed something special about us.

She explained. "I always knew I was different, but I kind of disregarded it after you and I became partners. I simply thought that everybody was in some way different. But here that difference is amplified by their machines. The priests fear our difference, and study it closely. I've discovered, talking with Diego Garcia who has no such powers, that the minds we have are dimensionally removed from 'normal' people."

Well, I didn't know about that, but with my recent experience in the inquisitor's chair, I'd be willing to accept almost anything. Shadow said that during my battle with the machine or whoever was on the other end of it, she'd helped and when we were losing, she enlisted the aid of the other prisoners with her mind. They'd come to our rescue, giving us time to regroup. As their sparks were snuffed out one by one, they fell unconscious here. Baldy and Lord Evan found out about it immediately thereafter and asked them about it, but no one would talk. However, this must have meant something to them.

The conclusion that our minds all linked in a mutual defense had upset them, and I feared that once Evan figured the ramifications, he'd separate us or perhaps execute us. But, inescapably, they'd learned something valuable. On the other hand, so had we.

Shadow and I talked most of the night, and later I drowsed off dreaming bad things.

In the morning when I awoke, Diego Garcia was next to me and Shadow.

"So you made it, compadre. Our plan worked, but look at where we are. In the middle of a mountain and well guarded. We are not much better off than when we started, and perhaps worse."

"We'll get out of this. Have they found out you are not autistic yet?"

"No, my turn has not come."

His sister came over and he introduced me to her. Elana was a classic beauty. Had Shadow not been around I would have had many impure thoughts about her, but I was constricted by Shadow's presence, mentally and physically. Not that I objected, you understand.

"The Lady Shadow, *señor,*" said Elana, "has helped us all. She has saved many of us from going crazy. She has showed us tricks to keep our minds in the proper place and how to face the difficult times when the brain burns and wants to explode out of the skull."

I looked at Shadow with new respect.

Elana continued, "And, too, she told us you were coming. Even before my brother was brought in. She said that she knew that Daystar would come and rescue us and then my brother came in and told us of you."

How the hell was I going to live up to my advance billing?

"And when you were inside the mountain," said Diego, "she whispered that you had made it inside and would soon be here."

Shadow had recognized my thought pattern.

"And it remains," I said to Diego and Elana, "for me to figure a way out of this mess."

"Sí," said Diego.

A crowd had gathered around us and most were presented to me; they looked upon me as the long lost key out of this hell. And here I was severely manacled and well guarded inside an escape-proof mountain.

The sentries above lowered buckets and some of the prisoners went to retrieve them. It was food and water. The food consisted of some type of mush, not very appetizing but apparently nourishing.

The prisoners brought the buckets to Shadow and all lined

up in front of her. She dished out the stuff equitably, insuring that no one got more than his share. It occurred to me that Shadow was the unspoken leader of this motley crew. I laughed to myself at the change in her. From a scared kid out of Destiny to a self-assured leader was a big jump. I even got jealous when several of the men stared an inordinately long time at her while she served them.

In disgust, I shuffled off into the only open door facing on the cavern, marked "latrine." I used the trench and returned, fighting down my feelings. I wasn't as mobile as I'd have liked to have been with the manacles and chains but I could get around.

After the meal, I asked Shadow and Diego if they had any idea of how to escape. None, they said.

Apparently, I or we had broken their machinery and the inquisitions would have to be postponed for a few days.

I rested and grew stronger, chafing at my bonds. I wracked my brain for a plan or method of escape but could only come up with one hazy idea. Quietly, I discussed it with Shadow.

"Shadow, have you tried your mind power over other people yet?"

She shook her head.

I told her of the beating I'd received in Evan's office and how the guard had backed off. "With our recent experience and all working together maybe we can knock off the guards."

"Sure," she agreed. "Then simply jump twenty-five feet into the air, say the magic words and your chains fall off, and casually walk several miles through a mountain full of laser-armed men, and there we are outside."

She had a point. All we had to do was overcome all of those obstacles and we'd be free.

"We need a laser of our own then," I said and our minds instantly fused and came up with the answers.

I called Diego over and a couple of the others and went over the plan.

"This is it. Tonight in the middle of the sleeping period and after the change of guard we break into four groups. Each group concentrates on one guard to knock him out or kill him. Then we form a human ladder up to the gallery and we've got four lasers. We burn off these manacles and run for the entrance tunnel. We may take a few losses but it's the only plan I can come up with."

After much discussion and disbelief, I convinced them that this was our only chance. They didn't think that they could do it, but their previous efforts on my behalf bolstered them. Shadow's influence finally swung them. We had nothing to lose anyway.

But it was not to be.

Toward the evening meal, one of the gates clanked and several guards marched in.

They unshackled me and made me go with them. Reluctantly I followed. We ended up in Evan's office again.

When I was thrust before him he asked, "Surprised?"

I shrugged, not knowing what was going on.

"*They*," he said, "have analyzed what little they could of your earlier performances and determined that you are a grave threat. You have the ability to command others to do your bidding and group mind power about you. Because of your arrival, our experiments with the others are no longer necessary. Only you are required for further tests." He laughed wickedly.

"Who are *they*?" I asked.

"Never mind," he said. "But you needn't worry about your friends. Tomorrow they will be marched outside and eliminated. They are no longer useful. We would kill them right now but we cannot dispose of that many bodies within the citadel." He turned from me to the guard detail. "Put him in the prepared room, bind him well, and sec that the entrance is open with no one going near. Four guards with lasers to be a safe distance outside the room."

My heart sunk. I couldn't go back to Shadow. They took me to another room off the inquisition cavern. It was dark and musky; it smelled as if it hadn't been used for a long time. They bound me with rope this time, wrapped around me from ankles to shoulders, gagged me, and threw me on a straw pallet.

Things were worse than ever. I didn't think that the prisoners could pull off the escape without my aid. I'd had the practice and they hadn't.

Unless I did something, they would all die, including Shadow.

CHAPTER SIXTEEN

I lay there discouraged and frustrated. All of our plans would amount to nothing. And Shadow would die.

Time passed and I felt Shadow trying to contact me. I concentrated and soon we had a tentative mind-link. I cursed because we weren't able to communicate with words. But pictures, concepts, and feelings would have to suffice.

Shadow was simply searching for me to see if I was all right. I blanked my mind and tried to replay the scene in Evan's office. Slowly, I mentally enunciated each word and underlined the thought that all the prisoners would be shot down. I think she got it, for with practice, we locked in more accurately and soon had a strange dialogue going between us. It's something you have to experience, like speaking in a new and unfamiliar language, body movements and gestures being just as informative as the words. But we finally did manage to communicate.

She paused for a moment to inform Diego and the other selected spokesmen of their impending doom. I used this opportunity to practice "seeing" through her eyes. Maintaining contact with her, and with her aid, I was actually able to view, in a smoky sort of way, what transpired in front of her. It took all my mental ability. Then, I could tell they all were justifiably concerned. Shadow had to spend extra time in calming them, but they acceded to her leadership. That was a good point, since I didn't want them panicking and spoiling everything with rash action. If Evan found out that we could communicate in that way, he'd waste no time and have them all executed immediately. I got the idea that Shadow was telling them much the same. Some of them passed the word around the chamber. Several of the prisoners began to withdraw into themselves, apparently crooning, beating their heads against the wall, rocking themselves, or remaining rigid in one position. One had an epileptic fit.

Shadow had to go among them and calm them all with soft words and firm commands. Soon the scene returned to normal without the guards noticing a different mood within the prisoner ranks.

Then she went to one side by herself to resume our conversation. I tried to put across the idea that they should go ahead with the original plan without my help. Shadow showed doubt that they could accomplish this without my mind as a catalyst but she agreed to try.

For the next hour she quietly coaxed them, building their confidence. Without the aid of Diego and Elana she couldn't have done it. More time was spent dividing the prisoners into four like groups, each with an assigned guard as a target.

We held a final consultation before the plan was enacted. Shadow was stalling for time to get the prisoners used to the idea, and the autistics who had withdrawn needed time to regain clear thinking processes. I thought that one day I could find a connection between withdrawal and mind activity so that the withdrawal forces could be harnessed. But this was not the time or place for experimentation, no matter what I'd had to do in that manner myself.

Four other guards came and relieved their counterparts. We waited for an hour to allow them time to establish a routine.

The time for action came and I strained at my bonds to be a part of it. I was frustrated and could only watch vicariously through Shadow's eyes. I feared that the effort it took her to let me watch through her eyes cost too much of her strength and ability, but I had to observe.

If they missed only one sentry, the whole plan would fail.

They all sat and eyed their assigned guards. I felt a growing aura from the cavern. The guards stopped moving in their random marching on the gallery. They began fidgeting and were visibly nervous. One sentry slumped against the wall and I knew this one was Shadow's target. I focused my mind through Shadow's to help, but she was so tied up with her own effort that I couldn't find enough power base to spring off. One sentry shook his head and moved about as if waking from a bad dream. I knew we'd lost him. He looked about as if attempting to fathom a strange situation. It was all over, a failure. I knew this instantly. Another guard pushed himself from the wall shuddering.

If these guards alerted others, all would be lost.

With an uncoordinated idea, I lashed out a blanket mental wave to the prisoners. Shadow caught it first and implemented it, whispering quickly to those nearest her.

The idea was simple. We couldn't overcome them, so we had to calm them, making them forget the momentary mental annoyance.

Soothing thoughts of sleep and rest funneled out from the prisoners. Almost immediately the sentries relaxed, all violent thoughts removed. We had hoped that each would think that he'd almost fallen asleep and would be reluctant to admit the fault to his comrades. It seemed to work.

Soon the guards resumed their individual stations and all seemed well. I cautioned Shadow to maintain a watch on them with several of the prisoners. They must remain mentally sleepy. If one awoke to the fact that his mind had been tampered with the show was over for us.

Shadow and I held a swift conference on this and she concurred. She assigned the groups to maintain their mental blanketing of the cavern. Perhaps eventually the guards would in fact fall asleep on their feet.

I ached to be there with her. She had to carry the entire burden and she was tiring. But there was nothing that I could do. Some of the prisoners were faltering now, and one of the sentries seemed to wake up and look around him in wonder. It was as if he had been pacing in his sleep. One of the four groups had drained its mental reserves below minimum. Or perhaps this guard was mentally stronger than the rest. I screamed at Shadow and she took up the watch. She was now involved in assisting two groups and I could feel her aura being stretched to its utmost.

With Shadow concentrating so heavily, I found myself limited in the view I had. She wasn't able to observe all of the action.

Elana moved next to Shadow and grasped her hand. I felt an additional power flow from them. As if I were part of their mutual brain pattern, I commanded that they reach out to each other and all join hands, adding physical strength to their mental powers. Several of the prisoners had passed out from the effort and some were simply not cooperating now. But those that could joined hands and the bond became stronger. All the sentries were under a blanket of mind control now, but it was merely a holding pattern. The prisoners could effect no stronger control, and they were weakening.

Occasionally, one prisoner would fall out of the circle and the others would scoot over and rejoin hands, completing the linked minds again.

I knew that it could not go on much longer. Already, Shadow was carrying a large portion of the battle herself. I tried my damnedest to assist her.

I had shriveled my awareness to the single mind link with Shadow. I hadn't paid any attention to my physical circumstances.

At the height of the battle I was rudely wrenched away.

CHAPTER SEVENTEEN

A soft scuffling noise interrupted my focalization. The mind link faded and was abruptly snapped. I didn't know what was happening and tried to ignore it so that I could assist Shadow and the others. But I couldn't concentrate enough to regain the lost contact.

It took a few seconds for my brain to regear itself to my present location and circumstances.

The room was still dark and stank of sweat and effort. I found that I was physically drained, the past activities and the present mind battle had taken their toll on me.

I tried to accustom my eyes to the dark and locate the source of the interrupting noise. Soon I found it. A stealthy sound came from the ventilator grating, high up on the far wall. Suddenly the grating fell to the floor with a muffled clang.

A small head popped out of the opening and looked around. It was the third monkey, red tufts of hair frothing from his ears. I had no idea what the hell it was doing here, just as I hadn't known what was happening at the tunnel entrance of the citadel earlier.

Apparently, the sentries outside my door were too far removed by Evan's worries about my control abilities to hear the clamor of the falling grate.

The monkey leaped down, scuttled to the open doorway, checked outside, and came over to me. He stood over me for a moment as I lay helplessly on my back. He gestured at me. I couldn't follow his reasoning, but now I didn't think he was inimical. All I wanted to do was to get back to Shadow and the battle.

Finally he gave up whatever he was trying to tell me and grasped my shoulder, trying to pull me over on my stomach. I rolled over, hoping.

He fumbled at the tight bonds for a few minutes. I couldn't believe that I'd found succor in the middle of the citadel, but I had.

However, the bonds were too tight for the monkey to untie. He continued trying, though. I remembered the razor on the thong behind my neck.

"A razor, behind my neck, on a thong," I whispered urgently.

He didn't understand.

"Like a knife, under my shirt."

He scratched his head, still not comprehending.

With an effort, I managed to work my chin beneath the thong at the front and give it a yank.

Then he got the idea. He pulled the thong and it stuck, the pouch catching on my shirt. But he was not easily thwarted. His little hands snaked under my shirt and wrenched the pouch around. Soon he had the razor in his hand and sliced neatly through the ropes binding me.

He stepped back and I sat up, limbs burning from returning circulation. I was free, but there were still guards outside this chamber.

I tried to reestablish contact with Shadow, but she must not have had the extra strength to receive me. I could feel mental waves ricocheting all over the place. At least they were still at it. If I could get out of this room, I could help them immeasurably and perhaps there would still be a chance for mass escape.

Time was passing swiftly. I hadn't much idea of what the hour was, but soon the sleeping period must end. We'd started our attempt after the midnight changing of the guard, at least an hour later. And some time had expired already.

I shot out a wide-beam reassurance broadcast, hoping that Shadow or one of the others would pick it up and continue the battle. Shadow would know that I'd broken loose and would come to her aid if possible.

Feeling my bones creak, I edged up to the opening and peered out. The cavern was empty save the consoles, quiet now, and four sentries, seated by twos on benches in the middle of the cavern and facing my door. Two of them drowsed while the other two carried on a desultory conversation.

I went back into the dark area and did a few exercises to hasten the reawakening of my body. I cleared my mind of all extraneous thoughts so that I could work on the four sentries.

The monkey sat aside and watched me. I wondered about him. The last time and only time I'd seen any monkeys was with the Prof. There must be some significance to his presence. And it was a strange monkey; obviously not of the family to which I was accustomed, that of Abraham.

I dared wait no longer. Again I approached the door. I selected the two guards who were awake, concentrating on putting them to sleep.

My temples throbbed with abnormally expanded blood flow and I could feel their minds. With the same plan that I proposed that the prisoners attempt on their guards, I directed soothing, sleeping thoughts at these sentries. The conversation seemed to die of its own accord and they listlessly sprawled on the bench. The eyes of one glanced uncomprehendingly around, seeking to understand what had come over him.

Fortunately for me I'd had recent practice, and I singled him out for extra effort. He tried to raise his arm, and it slumped beside him. Presently, he was fast asleep. The other one was easier. Then I directed my mind to the two remaining, those that had been drowsing, and gave them an added shot of command-induced sleep. Soon all four were breathing deeply and regularly.

I scanned the cavern again for signs of others present and saw none. To be sure, I added a quick mental sweep to verify: no one.

To shore up Shadow and the others, I blasted a thought pattern of jubilation to them so they would be encouraged. Shadow would know that I was now free.

Cautiously, I swung along the wall toward the stairs so as not to awaken the sleeping sentries. I kept a portion of my mind covering them, well aware of my tenuous hold. Any slight noise would ruin the effect and they would be on me, lasers blazing. I thought longingly of the lasers at their sides.

The monkey followed me out. He saw the sleeping guards and went over to them. I tried to motion him back, but he ignored me.

My razor flashed and I saw what he was doing. I was initially aghast, but could find no sympathy. So I helped. While he slit their throats, I clamped down on the remaining sentries to avoid their premature wakening.

Soon all four were dead; a ghostly silence reigned. Blood spurted from their necks, several carotid arteries pumping the juice from their bodies. Heads lolled askew. I ran over and soon held four lasers. I tucked three into pockets and belt and was on the way to the stairs. It was no time for trickery.

But I stopped and ran back to the room I'd been tied up in, gathered scraps of ropes, and ran again for the stairs.

The monkey followed.

At the top of the stairs, I paused and checked the corridor to the prison cavern. It was empty. I went down the passageway swiftly but quietly.

At the opening onto the prison chamber I halted and peeked around the corner.

The four guards were leaning languidly against walls in their positions. One was stirring.

Below, Shadow and Elana sat together, hugging each other, something contrary to their natural inclinations. Oddly, I thought that this mind-link business might be a breakthrough, indicating that autistics weren't merely mental deficients.

But all the other autistics lay sprawled about, moaning or simply curled up within themselves. Diego Garcia, the only non-autistic prisoner, not being able to assist in the mind attack, was moving about the exhausted prisoners, quietly urging them back into the fray. He wasn't having much luck.

Shadow and Elana were the only ones left holding the sentries. And they were tiring swiftly. As I said, one of the guards was breaking their hold.

I directed my recently successful technique at him and he promptly folded up and slumped to the floor. One at a time, I aimed at the remaining sentries. And one by one they went down. The monkey and I raced for them and I risked a glance into the prison pit. Shadow and Elana had passed out in each other's arms.

The monkey made quick work of four throats. I now was burdened with four more lasers. I stopped to tie two portions of cut rope together. Testing the knot, I secured one end of the rope to the base of the railing and was over it and down the rope in a moment.

Diego met me at the bottom.

"*Señor,* I am glad to see you!"

"Me, too, Diego." We clasped each other and I thrust six lasers in his hand. "Pass these out; keep one for yourself. Start the strong ones up the rope as soon as you can. Keep it quiet."

Most of the people were still down, but Diego went to work. The monkey perched on the rail and watched.

I rushed over to Shadow who was now propped up on an elbow.

"Robin. I knew you'd come."

I couldn't answer as I was too choked up. I crouched next to her and took her in my arms.

Time was a factor, and I tore myself away. Handing her a laser, I said, "Up the rope as soon as you can. Use this if you have to."

She looked at it distastefully. "I don't know how it works."

"Me neither, but I think you just point it and push this stud. And the thumb catch here on the butt must be the selector—from narrow beam to wide spray. Maybe we won't have to figure it out."

Diego was arranging things nicely. He had several of the strongest men already up on the gallery and they were spreading out to the various openings to serve as lookouts. Shadow got Elana going and the two of them went from one unconscious form to another, waking them, soothing them, and urging them to the rope.

It takes awhile for a hundred or so people to climb a rope. And some of them didn't possess the natural strength to climb it. Others were still too weak from their expended mental activities to respond, so we had to lash them in the rope and pull them up.

Diego Garcia was an effective organizer. He assigned the lasers to the guards, and directed others to carry those ten or twelve comatose cases. We would not leave any of our own to the mercy of Evan and his silent partners.

Eventually, all were on the upper landing. Shadow, Diego and I held a planning conference.

"Diego, do you have any idea how many NC people there are here?"

"No, *amigo*, I haven't been here long enough."

"I do," said Shadow. "From what I can gather, this is their stronghold. The whole base of the mountain is burrowed with tunnels, caverns, and rooms. I'd guess over a thousand, and I've seen well over a hundred different sentries."

"Damn," I said. "This must be a gathering of their hierarchy or something similar. They've just started their kidnapping and from what Evan said, they no longer need captives."

"Maybe," said Diego, "they are preparing for some sort of action."

"Yeah, but what could it be?"

Shadow and Diego shrugged.

Our problem was to sneak a hundred people through the maze and escape. "We can worry about the ramifications later," I said. "I came through last, so I'll lead. Additionally, Shadow and I can sniff out any opposition before they see us. Diego, you take the rear guard, pick four or five men with lasers, and keep the crowd moving and quiet."

He nodded. The monkey was clinging to my legs now, so I hoisted him to my shoulder. He still gripped the bloody razor. Shadow saw it and shuddered.

We double-checked to insure that the ambulatory cases were taken care of and started out. I kept to the upper landing, retracing my way in. We passed the cavern with the electronic inquisition equipment. No one was about yet, and the four slain sentries lay on their benches, as if asleep, but pools of blood belied their status.

The column of people was strung out behind us and I heard a gasp or two as they came into this chamber. Some must have undergone horror here, enough to break them down emotionally. When and if we got out of this, I'd have to find out what Shadow had gone through. At least they hadn't enough information, according to the conversation during my inquisition, to home in on those who had gone before me.

A vague thought of retribution crossed my mind. I would have liked to find Evan and pay him back for the Professor, but I discarded the idea as impractical. The living quarters must be elscwhere and I could have sniffed them out, but I had a bunch of people to get out of there. I didn't want to endanger Shadow any more than possible. I wondered how much longer we could stay quiet and avoid discovery.

We pressed on, Shadow and I mentally casting out ahead of us to discover anybody in our way. The other side of the inquisition cavern led us into a far passageway. I thought I detected a presence in a side room and looked at Shadow.

She nodded that she'd felt it, too. I motioned those behind us to stop and the whole chain backed up. Fortunately, they were quiet. I saw Elana clamp her hand across the mouth of one woman who was being carried and moaned in her unconsciousness.

Waving Shadow back, I stepped lightly forward. The passageway was well lighted, and light also shone from several open doorways. I got out my laser, studied it again to be sure I could fire it if necessary. The monkey squirmed on my shoulder.

The first door opened onto an empty room and I bypassed it. I got stronger emanations from the second door.

As I started to peek around the door, a sentry stepped out and collided with me. He bounced back, saw me, and shouted. Then the monkey was in the air and landed on his head and shoulders. The razor flicked and the sentry fell to the floor, gurgling. Another shout came from within the room and I glanced in. Several guards were in there. Perhaps this was the sergeant of the guard's command room. There must have been five or six of them within. They had frozen and watched their fellow fall with the monkey astride him. But now they were galvanized into action. One sprung for what I could only gather was an alarm and the others struggled to pull their weapons. Raising my laser, I pointed it at the guard trying for the alarm, a red switch on the wall, and pressed the stud.

Then Shadow was beside me, coolly firing into the room. Beams crisscrossed and the guards were falling. I didn't hold my fire on narrow beam, and with a little experimentation, I got the wide beam on and swept the room. In seconds, the insides, the flammable portions, furniture and the like, were aflame and no one alive remained.

The stench of charred human flesh filled the corridor and smoke billowed out. I couldn't see into the room any longer and shoved Shadow ahead, waved the people behind us forward and started off myself.

Then an alarm went off. A clanging bell sounded within the room.

A damn fire alarm! I hadn't seen one of those since San Diego.

But a red light rotated in the room and I guessed it was located near the clanging bell and shot it out. The alarm went off, too. So I speeded ahead, dodging people, to catch up with Shadow.

No other rooms along that passageway were occupied. I hoped that the fire alarm wasn't centrally controlled somewhere besides the guard room. Grimly, we hurried the pace.

As we came out on the gallery of the cavern with the machinery, I quickly mind swept the area. I found one or two presences within. I had no choice.

I stepped out onto the gallery and looked around. Two more guards and a couple of technicians were down in the cavern. The monkey scampered by me. The guards saw us almost simultaneously. People were panicking, spilling around me and running.

I snapped a shot at the guards and yelled for Shadow to lead them around the gallery while I held off the guards. She nodded and started off.

Continuing my fire to keep the guards' heads down, I was joined by two others in the vanguard of our group who had lasers. I got one of the guards and the other ran. He was cut down immediately. The two technicians scrambled under some equipment and hid. I discounted them as adversaries.

Running, I circled the landing, shoving people aside. A rotating red beacon was on in this cavern, too. So the fire alarm was wired together throughout the mountain.

We had very little time.

Shadow and I raced down the stairs and headed for the tunnel. People were running hard behind us. The end of our column came into view as I paused at the tunnel opening.

I saw Diego Garcia and a handful of men bringing up the rear and firing behind them. That meant we were pursued already. Nothing I could do about it, so I turned and ran into the tunnel. Shadow was beside me.

I grabbed her arm and said, "Take the right and I'll take the left. Check each room off the tunnel quickly—any doubt, hose it down with your weapon. We've no time for finesse, they're pressing Diego hard from the rear."

She nodded and we sprinted ahead of the panic-stricken mob behind us. Nobody could outrun Daystar and Shadow.

Two priests were sleeping in the front room and I shot them coldly from the door. It wouldn't do to have those priests wake up and see our procession stream by their door. Shadow was firing on her side of the tunnel now, and then sprinted for the next open doorway. My next room was empty and the next after that. I was ahead of Shadow.

She'd stopped at one room where someone had slammed and locked the door on her. Together we burned off the metal around the locking mechanism and I stepped in, spraying the wide beam. Half a dozen priests went down, and a needle-thin beam creased my arm. Shadow shot calmly over my shoulder and the priest fell from a hidden alcove.

We ran on, the monkey scampering along with us somehow. Soon there were no more doors and the tunnel darkened as it had on the inward trip.

I stopped Shadow and told her of the lack of light and the guards at the end of the tunnel.

"They have some apparatus for seeing in the dark," I said. "I don't know if it's night or day outside, so we must be careful. I'll go ahead, and you follow in a minute or so. If I draw their fire, you pick 'em off."

She squeezed my hand. I swung the monkey to my shoulder and ran off down the tunnel. Then, the light from behind faded, and I had to run with one hand on the side wall of the tunnel. I prayed there were no diverging corridors. The monkey held on for dear life, arms clasped around my neck. I still couldn't fathom his presence or his role in this bizarre drama, but I was thankful just the same.

After I judged I'd gone far enough, I slowed down to approach the entrance cautiously. One possible benefit to our situation was that the guards were alert for external intruders, not for people escaping from within. I cast ahead and found the regulation two minds a bit farther along the tunnel. They were not hyperactive, meaning, I hoped, that they weren't aware of our break for freedom. At least they weren't forwarned. I grasped my laser and stepped ahead as silently as I could.

My need for stealth had slowed me down perceptibly. I began to hear the sounds of the running people behind me. Their auras penetrated the air and screwed up my reception of the two guards.

If I didn't do something soon, they'd be on me and the noise would alert the guards. Boldly I moved forward, weapon outstretched.

I couldn't see a damned thing except a lighter patch against the dark background. I caught increased mental activity ahead of me.

A challenge rang out, not demanding, but a challenge nonetheless.

"It's me," I said. Well, weak, yes, but the only thing I could think of.

I felt Shadow's presence on the opposite wall.

"Who's me?" The voice was still unsure.

"Who the hell do you think?" I demanded.

All this time I'd been edging closer, trying to find a human outline. I was scared that they'd see me with their night-vision apparatus and I knew I couldn't stall them much longer.

"Step forward and identify yourself." The voice had taken on a commanding tone. But I located it with the last statement.

I fired, wide beam, and rolled aside, spilling the monkey onto the gravelly surface.

It was a good thing I did, for another flash whizzed over the spot I'd just been standing on. I thought I got the speaker, but I wasn't sure. The weapon flashed again and a laser opened up from Shadow's position.

I heard a cry and fired simultaneously with Shadow. Burned flesh smoked through the tunnel.

I scrambled forward, mentally telling Shadow to remain hidden, and checked for the sentries.

I found two smoldering piles. Unfortunately, their headgear had partially disintegrated, too, so it was of no use to us.

Searching quickly, I ascertained there were no more guards and stepped out into the starlight. The skies showed a hint of dawn, which was to our advantage. We still had a long way to travel with possible pursuit.

Shadow came out beside me and grasped my hand. The monkey hovered nearby.

Soon, the first people streamed out into the night with us. Glad cries of joy filled the night air. I sent Shadow to corral them and get them down off the plateau where they wouldn't be in the way of a fire fight should pursuit overtake us at the mouth of the tunnel.

I fought my way through the stumbling crowd, trying to find the rear guard and help if necessary. In a few moments, flashes lit the tunnel and were coming this way. I ran toward them.

In the intermittent light, I made out Diego Garcia, firing

coolly behind him. He and two others were walking backwards, keeping the opposition's heads down.

I fell in beside him. "How goes it, *amigo?*"

"Not good. They are pressing and we've lost a half-dozen good men."

"We're almost to the end of the tunnel, Diego, then we'll be free."

"It is a long way over rough country, *señor,* with those *bastardos* following."

"No sweat, Diego. We scatter around the tunnel opening and pick them off as they come out." I snapped a shot at a flash. Some smart ass had turned his weapon to wide beam and illuminated the tunnel. Apparently wide beam decreased the effective range because his shot didn't reach us. But Diego and I both nailed him with narrow beams.

"Diego, we need time to regroup our forces. Let the others go ahead, and we will crouch here and take their front men when they come upon us." I hoped to wipe out the enemy immediately behind us and give us time to set up a perimeter outside the tunnel entrance.

"Good idea, *amigo.* You hear that, Willy?" He spoke to a tall, thin black man at his side.

Willy fired again and said, "Got it, man. I'll set up a defense."

"Good," muttered Diego. "But please do not shoot me and Daystar when we come running out."

"I said I got it, man."

"Go then," Diego told him.

We all ceased firing and Diego and I split up, he taking one side of the tunnel and I the other.

The enemy advanced, still firing haphazardly in the center of the tunnel. We waited.

I searched out minds. It was difficult as they were all in a killing haze. This made the task doubly difficult as their minds overlapped with their desire to get us. Random thoughts bombarded the inside of the tunnel. I had to guess at least seven or eight.

I set wide beam and waited. Diego would shoot on my cue. We were making good skirmish partners, each knowing what the other would do.

I didn't want them exactly level with us, fearing that Diego and I might shoot each other in the cross fire. When they were but a few paces away, and we were just outside the circle of light cast by their shooting, I opened up and so did Diego. He'd set wide beam, too.

They walked right into it.

In a few seconds, it was over. Piles of stinking and burning bodies littered the tunnel. I could find no other thoughts present besides Diego's and called to him.

"That's all of them."

"Then, *señor,* I suggest we get the hell out of here before my nose falls off."

I agreed and we ran to the end of the tunnel and out into the night. I broadcast ahead of us so that our friends wouldn't shoot us.

CHAPTER EIGHTEEN

When we ran out of the tunnel, there was no one in sight; dawn was promising and starlight provided some illumination.

"Over here," came a whisper. Willy.

He had a couple of men hidden in the rocks with a good angle of fire at the tunnel entrance. The plateau trailed off here, down to the rolling hills.

"Where is everybody else?" Diego asked.

"Down below," said Willy. "And most of them are pooped out. They need rest, man."

"We've got to have a conference and decide what to do," I said, eyeing the opening suspiciously.

We left two men with explicit instructions and went downhill to the rest of the group. They lay on the ground, exhausted from the night's ordeal. First their minds had been stretched for an inordinate time and then they had been physically taxed. We were just realizing that we had a long way to go yet without water or provisions.

I fell to Shadow's side where she tended a wounded man. He wasn't going to make it, not without an arm. Fortunately, the lasers cauterized a wound simultaneously with inflicting damage. But the shock would kill him.

"How about some water, Robin?" Shadow said. "Some of these people aren't going to make it any farther without it."

I remembered a seep I'd found a short way off the upward trail. We, all ninety or so of us, left, moved the wounded and unconscious through the rocks to the seep. A small, natural bowl just barely fit us in.

After each one had assuaged his thirst, several of the stauncher joined us. Willy, Diego, Elana, and a couple of others who had emerged as natural leaders gathered and we held a meeting.

"I'm for making like birds and getting the flock out of here," Willy stated.

There was a general wave of agreement to this.

"It's a long way."

"To where?" asked another.

"Ah, but that's the question," said Diego Garcia.

I let them talk it out for a while. We needed to act as a group. The meeting and conversation were doing more than I could to alleviate the tendencies of autistics to be loners, as I had been. Additionally, autistics were not known to work together. But the long imprisonment had done a lot to promote cooperation, and I was surprised. Most were considerate of the wounded and were thinking as a team. Perhaps their mental joining earlier in my defense and overcoming the sentries had opened new vistas for them. Or I should say, us.

"There is nothing to the north," Willy was saying.

"*Sí*," agreed Diego, "and the west and east are equally unappetizing. That leaves the south, the route by which we came."

"With no food yet."

"We can find water," I said, "from locations where the kidnappers took their supply and others I found on the way up here. But food is a necessity, and I recommend that since we cannot find much forage on the land, the sooner we start out, the sooner we'll arrive. We're burning energy just by staying here."

"Let's hit the trail then," Willy said.

Shadow started to say something then held back, knowing from the tentative link we'd established that I wasn't through yet and would say what she had thought.

"We've wounded and unconscious to think about," I said. "But that's not what's worrying me. As soon as we pull out, that tunnel is going to vomit New Christians with a bloodlust. And all armed to the teeth. We'd have to fight all the way."

That stopped them all right. They saw what I saw, everyone splitting up and every man for himself, to be picked off one by one by the enemy or by fireworms.

But I was thinking two or three steps ahead of that. Here

we had an effective fighting force, hate-mad at New Christians and a cultural system that wanted autistics and others like them dead. They hadn't realized this yet, but over time the thought would crystallize. Sure, they'd all make it home. But were they prepared to go back into hiding? After they'd seen what they could do both individually and as a working team, would they be content to lead their normal withdrawn lives or to be discriminated against my family and friends again?

I doubted this and it led me into other areas of deep thought. Perhaps this was why Shadow and I had roamed so much. There was nothing for us in today's society; we'd made our own life and operated on our own rules.

I had to plant a seed, so I carefully selected my words, deciding that honesty would be accepted at face value and they could see mentally that I was lying if I tried that track.

"What are you going to do when we return to civilization?" I asked.

That shut them up. Each fell into his own thoughts. Their faces told me they weren't going to accept their previous lot in life.

Willy broke the silence. "Man, I think the first thing I'm gonna do in Tucson is burn down the New Christian Temple." He nodded to himself as if reaffirming his decision.

"Things will be different," Elana said.

All nodded agreement as if she had echoed their thoughts, which, with this group, was high on the probability scale.

"I have to ask," I interrupted, "if any of you knows why you were kidnapped?"

No one answered.

"That's what I thought. Have you considered the ramifications of your kidnapping?" I pushed on relentlessly. I didn't know why, but I knew that I had to break through a barrier here. "Why, I wonder, does the New Christian hierarchy preach death to mentally disturbed children and kidnap those that made it through the trying times we all had? And why now, all of a sudden?"

"That's true," said one, thoughtfully. "I never heard of anybody being kidnapped, but now they brought in a bunch of us and, if Shadow's friend is correct, they were prepared to kill us straight off."

"What have they got against us?" Elana asked, curiosity shining on her face.

Most of the remainder of the escaped prisoners had gathered around us now and were listening intently. I had my audience.

And Elana had provided my line.

"I don't know what they have against us, Elana, but I would pose the question differently." I paused for dramatic effect, and the hollow became quiet, individual conversations dying. I had all of their attention.

I raised my voice. "What are they afraid of?"

There was a stunned silence while the hidden meaning of my words sunk in. Shadow was happy, that I could tell, as she was with me on every step of the thinking I'd done.

I gave them a moment to consider my words and hammered my point in further. "Why were they studying autistic people—adults specifically? What do we have that is different from everybody else in the world, that, since they kill us off as children, can be construed as a threat to them?"

I hit home. I could tell that they were working it out. There was an immediate upsurge in mental activity, unshielded as yet, since they didn't have the control that I'd recently developed. Some of it was emotional reaction, but most reflected intricate thinking and weeding out of extraneous data, and correlating information to reach a logical conclusion.

I pursued them relentlessly. "And who the hell are *they*? Evan kept referring to *they* as if *they* were his masters. And *they* must be scientifically or technologically advanced, as you could tell from their setup in the citadel. I'd like to find out who's been hunting us and why. Someone has been searching for me, and Shadow, for years. I originally thought it was because I messed them up in Sacramento, but now I'm not so sure."

Someone in the circle of faces spoke up. "Say, I remember that. Was that you? You sure played hell."

"Could it be the Monitors?" asked another from the dark.

"Beats me," I said. Remembering the Professor, I doubted that *they* fit the pattern. I said as much. But that possibility was there. "Oh, I forgot, Evan made a reference to a Monitor spy, so perhaps Evan and his cronies fear the Monitors."

"I think," said Willy, "that we ought to head back, and

burn every goddamn New Christian church or temple along the way, starting with Taos, Sante Fe, and all the rest of them."

Some of the men murmured agreement. Willy was a good fighter and field commander, but he'd have to be well harnessed or he'd burn the country down around our ears.

Carefully, I chose my words again. "That's possible. But it isn't solving the problem. Those churches are obviously a manifestation of the problem. If a whole village becomes sick on bad water, you don't burn all the water buckets. You remove the source of the problem."

"Yeah," he said. "Let's go back in there and wipe 'em out."

Others joined in and shouted down his solution for obvious reasons. But I had them thinking, to what end I didn't know. An idea was creeping into my mind. In addition to being a battle-molded fighting force, we were also an intelligent crew who could put across ideas. After escaping the citadel, all had a growing confidence that came from new-found mental prowess, incipient though it might be. With ninety agitators spread throughout this part of the country, our "problem" or trait would be a force to be reckoned with. The first order of business would be to stamp out the barbaric process of killing mentally defective infants and children.

But all these thoughts were for naught if we couldn't escape our present predicament and identify who was trying to kill us.

I said as much, and the arguments tapered off into silence. But I had here an effective force of one kind or the other. They had been through the devirginating process of battle and had worked together physically and mentally. They were malleable. I'd figure out how to use this later, if they were still in the right frame of mind for it.

I was ready to get them rolling, as dawn had crept over us, when someone asked another question.

"You've said the word 'autistic' several times. Is that what I am? And if so, what is it?"

I hastily explained what I'd learned from my sister in El Paso. But the surprising thing was that many of those present already knew that autism was their problem. These people had grown up in more enlightened communities or were inquisitive enough to find out from some who were more learned than they.

I felt sorry for Diego, then, as he sat quietly during the entire conversation. It was his lot to be the only normal person in a group of abnormals. He endured the role reversal well.

We were planning our trek down the mountains to Taos when we heard shots fired and light bolts illuminated the shadows above us.

CHAPTER NINETEEN

Those of us with lasers raced up the trail and filtered into the rocks. The guards we'd left were pouring fire into the tunnel entrance. Smoking bodies lay out front, permeating the area with their stench.

"Hold your fire!" I shouted. "Don't waste the charge." I didn't know how long the laser charges would last, but one thing was certain: they weren't inexhaustible.

The situation remained calm for a moment, and one of those who were on watch told me that men had come out of the opening and they'd opened fire.

That was as far as he got.

This time the tunnel boiled out men and soldiers, coming in waves.

We sliced through them, wreaking destruction. It made me sick how Evan wasted life. They shot back, ineffectually, unable to see us from our hidden positions.

The sun peeked over a mountain crag and they withdrew, those left alive, into the cave mouth. I figured that we'd stopped them for now.

I crawled to where Diego and Willy were lying side by side, followed by Shadow.

"Diego, you and Willy must start the others out of here. One or two weapons can guard the tunnel. I don't think they'll try another rush soon; maybe not until tonight when we can't see."

"I will remain with you, *señor*."

"Me, too," said Willy.

"I'm not leaving you," Shadow echoed, and from her aura,

I knew she was determined. I could never make Shadow do anything she didn't want to do. I argued in vain with her for awhile, but nothing was settled and she would remain. Willy and Diego finally conceded that we weren't getting anywhere, and they'd go with the others.

"But you can find us water," Diego said in a last-ditch effort. "Without you, we may die of thirst."

"Bull, Diego. You saw where the guards found water on your trip up, and I will tell you of other landmarks to look for should those water holes be useless or insufficient. Besides, one thing both Shadow and I do well is run. We can easily outdistance any pursuers . . ."

"That's strange," Willy interrupted. "I found that I like physical exertion, too. Why, I can run . . ."

"Not now, Willy," I said. "Get those people on the road. We'll hold them off as long as we can and catch up with you. If we can find a good vantage point, we'll hold them at night, too."

I shot an angry thought at Shadow for not accompanying them, but she dutifully ignored me.

Diego and Willy shook my hand and they kissed Shadow on the cheek and left. For a long while we could see the procession wind its way down the trail and then they were out of sight.

Our present position was a good one for daylight operation. We had a complete field of fire, and those in the citadel could not escape without being sliced apart.

Shadow and I alternated watch, catching up on much needed sleep and making trips to the water seep.

Toward midafternoon, a couple of soldiers tentatively crept outside. I cut them down without hesitation. Now they'd wait for the night when they could use their night-seeing gear.

I worried about food. How long could we last without it? And we were in better shape than our compadres who had left. I guessed that if worse came to worst, Shadow and I could run in two hours a distance the rest of them would cover in a day. So we had to hold out for at least two days.

Near sunset, Shadow asked, "By the way, who was that monkey I saw you with last night?"

Monkey! He'd disappeared. I didn't think he'd gotten shot, but what had happened to him?

I told her as much as I knew of the little critter with the red tufts of hair coming out of his ears. "And that's all I know. I'd just seen him that one time, when I went outside, and then there he was climbing out of the ventilator vent. It was almost as if he were casing the place, checking out the layout of it."

I'd already told her of the monkeys that were with me and the Professor and we idly speculated on it.

But dark was growing. And with the absence of our friends, I sensed an increasing number of mental presences within the tunnel.

"They're going to come out after it's fully dark," Shadow observed, stealing my thoughts. Or perhaps I stole hers.

Life was going to be complicated after this, I thought, and damn it, Shadow said, "I think so, too."

Well, hell, at least it was somebody I cared about.

Shadow smiled at this thought. I didn't have to look at her to know she was smiling.

"We need to get a better vantage point to watch through the night," I said. "We can't see the entrance well enough and I don't trust my mind to tell me where they all are in the dark."

Climbing about, we gradually closed in on the tunnel entrance. At about twenty feet up on the mountainside around the tunnel entrance, was a cleft in the rocks. It was just large enough for two people to lie in and face the tunnel over a ridge of rock. We had an oblique angle, but it covered the entrance nicely. And the moon was out for now, illuminating the scene.

Within thirty minutes more soldiers crept out of the tunnel. We cut them down, and the remainder withdrew. Things were quiet until two or three in the morning when the moon had disappeared. They came running out in another charge, but our proximity to the tunnel entrance enabled us to fire more accurately, selecting our targets before they could locate us.

That ended the hostilities for the night. But we lay on guard anyway, nestled together. Fortunately, we had chosen our location for wind direction as well as concealment and proximity to the tunnel, so the wind swept across us onto the plateau, saving us the terrible smell of death.

Just before dawn, Shadow left for water. The loss of her body heat made me realize that the cold was eating at me. I moved to a more comfortable prone position, considering whether we could use the lasers to close up the tunnel. But based on my recent experiences, I didn't think they held enough power to do that.

Shadow returned and snuggled in closer to me. The smell of her freshly scrubbed face gave me a warm glow. And then we were in each other's arms kissing hungrily. I realized how much I'd missed her during our forced separation and a tender protective feeling crept into my mind. Then we were clutching passionately. The first time was clumsy, quick, messy, and totally unsatisfactory. Afterwards, Shadow rose and scampered off without a word. I regretted my impulsive actions, although in all honesty, she was as much to blame as I was.

I feared that this would mean a change in our relationship, and I wanted nothing to interfere with that. Nonetheless it was done, and I worried for awhile that she would simply disappear on me. But I could tell from searching with my mind that she was still about.

At dawn, I snaked out of the niche, got a hasty drink, and returned to our daytime watch post. After a while, Shadow joined me without a word.

I tried to explain that I was sorry, but she simply lay there, out of reach, not speaking. Her aura showed a carefully designed indifference.

We traded watches and sleep, and I worried about food. I was weakening perceptibly, and knew Shadow was not much better off than I.

In the early afternoon, they tried another rush, half-hearted, but still they came. The fighting woke Shadow up and with her help, I drove them back inside. We saw no more action that day. Apparently, Evan must have figured that he was boxed in and decided to wait us out. He knew we had no food and couldn't stay much longer.

That night we reluctantly returned to our hollow above the tunnel entrance. Shadow was hesitant, but the exigencies of the situation dictated that we do so.

With it returned memories of the night before. I turned them over in my mind, searching for the reason, if there was one, for the failure. Shadow and I got along so well that it was hard to believe that this was one thing we couldn't do well together. I thought back to my all-night conversation with Annette. Her research on autism had produced some startling facts, which I realized pretty well described my behavior. One of the subjects she'd held forth upon was sex.

She'd pointed out that interest in sex, for autistics, initially was generally limited to childish curiosity. But when the child approached adulthood, autistics sometimes seemed to lack the social skills to attract the opposite sex, and all combined to hinder the drive toward adult sexual activity. But from various signs, I guessed I'd been coming out of this phase lately. The constant companionship between Shadow and me had probably served to overcome some of the internal obstacles we had. Or perhaps the growth of our minds allowed us to become freer with each other. Needless to say, I realized that we were grown people now, with no sexual experience. I discounted lack of experience. But this thought led to another. We hadn't been concerned for each other's pleasure, or at least I hadn't. I'd just taken what I wanted and that was all. There was none of our usual communication, verbal or nonverbal, involved. We'd linked bodies, but not minds.

"I thought you'd never come up with it," she said, smiling. And it was better, much better, this time, when she came to me. We were together in mind as well as body.

Fortunately, the bad guys didn't try anything for the next couple of hours or we'd never have noticed them.

At least we'd found an acceptable way to kill time.

My belly was hollow, and I'd almost lost the desire for food. Water seemed to fill an empty void. I knew we were weakening too fast now and would have to leave soon. But I didn't want to. We'd found too much here to leave now. It was as if when we left, we'd leave something of us behind, now that we'd properly found each other. I regretted that we hadn't started this sooner. We tried to catch up on what we'd missed.

That morning they shoved one poor soul out. Shadow shot near him, not killing him, and he ran back inside. That would hold them for awhile.

In the late afternoon, we were in our position above the water seep, drowsing unclad in each other's arms, soaking up sunlight. Exhausted as we were, the urge came over us again and we coupled, mind and body, never seeming to get enough of it. Shadow was developing an enormous appetite.

I lay back, sweating profusely and heard a shout. I scrambled to look over the rim, tumbling Shadow aside. Soldiers had fanned out all over the plateau.

We'd blown it. I snapped a shot and dived behind a rock. The damn thing was hot from the sun and scorched my naked body. Shadow crouched behind an outcropping and fired, too. We got a few of them, but the large remainder found cover in the surrounding territory.

If we didn't do something quick we'd be trapped.

CHAPTER TWENTY

Fire sizzled in our direction. We had to keep low and out of sight or get caught in one of the deadly beams. I risked a glance out and more soldiers were pouring from the tunnel.

They'd established a beachhead and were consolidating their positions.

We were finished here, and dead if we didn't move soon. I fired a couple of random shots to keep their heads down. "Get our clothes," I said, "and run down the trail. I'll cover you and catch up as soon as you're safe."

"No. Not without you," she said. *Dearest*, she amended mentally.

"Do it now," I said, putting command into my thoughts. "Damn it, woman, we ain't got time for this foolery." I was getting angry.

She caught that all right. She scrambled down the hill, nude body glinting in the sunlight. I snapped another random shot as she dressed. She picked up my clothing as well and made for the trail at an angle that would intercept it behind the brow of a hill. Soon she was running lithely and disappeared from sight.

And there I was, naked as a village infant, fighting a horde of soldiers trying their best to kill me. Another glance showed me several of them moving toward my position. I nailed two of them and fired a few more shots about, warning them they still had an able adversary.

Then I scuttled down the hillside, scraping myself and burning my limbs on hot rocks. After that I didn't look back, and ran with my best effort. It was difficult, as the rocks and terrain didn't make as good a surface as the trail, but I managed, leaping boulders, ravines, and small arroyos. Soon I was behind the crest of the hill and on the trail.

No one had shot at me, and I relaxed, my shoulders going into the ground-eating stride that I was used to. The trail gouged my feet, but there was nothing I could do about it. I was panting heavily and unable to run at my normal great speed. A couple of days without food might cleanse the soul in some cults, but it didn't provide the sustenance a body needed for intense physical work. I slowed and made out Shadow a few hundred yards ahead.

She felt my presence and turned around to await me. Mentally, I told her to resume her way and she did so.

Finally, I caught up with her and judged it safe to stop. Pulling on my clothes, I tried to regain my wind.

"We need food, Robin."

"I know. But we've got to stay ahead of them."

We ran on into the late afternoon. Once the body got accustomed to the pace, it ignored functional protests and covered ground.

As the day paled into night, we stopped and rested. After awhile, and a drink from a nearby underground stream, we began the trek ever southward.

I didn't think we'd make it through the night in the debilitated condition that we were in.

Shadow agreed. "Besides, on the way up here they never traveled at night." She stopped. In a determined voice she said, "And I'm not going any farther without food."

I was exasperated. "Where the hell do you think you're going to get some? Is there a cantina nearby that I missed?"

"The New Christians will have food."

"So what? Shall I just go up to them and ask for it?"

"No, dummy. Who can move through the night like another dark shadow?"

"They say we can."

"There you go."

So we did. We faded into the surrounding country and backtracked. They were quite a way back, too, I might add. We'd outrun them by miles, even in our weakened condition. One benefit of this incursion was that we'd have intelligence on their numbers at least.

They'd camped right on the trail and around it. I spotted a

half-dozen sentries located several hundred yards outside the perimeter.

We had to wait for the main body of them to fall asleep before we made our move.

I cautioned Shadow back and for once she did what I wanted her to. Hours passed and most of them were asleep. The guard changed and I was able to see where they all went. The changed guard fell into their blankets and were soon asleep.

I wormed my way down to the trail, not coming closer than within ten feet of any sentry. I'd seen the food packs, and crawled toward them. Approaching the camp, I had to tread my way through rocks and scrub. But a dry arroyo provided a quicker way, once I passed the outer ring of sentries. They were overconfident; they hadn't worried about infiltrators and took few measures to protect themselves.

I snaked across some open ground, flitting among the shadows. The soldiers must have been tired; they didn't move much, other than normal sleep movements, and they hadn't lighted a fire. Perhaps they didn't want to advertise their location. I estimated over a hundred sprawled about.

Finding the provisions, I rummaged about in them furtively, insuring that the one pack I'd carry had plenty of concentrated rations. With one glance, I could tell that the soldiers at least ate well.

I heard a thump and froze. A nearby empty blanket caught my eye and I casually rolled myself in it and peered around for the source of the noise. No one was moving. It must have been a guard. I waited a few more minutes and went back to the pack, dragging the blanket with me for camouflage. I stuffed it full, and took another for Shadow. A large water bladder added to my loot and I had to stop there as I didn't think I could carry any more.

Ready to make my break, I cast around for signs of awareness, but all the sleeping soldiers had their minds open and this clouded my scan.

Somehow I strapped on the packs and water bladder and scuttled out of there before someone woke. Retracing my path, I searched for the sentry, but could find no mental sign of him.

Where he should have been Shadow sat calmly on a rock. The sentry lay at her feet dead, head lolling at an odd angle from a broken neck. Before her on the ground lay six lasers and six knives.

"Oh, shit," I said, not helping myself. "The sentries?"

"All of them."

It figured.

We each took a knife and jammed the other knives and lasers into the packs. Shadow took one and I picked up the heavier pack and water bladder. We'd get out of here and have a meal.

Recalling that the trail made a dogleg to the south, we agreed to cut overland and avoid a wide swing. Perhaps we could catch up or even come out ahead of our friends. But we were dog tired then and had a hard time climbing. If our *compadres* were in as bad shape as we were, then the New Christian soldiers would catch up with them in no time—especially since there were days of travel ahead of us.

Reluctantly I stopped and explained the problem to Shadow.

"Let's do it then," she said.

We dropped our packs and drank some water quickly, wanting to return before the dead sentries were discovered.

In a little while we were on the crest of a ridge overlooking the trail. I estimated that our lasers would shoot that far to the camp. We split up so as not to draw concentrated fire.

Shadow was a hundred yards from me and most carefully concealed under a protective overhang. I spied at the camp through a niche in the rim.

Gauging the positions of sleeping men below by mental listening, I calculated the center of the camp. Shadow would fire in a crisscross pattern to me.

I gave her the signal and opened up on extreme narrow beam. Some brush ignored swiftly, and we had our target. I swept up and down in bursts. Shadow fired her weapon from right to left.

Screams erupted into the night. As I fired, I could see a great deal of motion below, and then panic reigned. We cut them up pretty good, before they organized resistance and fired back. Most had scattered, those that still lived, into the surrounding land, seeking cover and returned our fire. In the night it was easy for them to identify our positions, so soon the place was too hostile for us to remain there. I noted that Shadow had shifted positions and was calmly firing at the winks of light below. I called her off and we retreated.

At least they'd follow more cautiously from now on. Possibly we'd damaged them sufficiently to cause them to return to the citadel for reinforcements.

We reached our packs and strapped them on. From flashes of light, we could tell they were still firing at imaginary opponents.

I wanted to get a couple of hours away before we rested. The going got tougher and we were lucky to make five miles. But we did avoid fifteen or twenty miles of trail as we crossed a range of foothills. We decided to call it a night and stopped to rest.

Mountain cold had set in, but I didn't want to risk a fire. We huddled under the one blanket I'd stolen and Shadow tore at the packs, breaking out food. There was so much we had a hard time deciding what to eat. But we managed to gorge ourselves anyway.

After awhile I said, "We should get going. Diego and the rest have no food. We can share this."

"I'm tired. Let's sleep the rest of the night." But I also caught a wistful thought from her. She thought, possessively, that we didn't need them any longer and that this was *our* food, and why shouldn't we just go our own way?

Then images of wounded friends came upon her and she guiltily put her previous thoughts away. "I suppose you're right. But I'm not going another step without sleep."

I started to protest, but she had a convincing way about her.

We awoke entangled in our one blanket at midmorning. I scanned the area with my mind and found no other presences. So we were still safe.

The path we made through the mountains would make an entire story, but suffice it to say, eventually we intersected with the original trail, skipping many miles of travel by going overland, and thus we didn't encounter any of the bodies.

CHAPTER TWENTY-ONE

We came down the trail the next day, and there were no signs of recent passage, so we backtracked to a nearby water hole and waited.

That afternoon they came straggling up, a long line of exhausted people. Their minds echoed total fatigue. Their numbers had dropped by more than twenty, due primarily to previous wounds and thirst. Those left alive just let the others lay where they fell.

Willy was leading; with a jaunty gait he came swinging up. Shadow had spread the food out on the blanket into portions. It would all be gone soon.

Willy said, "Well, I'll be goddamned," and fell into the pool.

Others crowded around now, and I saw Diego and Elana come in last, supporting someone between them.

Shadow passed out the meager rations.

We had enough, stretched, to make this meal and perhaps a puny breakfast.

When everyone had eaten and drunk his fill, I briefed them all on the soldiers following us and what we'd done. "And so," I finished, "I don't think that they'll catch up with us, even if they do obtain reinforcements. But we'll have a rear party to make sure that very thing doesn't happen."

When night fell everyone simply went to sleep where he sat. But I did notice that most of the women had paired with men, much like Shadow and I had done so long ago. There was a free and easy camaraderie building up, and I welcomed it. Something was growing here between and among us, something wholesome and something that presaged a different environment for us.

Shadow had given our blanket to an injured teenager, and his "girl" hovered about him, thanking Shadow to excess. Like several other couples we saw, we found our own sleeping place well away from the main body.

Lying there holding Shadow, I wondered what we'd do next. I had plans of a hazy sort, but between here and there I had nothing.

Shadow could simplify anything to basics. "We have to get these people, our people, to safety first—food and shelter."

"You said it, kid, when you said 'our people.' That puts a different complexion on matters, doesn't it?"

"Certainly. Do you think life will be the same for them now? They're discovering things within themselves they didn't dream existed." She paused for a moment. She'd always been more emphatic than I had and could gauge a mood in an instant. I'd sensed a difference in their mental behavior as well as their outward conduct. These people were changing, they had more self-confidence, and were battle tested, both figuratively and literally.

Shadow continued. "And you know, I've been thinking. You were the catalyst." I moved to interrupt, but she held up a hand. "Outside the tunnel you wondered why the New Christians had all of a sudden started kidnapping autistics. I think it's all tied in with you, coincidental with the NC search for you. I, and all the others, would never have broken the mental barrier but for you. You encouraged me, coerced me, if you will, into a type of relationship that threw us together and, just like magic, we were communicating without talking."

"I didn't make anybody talk without speaking," I said. She'd pointed out without saying it that I was different, even more so than the abnormal people around us.

"No," she refuted my thoughts, "you grew up into what you are faster than did everybody else. And since I was with you longer, I picked it up, the trick or whatever it is, before they did. But nonetheless you were the agent for breaking us out of our mental blocks. Most of these people matured in a world that wasn't their own. But not you," her voice was accusing, but loving all the same, "you had to traipse about the wilderness on your own, creating your own special world. And you possessed, or developed, skills that took advantage of your situation, like finding water. You're special, Robin.

But you're my special Robin." Her grip on me tightened possessively.

"Not without you, I'm not," I said and tasted the salt of her tears.

I thought for a long time and sometimes sensed Shadow at the edge of my mind looking in. I thought she'd be long asleep by now, but I was wrong.

"Yes," she said. "I'm still awake."

"Go to sleep."

"No," she said. "I'm still thinking about it. So you're special. What does that mean? That is, over and above the differences you've exhibted lately. We all have the mental talent to do what you, and even I, have been doing." And I saw it dawn in her mind. "What can you do that we can't?"

I said what was in her mind. "Fireworms."

"Right. And what did you tell me the High Priest was excited over during the questioning?"

"Fireworms."

"And what did you do in Sacramento so long ago?"

"Fireworms."

"Then what the hell is the goddamn connection?" It was the first time I'd heard her use profanity and the shock of it emphasized her point.

"I don't know, love, I don't know. All I know is that twice in my life I've been swallowed by Mother fireworms and the next thing I knew is that I was wandering about in the desert somewhere, alone and naked. Try as I might, I can't recall anything in between. It scares me, Shadow, it scares the living hell out of me."

"I'm with you." Her aura enveloped me and I felt better for it.

"But you have a point. It must all be tied in somehow together. Fireworms. *They*. New Christians with a fatal grudge against abnormal children and autistic adults. Unfathomable technology. Hell, we've got more lasers with us tonight than I've ever heard of. There must be some connection. If I could only remember . . ."

"I don't know. I remembered wisps of my life as a child before the fireworm ate me; then I was able to recall almost everything. But I can't even get a hint about the times after the fireworms ate me until I woke up in the desert. Damn! If only I could remember."

My blood was racing and my head hurt with the effort.

Shadow's mind moved in and softly guided me into a rational thinking approach. Jointly, we explored the recesses of my mind, the dark places I'd never consciously been before. It was like moving through a veil of gelatin; our wanderings slowed and almost came to a stop as we fought the unfamiliar substance. There were ghosts of some kind behind that wall, but they only taunted us. We strove forward, hand in hand, until we could go no farther. We had stalled out, unable to take another step.

Slowly we withdrew and I came awake, a rough hand shaking my shoulder.

It was Willy. "Your turn for sentry duty."

"How'd you find us?" I asked.

"Man, I don't know what was going on in your mind, but there was a red haze over here, laced with laser-like light, the mental activity was so thick. So I kind of figured it was you-all."

I'd have to learn to shield my mind asleep as well as awake. But the aura was probably a result of my searching with Shadow, not of ordinary thoughts.

Now Willy was fast gaining a talent, too. It gave me cause to think.

I had the grave watch. We had only two on duty, one north and one south on the trail, since we'd sense any intruder's presence before arrival.

Groggily, I moved to the north position, a half-mile or so up the trail. Trying to work the cobwebs out of my mind, I ran a few miles north without finding any traces of pursuit and then returned and sat on a rock, awaiting dawn.

Since the enemy—and I was freely calling the New Christians and their cohorts that now—was nowhere in the vicinity, I went to the south sentry and arranged to let the group sleep as long as they could. It was well into midmorning before anyone stirred.

We saved the remaining rations for that night and struck out south.

The next day I was doing duty helping to carry a wounded man when one of the advance scouts ran back to the main group.

"Priests," he shouted. "Dozens of them. Willy is holding them off."

CHAPTER TWENTY-TWO

There were some fourteen lasers that we'd stolen, and everybody started to rush forward.

Shouting at the top of my lungs and brain, I stopped them. Shadow helped organize them. Those without weapons I had secrete themselves in the rocks beside the trail. Then I sent two men, each with weapons, to guard both our flanks and rear. With the rest, I ran forward to find Willy.

But Willy needed no help from us. The party of priests, it turned out, was unarmed. There were some thirty or forty of them, and Willy and the other advance party had sensed them before they'd seen them. Willy and the other had climbed into the rocks and ambushed them callously. They'd been in a tight bunch, and Willy and his partner had made short work of them.

Although there was no reason to kill them, Willy's actions were understandable after what he'd gone through in the hands of their fellow priests.

When we arrived, two or three of them were shouting for mercy, the rest dead, smoking on the dusty trail.

I ran up, not knowing then why, but threw myself in their line of fire.

Willy shouted down at me, "What the hell, man?"

"Hold your fire."

"Let me kill them."

"No. Look how much food in their packs you've ruined already."

"Oh." Willy grinned slyly. "Well, man, take their packs off and I'll put 'em out of their misery."

Others were around me now and I judged that the explosive moment had passed. "Come on down, Willy."

He grumbled as he climbed down.

The three priests left alive were cowering together. One had been sliced up pretty bad. We took all their food and paused for a noon break in our trek. Some of the rations the dead priests carried were not damaged and we were able to make a decent meal. Of course, we didn't offer any to the captive priests.

"Willy," I said, "it's time to find out from our friends what they know."

There was a gleam in his eye and he knew why I had picked him.

Several of us moved from the main body, but more of them followed; I couldn't exclude them since they had as much riding on this as I had.

With strips of cloth we bound them.

"Willy, we have to make sure that we don't kill them," I said to scare the shrinking priests.

"Why not?" demanded Shadow innocently.

"You bloodthirsty little wench, I'll handle this."

Willy was toying with one of the priests' knives, checking the blade. It was sharp.

I addressed the eldest priest, knowing he would be the hardest to break. He had snow-white hair and a fanatical gleam in his eyes.

"Where were you going?" I asked.

"I'm not going to answer any questions." His voice had a determined timbre.

"The citadel?"

He looked surprised.

"No use going there," my tone noncommittal, "we just looted the place and sealed the tunnel entrance."

"Then you don't need to know anything from me if you're so smart."

Damn. Wrong track. "Who is Lord Evan's partner or boss? Who are *they*?"

Willy was standing on the form of the remaining uninjured priest, a young man, barely out of the neophyte stage. He quivered with dread. Willy could be ferocious when he wanted.

The old priest didn't answer.

"I'm going to lay it on the line, old man, and I want some

answers. Our people have been ritualistically killed for some time now; all those you see were kidnapped by Evan's minions and threatened with death; they were tortured. And I want the answers. Are you going to talk and walk away free or are you going to remain silent and die?" I had to find out something from them.

"I will not talk."

"Willy," I said.

Willy stepped off the young priest and reached down with his knife and coolly slit the old man's throat. That wasn't exactly what I had in mind, but it was too late. I only wanted to persuade him a little bit.

Blood spurted onto the dust and was soaked up immediately.

The young priest cried out. The wounded priest fainted.

"Damn it all," Willy said. "These SOBs ain't got no guts whatsoever. Pity."

I moved over to the young priest. "You're next, fellow. What's your story?"

From somewhere he dragged up courage. He said nothing.

"Let's do this one different," Willy suggested.

"Good idea, Willy, else soon there wouldn't be any priests left to answer my questions."

"Let me handle it for a moment." He went to the unconscious form of the injured priest and dragged him next to the young priest. "Look here, man." His face trembled, but his eyes went to Willy. Willy lifted the hand of the wounded priest and sliced off his thumb.

The young man gulped but said nothing. Willy shrugged and cut off the rest of the fingers on the right hand. The young priest screamed in sympathetic horror.

"Ready to talk?" I asked. This was getting too grisly for me, but I had to have answers. And, too, somehow I didn't think any of these priests would leave camp alive. I didn't much care, but wanton killing wasn't my way, contrary to some of the storics that have grown about me.

Shadow and some of the women left, looking pale.

"Look again," Willy commanded.

Seemingly not in control of himself, the priest turned his eyes back to Willy's terrible visage. Willy stuck his thumb in the corner of one of the eyes and a wet, moist popping sound came, and out popped the left eye. Willy severed a tendon and dangled the obscene thing in front of the young priest. His eyes rolled and he fell back muttering.

It was then that I noticed the injured priest was dead.

"Yea, though I walk through the valley of the . . ." the young priest murmured.

Willy interrupted him by dropping the eyeball on his chest. The young man jumped to dodge it, but failed and the eyeball rolled grotesquely onto his stomach.

"I know that poem," Willy said. "But I like my version better. Yea, though I walk through the valley of the shadow of death, I will fear no evil, for I am the meanest mother fucker in the valley."

I had no doubt of that now.

"I'll talk! Please, God, don't let him near me."

Willy turned away to hide his smile.

"Willy, how about excuse us for a few minutes?" I asked. The old hard-sell soft-sell routine.

"Sure." He sauntered away.

"Talk."

"We were going to the citadel." The young priest's voice shook and he had to try a few times before the words came out right. "We'd been called in."

"You have communication with the citadel?"

"Yes."

That meant there would already be an alert out for us. Knowing glances passed around the circle of people, they'd caught the implication as well as I had.

"Where are you from?"

"The church in Santa Fe."

"Why were you called in?"

"I don't know. Only Simon knew." His eyes indicated the oldest and dead priest.

"Why do the New Christians promote the killing of mentally disturbed children?"

"It's policy with Biblical precedent. There is not enough food and care for them. They tell us that the children are dangerous to the order."

"You don't know?"

"Just what I've told you."

"Who provided the church with communications equipment?"

"I don't know, it came from the citadel."

"Who gives Lord Evan his orders?"

"It is said that he speaks with heaven."

This young twerp didn't know anything. "Why were you called into the citadel?"

"I'm not certain, but I think the High Priest is preparing for a Holy War."

"You don't know again?"

"I'm telling you everything I know. Please don't kill me."

Willy was standing to the side but not out of earshot. I motioned him over. "This guy isn't answering my questions. You heard what I asked him?"

He nodded.

"Think you can take it from here?"

"I got it, man."

I left, knowing that if there were any more answers, Willy would get them. Most of the others left with me, too.

Shadow came up to me. "Robin, you mustn't let Willy have that man alone. He'll kill him." Her mind said that she didn't understand my sudden cruel streak.

I took her hand. "Look, my love, when they kidnapped Willy, if you don't know, they murdered his whole family. His mother first, then his four sisters and his father. His family wouldn't let the kidnappers have him without a fight. I'd say he has just cause." But down deep inside of me I was sick with what Willy might do, although I felt helpless to stop him. When they'd killed the Prof, I'd had more vengeance than Willy was ever likely to.

I got the procession back on the trail and we left Willy with the priest. We could hear screams for a mile. They would haunt my sleep for a long time.

Presently Willy, running, caught up with us.

"I didn't learn anything else, man."

"Okay, you tried."

"And, man?"

"What?"

"Thanks." He looked depleted and dispirited as if in his actions he hadn't found the answer he was searching for. Oh, yes, he would have to fight it within himself for a long time, and maybe he'd finally find the answer.

I felt an urge coming on and knew I had to run. Swiftly, I told Diego and Willy that I was going to run ahead of the advance party in case there were other priests and the like on the trail. I'd meet them at the watering place of our stop that night.

Shadow was helping with the wounded teenager, so I sprinted out.

Soon I passed the advance guard, waved, and found my stride. I felt better already.

I had to think this whole thing through. Shadow had crystallized most of it for me, but when the priest had said "Holy War," I had caught something. What was it?

Suddenly I cursed myself for not thinking of the obvious. What had Evan done to us? He'd tried to monitor our minds. I had some power and the others had it, too, but less than I did. Why the hell didn't I try to read those priests' minds? What an idiot. But what was that thought that brought all of this to a head?

Something I'd intercepted without consciously knowing it. I strained my mind, aided by the cleansing blood that pumped rhythmically with every long stride.

I kept coming back to the "Holy War." Who would the New Christians war against? Not current society since the New Christians were free to set up shop anywhere they pleased, and in fact did have branches throughout most cities and communities. Other areas, such as Mexico? No, New Christians were there, too; besides, logistics wouldn't allow prolonged war in these days.

That left two possibilities. One, the Holy War could be against autistics. Only, that argument lacked substance. The New Christians already had a program tantamount to genocide. I thought it odd that I was already isolating autistics as different from all other people. It was becoming automatic. But the kidnappings had been an extra step in the NC program, a clean sweep, as it were. Killing autistics could be part of the NC overall goal, but I didn't think it would be the large portion.

So, by deduction, their Holy War had to be against an outside agency, and one that was easily accessible to them, especially if they were gathering at the citadel. Who could that be?

The only other party remaining unaccounted for that would explain the New Christians' drive for power, or whatever their target, was the Monitors. But they were an alleged benign, spacefaring race, orbiting the earth in a spaceship or two, doing their job of monitoring.

The more I thought about it the more I liked the idea. Then I remembered the lasers. Sure they'd come from off-world. No one on earth that I knew of had the technology to produce these weapons. Was it the Monitors who provided the New Christians with them? I didn't think so. It didn't fit their reputation. If they wanted to conquer the world, they could just land their spaceships and take over. Besides, Evan had accused the Prof of being a Monitor spy and suspected me of the same.

The fact remained that the citadel was chock full of technology and equipment unheard of. Since the Monitors were ostensibly friendly to Earth, the inevitable conclusion leaped in front of my eyes.

A surrogate war. *Two* alien races, one against the other, using Earth as a battleground. But why? Why couldn't they simply fight it out in the stars or in space above the Earth? One answer only there, too: a battle for possession of the Earth.

Every time I came up with the logical answer I had dozens more questions. But a few things did fall into place. Evan talked to them via radio, meaning *they* weren't present on Earth or they would have been in the citadel, their bastion. Therefore, the environment was not suited to their form of life.

Or not suited yet. I recalled the Professor exclaiming at times that the Earth was reclaiming herself. There was more than one war being waged here, or was there?

And where did the fireworm, a non-terrestrial organism, fit in?

It was all there if I could find answers enough to fill in the blanks.

No longer could I ignore the significance of myself and fellow autistics. We were a part of all this; be it a minor hinge point or not, we were still involved. But why?

I did not know.

In the back of my mind I was evolving a plan. As I ran, the idea solidified, and I organized it. It would depend on the cooperation of the escaped prisoners.

I could feel an urgency, a knowledge that things were coming to a head and that I must take some kind of action.

The plan hazy, I must determine where I was going with it. Again, I thought that the action would be close to the citadel, within a reasonable traveling distance.

One place that I thought of was the vast central wastelands, or Centralia, which stretched across the center of the continent. I had brushed the southern and western fringes of it all my life, but there was nowhere to go inland. Or was there?

Then I had the answer! The Carlsbad Taboo. Reputedly still radioactive, half-life still going strong; no one went there, not even desert rats such as I. If it was still radio-active, why weren't other nuclear-strike areas taboo, too? I'd even heard of water prospectors attempting to invade the periphery of the forbidden zone, but they never returned. Consequently I had steered clear of it. El Paso was about as far north in that area as you could go. And it was within striking distance of a few weeks from the citadel.

A chilling thought hit me. The first time a Mother fire-worm had swallowed me, I was outside El Paso. The second time was when I was way north of San Antonio, only four or five hundred miles of desert from El Paso and Carlsbad.

My head swam with thoughts and more questions. I wished I had a priest to query.

CHAPTER TWENTY-THREE

Tired, hungry, and sore, they weren't in the mood for what I had in mind. But that night I put it to them.

When everyone had rested I addressed them.

We were a couple of days out of Taos, and now was the time. Most of them had shed their clothes and bathed unashamedly in the stream I'd found. Now rested, thirst quenched, they were ready to listen.

"Have you thought of what you'll do when you return to civilization?" I paused for the words to sink in. They'd been running for so long that they hadn't had the time or the strength to consider their circumstances. Thoughts of uncertainty filled the air about us.

I had to get them in the right frame of mind for my proposition. "You are aware, of course, that the New Christians all by now know of our escape and that we're all marked?"

A murmur of worry greeted my words. Some had thought it all out, of course, but these didn't know what they would do.

Willy spoke up hesitantly, "I was gonna start burning churches and killing priests, but I ain't so sure it's the right answer now."

There was still some resentment of our captors but it was fading.

"Let me put it to you this way," I said. "Every one of us, if found by New Christian priests, will be marked for death. We can't start our own country, that's obvious. So we're all now like bastards at family reunions. Normal people shun us, save for a few families, and in those cases autism places hardships on the families. Everywhere you go, there will be New Christian priests, a hierarchy dedicated to the death of all autistics. Can you, with your new knowledge and abilities, abide in a society that condones behavior such as this?"

I had them thinking. It was a bleak picture. I sensed a common aversion to the idea of returning to the old way of life.

"But what can we do?" said one.

"Are you trying to tell us to overthrow the New Christians?" Willy asked. "I've already tried to kill every New Christian priest I've seen, and it's taken a toll on me. I ain't so sure that's the way."

"It isn't," I responded, silently thanking Willy for the cue. "We must find out why they are against us so and take action to remove the cause of their hatred. The root of our problems lies with the reason that they are trying their damnedest to kill off all autistics."

Elana said, "But it may amount to the same thing. Consider that if we do find the cause—and I think you have an idea as to what it is—will our eliminating the problem not amount to killing off the priests anyway?"

"I don't think so. Cut out the fangs of a snake and he is no longer dangerous."

"What can we do?" asked Diego. "We are no more than seventy starving people."

"We can do a great deal. I have thought this through, and with a few assumptions, I think I have part of the answer. But it will take more than seventy of us to solve the problem. A hundred or so autistics were kidnapped from only a few towns and cities that we know of. How many were missed? How many cities were untouched? How many autistic children will live to grow up if we stop the killing? Ancient figures indicate that four or five children out of every ten thousand born are autistic."

I stopped to let them think this out. I knew we didn't have enough time to save children and let them grow into warriors. But we should, if the plan succeeded, create an environment where those children could grow up and become a viable part of society.

I hadn't shielded these thoughts and most of the group caught the essence of them. I think that this, more than anything else, sold them.

"Let me outline my deductions for you." I told them of my

suspicions of alien intervention. To their credit, aside from a few ridiculing comments, they accepted my reasoning. I went through the technological capabilities of the citadel, the alien fireworms and lasers, all of it I'd thought out.

I finished, "I do not have all the answers, but I do believe that the 'Holy War' will be against the Monitors or some agency of theirs in the Carlsbad Taboo. The obvious conclusion follows that if the 'Holy War' is successful, then the future of autistics and other inhabitants of Earth, too, is doomed. We are trying to get back into a cohesive society, where technology can aid man as it's supposed to. One of the tenets of New Christianity is to dispose of all technology. Can this be a forward-moving people? Hell no. I say again, there is some other force at work behind the New Christians and they are seeking to remove the only stabilizing influence the Earth has left. It is up to us to stop them."

"Man," Willy snorted, "are you saying that we gotta save the world? If you are, then I know you're crazy."

Others agreed with him. I couldn't blame them. The world I was seeking to save had dealt them all a dirty hand and covered them with manure. They couldn't care less.

"No, Willy. If I could, I suppose I'd try to save the world, to whom neither I, nor any of us, owe much allegiance. But if the world is 'saved' as a fallout benefit of our saving ourselves, so be it."

I was losing them. All they wanted to do was go somewhere and eat their fill and lead their own lives, unbothered by anybody.

Shadow sensed this, too. She stood and commanded their attention, opening her mind as well as using words.

"Sure, go ahead and desert him. He only taught you to use your minds. Go back to your hovels and let your expanded horizons atrophy. You don't owe Robin a thing. He only risked his life many times to save you when he could have gotten out himself and left you all to rot. Leave him, he only wants to save countless unborn children from horrible deaths. Leave him when *he* needs your help. But don't forget to take a drink of his water, there in the stream that you would have bypassed. Sure, go ahead. *We* don't need you. But I need him. Not just for survival, either. Loyalty works two ways, you know. Robin will hurt when you leave him, but he'll get over it. He's found something here with you, a new mankind, and his hopes, and the hopes of all people for a decent, unkilling world, will be dashed. But what's that to you? You don't owe him any loyalty, not after what he's done for you. True, he's a dreamer. Go ahead and prove it. Let him nurse his lonely dream, wander the deserts forever thinking of what might have been." She sat down, disgusted.

She'd hit them below the belt and she knew it and I knew it and some of the others knew it, as I could tell by their sly smiles.

Willy stood up and looked around. He was dead serious. "I don't know about all this crap, but what the lady said was right. I ain't gonna skulk around as a bum, trying to scrape up handouts for a meal. I invite all of you who ain't with me and the lady and the man to get the hell out of here now so's we can plan what we're gonna do."

Nobody left, and Willy favored them all with a furious glare. He turned to me. "The floor's yours."

It was all pretty good drama, but the loyal hard core of my friends had swayed the rest. They were sick and tired of being on the dodge; they were tired of persecution and murder. And they didn't have any answer to their problems. They were stuck with me.

"Here it is simply," I said, taking a deep breath. "I'm going alone into Carlsbad to seek the answer."

Like hell you are, thought Shadow.

"I want the rest of you in your established pairs, or teams, to go out into neighboring communities—those which you are familiar with, or others, if you please—and recruit autistics like us. From San Diego to New Orleans, I want you to raise an army of autistics. We can work out the details later. Those cities, I feel, are the parameters of time, all the time we have to act. Gather as many as you can and head for El Paso. There is a liberal government there, and we won't have any problem. I'll grease it before you all arrive. Should there be a problem, I'll try to buy our way in. But the center of our activity will be the library. See my sister Annette for information, or there will be one of us there with instructions. Should I need you before the agreed-upon time, I will send word with the Newsbringers. They will call you to El Paso. The code words will be 'Midnight High.' If you hear a Newsbringer or see a notice to this effect, head immediately for El Paso. If I am not there, go to Carlsbad. Your lasers should insure safe passage."

Diego stood up. "*Señor*, we are as penniless orphans without means of accomplishing these tasks."

"That's phase one of my plan," I said. "We do need food and means to pay for it as soon as we reach Taos. I suggest the following: first, we enter at night. Recall that all New Christian priests will be on the lookout for us. We simply break into each church we find and steal their funds. It is simple, they owe us, and we collect. Should this not be possible for reasons of security, I will write a draft for each of you that should be honored by any Chinese merchant. I have Chinese connections and some wealth—" I hope, I added mentally. Robbing NC priests would also provide an outlet for their built-up frustrations.

"We should hang out signs that we're hunting for autistics?" said Willy, ever practical.

"No, that's the simplest part of the whole operation. Use your mind and scour the town. It shouldn't take much longer than a few days to sniff out, mentally, any other autistics. A little practice and you have the trick. It's almost what you've been doing since you were inside the citadel."

Some nodded and others marveled at the novelty of the idea. This approach had another benefit: it kept their minds at work developing their incipient powers.

The rest of the night was spent in planning details and tactics. I found, as have others, that the action is the least part of any battle. Planning, strategy, logistics, manpower, and myriad other details overwhelmed the actual fighting.

The time frame I sought gave those that had to go the farthest distance a few days at that location, and time to return to El Paso. I knew that some wouldn't make it and others wouldn't be able to recruit any autistics. But we should be able to gather an appreciable army. I emphasized to them that their main function was to train their recruits. This would give them their best recruiting inducement, the ability to be a part of something important. I also relied on the ever-present discrimination.

A veil of absolute secrecy had to be maintained.

CHAPTER TWENTY-FOUR

It was a starving and tired seventy people that stopped outside of Taos two days later. About half of them could go no farther and sank to the ground. I'd found a water hole, and we made this our camp. I didn't want too many of our people flooding Taos.

Along with Diego, Willy, and a half-dozen others, I made for the outskirts of town. There was only one New Christian Church here, Taos being a small town. It was the same one that had held Diego a prisoner so long ago, it seemed.

He briefed us on the layout as he remembered it, and we stayed away from town until late that night.

Then by twos we approached the church from different directions, covering all entrances.

I went in the double doors in the front, with Diego at my side. A quick scan showed only a few people inside. Lasers hidden inside clothing, we walked down the aisle past rough-hewn benches. The priests' living quarters were in back, along with a few storerooms, one of which had held Diego and some other prisoners previously. By the time Diego and I got there, Willy had entered and captured two priests and an apprentice. They cowered in a corner, covered by two lasers.

We went through the church, and in the storerooms we found a great deal of food.

Willy observed, "This must be a major jumping-off point for the citadel, so they keep concentrates here to supply the troops going north."

It made sense to me.

I knew I'd have to face a dilemma, so I stalled as long as I could. I didn't want to have to kill these priests, but they were our sworn enemies and could make trouble for us should they be left alive.

I faced them. "Where's your money supply?"

This time I was ready. I'd concentrated on the seeming senior priest and when my question hit him, there immediately popped into his mind a picture of a swinging panel behind the NC logo above the pulpit.

Needless to say, he didn't answer.

I told Willy to check it out and he returned in a few moments with a sack full of water credits and some electronic equipment.

"Look what I found."

"Their communications gear for talking with the citadel, I assume?" Seemed a stupid observation, but I was still monitoring the senior priest and his mind confirmed my thoughts. "It looks portable." It must have contained its own power source.

"Yeah, but I wouldn't know how to operate it."

We all tried to figure it out but couldn't. The priest's mind showed a long sequence of actions to work it, and a series of times, codes, and frequencies. One frequency, a command channel of some sort, overrode the others.

I flipped it on, twisted the right dials and set it on the command frequency before I forgot. We'd carry the radio and listen in on anything that came along.

The priest was not stupid. He was wondering how we'd figured where to find their cash box and radio; also, he was unnerved by my ability to use the radio. A suspicion was growing in his mind.

Willy saw the byplay of the priest's eyes, going to me in fear. He read part of his mind, too. Willy was increasing his proficiency.

"You know what that all means, don't you?" he asked me.

I nodded. The three priests would have to die. We couldn't risk exposure. I think the senior priest realized it at the same time, because a fatal depression came over him.

"What do you know of the Holy War?" I asked.

His mind flew to it and then he tried to block it out, ineffectively.

"See if I got it right, will you?" said Willy. "It's to be within the next three months, preparations are well under way, and he doesn't know the location, but he suspects . . . I didn't get it, something like caves. Could be Carlsbad . . ."

The priest's mind reflected horror, as if his soul had been raped. One portion of his mind was logically grinding out the thought that he'd been right: we could read minds. The other part of his brain screamed, as if it were penned up with nameless devils. I guess the experience could be disconcerting.

We questioned them further, about possible aliens, the citadel, the Holy War, and other things. They didn't know any more than we already did.

"Man," said Willy, "if we don't hurry up and get out of here with this food, I'm gonna eat it through the packaging."

I agreed, dreading what came next.

"You want me to do it?" asked Willy.

"No, damn it. It's my job. You've had your share. I just wish there were another way." There are times when you can't delegate distasteful jobs. This was one of those times.

The smart priest knew exactly what we were talking about. "I won't tell a soul—and neither will they." But his mind said he was lying. So I shot him; a swift and merciful death was dealt to all three.

We found a barrel of lamp oil and splashed it around to hide evidences of murder and theft. I broke a lamp in the oil as we left. We were all buried under the weight of food packs and a radio.

We spoke not a word on the return trip, but our arrival was greeted with glee. With an overabundance of food now, people fell to eating and gorged themselves. They'd regret it later, when stomach cramps from the large amount consumed hit them. Shadow and I ate sparingly. She didn't question me as to what had happened in Taos, but it was still clear in my mind and she read it like an open book.

"You did what you had to do," she said simply.

"Yes, but it doesn't make it any easier." Why had I cut out such a mammoth task for myself?

The following day we made for Santa Fe. Outside the city we split up. Last-minute instructions took several hours.

Santa Fe was a large enough town to absorb us all individually, but some circled the city and continued on their way. Santa Fe was the city where we all went our different directions.

Diego and Elana Garcia, Willy, Shadow, and I all retraced the trip to El Paso. Willy said he'd rather accompany us than go to Tucson. We'd decided that Willy and Elana would be our agents in El Paso, Diego unable to help with the recruiting, and Shadow and I would head north for the Carlsbad Taboo.

I had in mind to try something. Elana would remain in Santa Fe, and Willy would accompany us to the edge of the Taboo. He'd serve as a mental communications relay to Elana and Diego in the city. They'd be the focal point of our gathering army. I just hoped it would work.

Practicing the idea, I attempted to keep in touch with as many groups of our fellows as I could on the trip away from Santa Fe. Eventually, they all faded out of my range, but the practice helped.

I had an idea of posting Shadow farther on into the Carlsbad Taboo to relay to Willy and then to Elana in El Paso, but she intercepted my thoughts and said no.

We'd work something out.

First, I had two important tasks to accomplish in El Paso.

CHAPTER TWENTY-FIVE

Annette was surprised to see us. "So this is Shadow?"

She was gracious to Shadow, who, while feeling somewhat a country girl in the presence of the elegant Annette, nonetheless carried herself regally.

Annette wanted to know everything.

"Do you have writers that can transcribe my words as I speak them?"

"Yes."

"Do you trust them?"

"They do what I tell them to." Librarians are a society of their own and generally answer to no one.

"Just so long as they aren't New Christians I'll trust them," I said, "for if my, our, mission results in our deaths, I would want others to be aware of what we know. Our story is important."

"We will start on the morrow," she said.

"We have a month, at least, before we head to Carlsbad, but tomorrow we have something special to do. Shadow and I are going to get married."

"I'll be damned," said Willy.

"Me, too," said Diego.

"Oh, wonderful," said Elana. I noticed her eyes flick toward Willy. I declined to check their minds, and caught Shadow trying to read them. She backed off when I reprimanded her wordlessly for snooping.

Hah! she thought at me haughtily.

The ceremony was short. With Annette's connections, she was able to arrange for the Mayor of El Paso to do the officiating. This served another purpose, which I didn't broach then: to acquaint me with Hizzoner. Knowing him could become important later.

Annette and Elana had dressed Shadow up in frilly Mexican lace and she was truly beautiful. I'd never seen her in a dress before, and it was an amazing transformation, a strange difference from her usual travel garb. Shadow was certainly no longer a skinny kid, clinging to a life-style with me because she feared any change. Her childish freckles had turned into smoothly tanned skin, which was too bad for I kind of liked her freckles. The word dignity sprang uncalled into my mind. Shadow always had dignity, but through it all, I could tell that she'd still be my best friend in addition to wife and lover. I was happy then. The partnership would endure and grow. My misgivings, what few there had been, were gone.

I'd bought some new clothes and felt ill at ease during the ceremonies. I wasn't real sure what Shadow saw in me, for I was no more a gangling kid. I was big and strong from carrying the Prof as a youngster and the hard life since. My six-two frame carried just under two hundred pounds and none of it fat. I wasn't pretty, for certain, and, to be more than charitable, I had a strong face.

Only our friends were present as witnesses.

Shadow fairly glowed, physically and mentally.

We kissed coyly at the end and went on our honeymoon, which lasted until the next morning when I went to work with a couple of Annette's librarians.

I was determined to get the story down should bad fortune befall us. If my suspicions were correct, then something fateful was about to happen. And knowledge of the events couldn't hurt our cause should we disappear forever.

Willy, Elana, and Diego went to work recruiting. The New Christian sweep through El Paso had only caught up a few of the autistics. Many more were uncovered. But as I said, I was busy chronicling this story so I couldn't be much involved. Annette sat through the whole thing and was amazed at the adventures we'd faced. Being a Librarian, she was much in the know on current events, and when I finished she said she was forced to agree with my conclusions about a surrogate war. But she thought that there might be unplumbed depths that I hadn't considered.

"Don't you think I haven't worried about that?" I asked

crossly. "That's one reason why I don't want Shadow to go along."

"I belong at your side."

"Or the other way around," stated Annette.

Sometimes at night Shadow and I would haunt the outsides of the New Christian churches in El Paso and Juárez. There were three of them and the main temple in the city was the most important.

I didn't want to upset our plans by disclosing our presence, so we surreptitiously spied on them. There wasn't much going on, but we sensed a growing anticipation.

Diego monitored the radio, but most of the transmissions were in code, except orders for supplies for the citadel. Their consumption was increasing daily. There must have been many supply trains up into those mountains. I cursed myself for lack of foresight. We could have left an ambush team behind, playing hell with their supply caravans. But that move would have tipped our hand, and it was just as well we didn't.

Elana and Willy worked well together. In one of our nightly meetings I was taken outside Juárez to a spring and found that they'd recruited twenty-two autistics. Elana was going full force on the training, and Willy continually swept the towns for more "volunteers." They were making an efficient team.

One day, the orders for supplies to the citadel ceased. Nor did they ask for any the following day. I called a council of war.

"The coded exchanges are increasing," said Diego.

Willy slipped out of camp and went away for an hour.

He came back, blood splattered on his shirt. "It's on," he said. "The priest I questioned knew next to nothing, but he did allow as how some plan had been enacted. The El Paso church is to send supplies to a certain location to the north of here."

"They're staging their operation," said Shadow. "The citadel is marching from the mountains to the north of El Paso. That puts them in a direct route for Carlsbad."

"This is it, then," I said. "Find all the Newsbringers you can and bribe them to leave now. Pay them extra to hurry. Get them fast horses if they have none. They are to publicize 'high midnight.' "

We worked late that night, figuring routes for Newsbringers to cover as much territory as possible. The original date we'd set would be here soon, but we couldn't take any chances.

The next morning Willy, Shadow, and I set out for Carlsbad.

CHAPTER TWENTY-SIX

The Carlsbad Taboo lies slightly north of El Paso and maybe a hundred and twenty or so miles east. We struck directly for it, covering ground at a fast pace. We packed lightly, figuring that maneuverability was more important than a safety factor of food.

At about fifty miles out we lost contact with Elana. I wanted Willy to stop there, but he resisted strongly, saying that he was trying a new procedure. Willy had no trouble keeping up with our mile-eating jog.

The second night we were perhaps one hundred miles from El Paso and had made camp. Willy had us hold hands and concentrate. It was something he and Elana had instituted. The new communications worked, for soon we were in contact with Elana. She had all of their recruits joining hands and concentrating together. Since her reception/transmission was the strongest, we could almost talk with her word for word.

Willy explained that they were going to try to contact other parties of our friends in the same manner. This buoyed my hopes.

The land was gradually changing. Ordinarily arid, it became almost hostile. We saw human skulls propped on rocks and saguaro cacti as warnings. Nothing grew thereabouts, save those plants that needed little water.

The sun was inordinately hot, or so it seemed. And the fireworms. I sensed them all about us, but they did not intrude. I feared for the safety of Shadow and Willy. I knew they'd be safe as long as they were with me, but I didn't think I could stand off a concentrated rush.

At midday, I found a water source that was continuous in a deep ravine. The fireworms seemed to be fewer in number around the water, so I insisted that Willy remain there. He didn't like it, but the increasing number of fireworms convinced him. I tried to get Shadow to stay, too, but she rejected that suggestion.

As we parted I said, "If fireworms approach you, Willy, use your mind. I have a suspicion that they are semi-intelligent and might heed your wishes. It's something that I can't explain yet, but try it anyway. Your laser isn't going to help if they flood down on you."

"No sweat, man." We shook hands and Shadow kissed him.

Shadow and I took up the journey once again. I worried incessantly about the supposed radiation, but there was nothing I could do about it.

Shadow peeked at my thoughts, since they must have been flying about unhindered.

"You'll note," she said, "that there are desert animals about, notably snakes and some birds of prey. And I think I saw a jackrabbit or small kangaroo earlier."

"So?"

"So, if the Taboo is dangerous to life, wouldn't they be affected, too?"

"Yeah." She was right. My thoughts were easier after that. Additionally, the nuclear weapons used during the Holocaust were supposedly clean. I'd always wondered at the radioactive taboo.

But we didn't really know what we were looking for. We just headed for the center of the Taboo in hopes of coming upon something.

If the fireworms were numerous before, now they were rampant. About us the ground swelled with motion. Occasionally we could see them swarm to the surface, crawl about, and move around us curiously.

I was feeling them out, trying to project innocence for safe passage, when Shadow interrupted me.

"What'll we do, Robin?"

"About what?"

"Didn't you listen to Willy?"

"No, I was busy with the fireworms. What did he say?"

"He'd scanned the area and there's a large body of men approaching."

"What could it mean?"

"He's going to check it out; they aren't far from him."

We paused to rest in the shade of a rock outcropping and worked together to reestablish contact with Willy.

He was intent on dodging fireworms and covering territory. He couldn't concentrate for us and seek out the people he had sensed simultaneously. But he did keep open a corner of his mind so that Shadow and I could maintain contact. I could tell that he was running freely—that's a state of mind familiar to us; it lends itself to a higher plane of mental activity.

For an hour he ran, then he topped out on a long rolling hill. And there they were below him. His mind exploded with curiosity. I could sense him funneling his view to us.

Below him, a large group of men marched in a wedge-shaped column. Occasionally, a laser beam would flash out and a fireworm would die. There must have been hundreds of them.

The mob was laced with New Christian red and black, meaning that many priests were there, too. They were too far away to recognize individuals, Evan in particular.

We'd been tricked. Somehow they'd misled us into believing their timetable was much slower.

Willy, Shadow, and I were thinking together.

"Perhaps the New Christians below spied on us," thought Willy.

"Looks that way," I thought.

"But they didn't take any action to stop us," Shadow inserted. I could tell her brain was working fast and furious.

"Maybe we aren't important," Willy replied. Our transmissions were getting better the more we practiced each hookup.

"There's another answer," I thought aloud to them.

"What?" simultaneous from both of them.

"They don't know about us, specifically, and were tricking their targets, the Monitors or whomever. Subterfuge that would confuse their first enemy, the object of the Holy War, and we fell for it, too. Perhaps the Monitors had their own spies, and to fool them, Evan and his army wove a cloud of intrigue and false trails."

"Sounds possible," Willy thought, but doubt was in his mind.

We simply didn't understand. We were into something way over our heads. Was I a fool for intruding?

"You forget," thought Shadow, "that the New Christians have a higher sponsor with full technology. *They* could be doing the thinking and planning for the New Christian strike force."

Now that thought was a helluva lot more logical. If the supposition about the surrogate war was correct, then the men involved, New Christians specifically and we in an ancillary capacity, were mere puppets. It was an unsettling thought.

But we were too deep to back out now.

"We've got to beat them to their target," I thought. Our time had run out.

"I can delay them," thought Willy. "Harass them from ambush and concealment. It would slow them down."

"Not for long," I replied. "And you'd guarantee yourself an early burial. No. Contact Elana and have her reach as many incoming groups as she can. Start them on the way, meet them, and follow our trail if you can."

"How are they going to do that?" asked Shadow, "when we don't even know where we're going."

"We'll follow the New Christians," thought Willy. "They seem to know exactly where they are headed."

"So we simply keep ahead of them on their present course and we get there first," Shadow added.

She was right. I wondered why I hadn't thought of that myself.

"Sure. Then what will you do when you get there first?" Willy thought. "You don't even know where *there* is, or who."

"Robin will think of something."

"At least we can warn them," I thought.

Willy gave us a last view of the column, then disappeared over the brow of the hill and ran toward El Paso.

Shadow and I headed into the unknown.

CHAPTER TWENTY-SEVEN

In sandy places, the desert seethed with fireworms. For now, they weren't inimical to us, but I knew they would be to the New Christians. This may slow down the advance of the enemy. But then, I thought, if Lord Evan's alien superiors sent an army after the Monitors, they must have provided weapons to combat the fireworms, else their invasion would be for naught.

With these unhappy thoughts, we jogged ahead.

I'd fixed the New Christians' direction of march firmly in my mind and was certain we were on the right track. I no longer worried about radiation. The advancing army dispelled that old tale.

I sensed another mind present, but one on a different level than I was accustomed to.

"Look." Shadow pointed.

Perched on a rock a quarter mile in front of us sat a monkey. Another monkey! Now I knew there was a hell of a lot more to this whole thing than I'd ever suspected.

As we approached him, he rose. He could have been the same monkey that rescued me in the citadel. Red tufts of hair bristled from his ears.

When we reached him, he hopped down off his perch and we stopped.

He motioned to us, turned and made off along a draw. "He wants us to follow him, Robin."

"Yeah, I noticed."

We followed, cautiously. He led us across some rough territory. If the New Christian army was coming this way, they'd be enormously slowed down getting that many men through such terrain.

The monkey trotted ahead of us as we traversed a series of rugged foothills. Fireworms were out in the open now, not hiding beneath the ground. The land was full of them.

Climbing almost constantly, after a few miles we came out below an enormous cavern. The opening seemed to fade down into untold depths. Shadow grasped my arm for reassurance.

Outside this cavern sat six huge, bulbous Mother fireworms, sunning themselves on the rocks. The opening seemed some forty or fifty feet high and perhaps a hundred feet wide, dwarfing the tunnel entrance to the citadel.

The monkey scampered between two Mother fireworms and into the opening.

It was darker inside, but some source of light was evident. The place *smelled* alien. We were following a paved, hard-worn pathway. It descended, spiraling occasionally, into the great caverns. Bats hung from the roof along the way. Crystalline structures seemed to grow into plants, myriad colors reflecting from within. I recognized stalactites and stalagmites in abundance. Water had dripped here for millions of years, building great pillars of minerals and limestone. The minerals tinted all the nature-built sights, giving a weird range of color.

We continued descending. I couldn't guess the depth too well, but it could have been close to a thousand feet beneath the surface. I did know that we walked almost a mile in the descent.

Debouching onto an almost level place, I realized we were in a large room. And something else was in here with us, too. My mind felt as if it were swimming in thick soup.

Several monkeys tended some pulpy-looking plants in a green pool. They looked up when we entered, then continued on with what they were doing.

"Welcome," echoed a collective voice in my mind. It was a combination of concepts, pictures, and ideas that coalesced into words.

The thoughts and concepts that I received were completely foreign, unlike anything I'd ever experienced. I had found them, the Monitors. Now that all our troubles were gone, we'd warn them of the approaching New Christians and the Monitors could eliminate all problems in one sweep of advanced technology. I felt momentary regret for some of the New Christians who must be innocent of any transgressions save following Lord Evan's orders. Nonetheless, a warm feeling of positive personal accomplishment washed over me.

Shadow shivered and hugged me closer. It was cool in here, thirty or forty degrees colder than outside, but not anywhere near freezing. Perhaps my confidence was misplaced: Shadow wasn't shivering just from the chill.

"Hello yourself," I said out loud.

"Welcome Robin and Shadow," echoed the voice again. It kind of bounced around in my skull, like a marble in an empty cup. It took some getting used to, but I could decipher it.

"Can you hear my thoughts?" I asked.

"Certainly."

"Where are you?"

"In the pool."

"I see only plants." A thousand colors of the sea swirled within, and crabs scuttled about scavenging. I'd seen sea anemones while swimming near San Diego, and these Monitors could be cousins if the anemones were interlaced with bright coral-like growth. Mists swirled from the pool indicating that the water was warmer than the air around us.

"You see, then, me/us," the voice said.

I strangled my surprise. "You're water creatures?"

"Here it is necessary to live in this solution. Although water is the base, it is not water as you know it."

"Who are you? Which one of you am I talking to?"

"We are one, I am all."

I'd have to think on that one for awhile. "Aren't you the Monitors?"

"Yes, as you sometimes call me/us. You may discard the idea that the monkeys are the intelligent species here. I/we assure you that they are merely servitors, able to move around in your environment, so I/we employ them."

Indeed, I had harbored the idea that the monkeys were the sentient creature here.

"Look," I said, "are you aware that there is an army headed this way?"

"Yes. That is the reason you have been called here." The voice was supremely confident.

"Hell. We came of our own volition."

"Did you?"

"Seems that I don't know anything anymore. What do you want from us?"

"Primarily, you will be my/our communications device for negotiating with the New Christians when they arrive. You see, I/we can only communicate with you or one like you after much practice and training. I/we cannot communicate with the backward humans."

Backward? But that wasn't the question right now.

"Negotiate? Communicate? How about fight them!"

"I/we do not fight, being nonviolent in nature. The *Others* take advantage of this racial trait of mine/ours. However, after millennia, I/we have learned to work around problems and solve them without recourse to combat."

"Is that anything like using other peoples to fight for you?" I shouldn't be getting upset now as the situation called for clear thinking.

"Not precisely," it said. "But you must now follow your guide. He will take you to another part of this place where the remainder of me/us reside. I/we serve as a sentinel in this room, which I/we must prepare to abandon, since it is merely the entrance to my/our establishment. The New Christians will kill all in this cavern upon their arrival, before I/we can initiate negotiations, and the monkeys are removing the parts of me/us which rest here."

Shadow was listening through me, and I sensed bewilderment from her. Well, we were both in the same boat.

The monkey led off again. We went through a partition seemingly made of onyx. Another room opened to us, but this time it was circular. A line of monkeys silently filed through here carrying items out into and through an adjoining chamber. There were delicate formations in this room, but we continued on. We followed a trail thronged with monkeys. There were no fireworms down here that I could see.

Eventually we made our way into a giant cavern, one I estimated to be more than a quarter mile in length. Stalagmites, tall and lofty, dotted the floor in forests. Many pools, some natural and some manufactured, lay about. More of the Monitor/anemones floated around within these pools. An alien mind probed into my brain and I automatically raised a shield.

Monkeys streamed in and out of this great room, coming from recesses and tunnels to the sides and below. I had the feeling that there was an immense source of power beneath me.

"Yes," said the voice. "My/our equipment and power lies interwoven throughout caves around and below here. I/we draw upon it what I/we need." My shielding hadn't been as good as I thought. I added another barrier in my mind and cautioned Shadow to do the same.

The monkey led us to a corner, inset in limestone, where we found food and potable water. We ate and I tried to think this through.

Shadow leaned against me and whispered, "I cannot follow their communication save through you. What strange manner of creatures are these?"

I shrugged, mind whirling. Something was eating at my brain. I blocked it with little trouble. The mind war at the citadel and the practice since had added much to my mental skills.

Another, deeper voice echoed in my mind and I isolated a channel for Shadow to use, so that she could be part of the exchange.

"Robin, are you not curious about why you were brought here?"

"Yes, but I'm beginning to think I'm not going to like it."

"You've been here twice before."

"I'd guessed as much. Why and how?"

"Concisely, you were chosen for study and experimentation. Years ago when you were a child, transmissions from your brain were relayed by the fireworms to me/us. You had the strongest mind I/we had yet encountered on Earth, so I/we brought you in, by a Mother fireworm traveling mostly underneath the surface. You were held here and studied; I/we kept you alive and repaired the damages to your body. And improved it only in the sense that your self-recovery mechanism was enhanced. You may have guessed something of the sort since you have not been physically ill from virus or disease. On the second occurrence, your body was healed of its wounds, and further studies made of your advancement."

I hadn't noticed that I'd never been sick, but it was true.

"For what purpose did you want to study me? And what are you referring to when you say that I had the strongest mind you'd encountered?" I knew my mind was strong, and improving almost every minute, but why were they interested?

"I/we need you," they answered. "You represent a new level of maturity for humanity. Your 'autism' is a metamorphosis in the evolution of the human race. By saying this, I/we mean that autism provides an adaptability quotient to each man depending on the needs of that man."

"You mean," I asked, thinking furiously, "autism is a sort of a transition to the next stage of mankind?"

"Yes. Man is at the point of change now; autistic behavior, and all it entails, will eventually enhance the breed, make it adaptable to changing circumstances such as you have on Earth now. Your water-locating abilities are one example. If not allowed to die out, autism will spread until all humanity has passed through the stage and entered the following phase of growth."

That was a tall order to swallow all at once. Shadow seemed shocked. "So you pulled me in to study me?"

"Yes."

"You stole I don't know how many years of my life for study."

"You would have died had I/we not intervened. And I/we wanted to be sure you were capable of fending for yourself, avoiding the bad time of autism."

"You owe me eight years." The immensity of the thing struck me like being kicked in the head by an ox. I was mixed up emotionally; I didn't know whether to be mad or glad, but I didn't think I liked being a guinea pig for them.

"Where did you keep me?"

"Here, within the caverns. Your mind was kept on a low-activity level; you were fed and taken care of by the monkeys; and when you were released back in the desert, you were under a preplanted directive not to recall anything of your visit."

I remembered the gelatin wall that Shadow and I had come against when we searched for the answer. It sort of matched the mental soup that surrounded us now.

"I don't like this, Robin," whispered Shadow. Her instincts were better than mine. I trusted her.

"You must have had some end purpose in studying me," I said, worry nagging at me.

"Certainly. We needed someone strong enough to fight the Others, those that direct the New Christians in the citadel."

Now we were getting somewhere. If the Monitors were against the NCs and their allies, they couldn't be all bad.

Too, the Others must equate to *they*, Evan and the New Christians' overseers.

"Who are the Others?" I asked.

"The Others are the only spacefaring race, besides my/ourselves in this portion of the galaxy. They are aggressive and domineering. They mean to enslave the human race, make puppets and food of them. The Others are completely antagonistic to me/us, the Hemn, as I/we call my/ourself. They seek this world, the Earth, both for its resources, people and mineral, and for its strategic effect on me/us, the Hemn."

"Slow down now," I said. "The Others want the Earth?" I thought quickly. "And our resources? Can't they find what they want on another planet without bothering Earth?"

"No. Conditions must be absolutely right for them. There aren't many habitable planets in this section of the galaxy that meet their needs. They must have a dry, arid land with people. If humanity regains its once proud posture, the land will turn green, with a high-humidity atmosphere, and they cannot use that environment."

"What do they need people for?"

"They eat them."

"Come on now, this is getting farcical. Why don't they simply eat the people now, if what you say is true?"

"They don't simply eat people. First they select an appropriate organism, in this case humans, prepare them as a race in total, change them into a type of plant, then harvest and process them at their convenience."

I almost laughed, but a shudder from Shadow told me this was dead serious. "I recognize that a race that conquers space is technologically superior to us, but this is almost too weird to believe."

"You want a simple, biological explanation?"

"Correct."

"To enlist your aid, I/we will explain. The Others have a servitor race that helps them. It is parasitic in nature and about the size of a grain of sand. The Others plant this small parasite in various organisms, in this case humans, and the parasite controls the host's body and mind. It lodges in the brain and, in essence, remains dormant, but for the controlling function, until it is externally triggered by the Others to root and become a plant. The Others do not activate it from the dormant stage until environmental conditions are correct for growth. As stated earlier, this environmental necessity is dry and arid, and for sufficient host bodies to meet its needs."

"I'm not up on biology or physiology or horticulture, but it seems to me that the change from human to plant will take quite a bit of doing."

"It is not only quite possible, but it is done on several planets under the Others' control. There is even a similar growth here on Earth. On an island you call Zealand, thousands of miles south and west of here in the Pacific, there is a fungus which afflicts a certain insect. Eventually, the fungus spreads throughout the insect's entire structure. When the insect dies, the fungus remains alive as a plant, which visually resembles the original insect. The Others' parasite needs a certain vessel to accomplish its function of turning into a plant for the Others to eat. The human body, among others, fits the criteria well."

Hell, nothing was making sense anymore. The whole world had turned upside down for me and I was falling off. I had to struggle to get my thoughts back on a coherent path. Shadow had closed her mind and was funneled into mine. We were thinking as if one now. We had to get to the meat of the situation.

Taking a deep breath, I said, "All of this aside, what's it to you? That is, what is your stake in this? It is said that the Monitors are a benign race who mopped up after the Holocaust and have helped man emerge from trying times, giving aid when desperately needed. I ask why."

"I/we do not wish that the Others gain ascendancy here on Earth. Their plans must be blocked."

"It would seem to me," I said, choosing my words, "that the Others could be fought on the planet where they live, or in space. It would not then be necessary to battle on Earth for possession of Earth."

"You must understand, Robin, that conditions are not always as they seem. Intergalactic warfare is uneconomical. Their home system is not environmentally structured for me/us. Additionally, you misunderstand the intricacies of space flight. With faster-than-light drive, it is impossible to battle. Ships move faster than weapons can fire or travel. No, this millennia-long combat between the Hemn and the Others has eroded into a great war of attrition, fought on mutually disputable terrain: that of inhabitable worlds. Also, our technologies are incompatible, the Hemn and the Others. This fact makes physical contact and cooperation unproductive. We, the Hemn and the Others, are too alien both technologically and culturally, either to understand each other or to compete on the same level. It is as if, here on Earth, the land and the sea were sentient, each trying to claim all the living space, but could not communicate or live together in harmony. For all purposes, we do not actually engage in combat. Remember, the Hemn are nonviolent to an extent. And, again, that is where you come in. You can communicate with the humans who are infected with the parasite and are doing the Others' bidding. And I/we can communicate with you. You are in the middle, a necessary tool for me/us."

"Have you no defenses or weapons?"

"Certainly all defensive in nature, since I/we do not physically combat any race. But their weapons may counteract these. And their agents, the New Christians, are humans, and mobile. I/we cannot move from my/our environment in this solution. You see, I/we are at a definite disadvantage."

"How about the fireworms? Can you not use them as a defense?"

"This is true and I/we will. The fireworms are programmed specifically to pursue those humans who are inhabited by parasites, those you call 'cursed.' However, ion guns and lasers will kill them easily."

"So you introduced the fireworms to Earth for that purpose? Think how many lives not inflicted with parasites they have taken. Was it worth it?"

"Again, you are too easily misled. The fireworms were bred for an altogether different purpose, though they do serve to eliminate parasite-infested organisms. Their prime function is twofold: first, the fireworms are designed to assist in maintaining the carbon dioxide-oxygen cycle; second, their activities in desert areas serve to make the land arable, much as earthworms do in garden patches. But this is not an overnight thing; it takes centuries and centuries. There are now indications that the process is working up to expectations. Fringe land around the edges of the deserts is now becoming usable. Gradually, reclamation will increase until most of the land that can possibly be reclaimed is arable. Then the fireworms will die off."

"The land around the citadel is mountainous and laced

with much rock. Can this be the reason why there are no fire-worms about that place?" Shadow asked through me.

"Partially. The other portion of the answer is the Others. They have provided the New Christians with an electronic device, ultra-sound to be specific, that drives the fireworms off or kills them, if exposed long enough."

"That's why there were monkeys infiltrating the citadel," I said aloud, thinking of one of the things that had bothered me.

"Yes. Those monkeys were programmed to aid you to the extent of their ability should you not be able to cope with the situation."

My mind was leaping around like a firefly at night. "Was Professor Rosmanov your agent?" Remembering the mon-keys, I was suspicious.

"Only as an information gatherer, though I/we believe he had different motives."

The Prof was his own man and probably would have played both ends against the middle, the middle being his position as a loyal human. Both ends then would be the Hemn and the Others. I reserved judgment on the Prof.

"How did you enlist him?"

"He was curious about the world around him. When but a young man he was suspicious of this area, the Carlsbad Ta-boo. With disease in his legs, he trekked here upon a camel. I/we seized the opportunity he presented. I/we could not save his legs, but I/we were able to arrest the disease. He was programmed not to be specifically aware of what had hap-pened, and to observe and report through a complicated process involving transferring thoughts to certain monkeys bred for that purpose. Then he was released elsewhere with a contingent of monkeys." These words were what I translated. I saw a panorama of the Prof striving to impart thoughts and data to a monkey, and sending that monkey off into the wilds. A Mother fireworm would pick up the monkey and deliver him to Carlsbad.

The Hemn continued, "But I/we think that Rosmanov may have suspected more than he was programmed to know." Good old Prof! You couldn't fool him often. He probably complied with the programming simply to maintain the con-tact so that he could eventually understand what he had be-come involved in. Additionally, I'm sure he realized that the New Christians were dangerous and would have chosen any ally against them. Plus, I recalled, he had spoken well of the Monitors, so perhaps some of their conditioning remained in him.

"And you placed Robin in the desert where the Professor could find him," Shadow said.

"Correct. The Professor's monkeys were instructed to be on the lookout for Robin at the time."

It was all coming together for me now, and Shadow shared these same thought processes. Something tugged at the edge of my consciousness; illusively it fled, and I couldn't grasp it in time. Shadow caught it though, and what it said was that there was a flaw here. What did that idea mean?

The soup closed in and tried to steal the thought from us, but, with Shadow, I fought to hold it. I was becoming accustomed to the Hemn's way of thinking, and if I could only find the key, I could thus get a handle on the situation. We had been skillfully maneuvered away from some vital fact.

The fireworms! And the Monitors. They had been here ostensibly for centuries and perhaps longer. Why? I had asked the Hemn what their stake was in the Others' conquest of Earth, and they had answered; but their answer evaded the question partially. True, they had said that the Hemn and the Others were antithetical to each other and dueled on different worlds. But why were the Hemn dueling for Earth? The Hemn had said they were nonviolent, but when pressed, stated that they didn't "physically" combat the Others.

The soup turned to gelatin, thickening rapidly, and I don't think that my mind would have worked were it not for the intimate partnership between Shadow and me, our mind-fusion.

I struggled on. Thinking was difficult, so I asked, "Your reason for negating the Others' presence on Earth?"

"I/we are benign." There it was again. "However, the Others are mortal enemies to me/us. I/we would not have them expand."

There was a reddish haze behind that simple explanation. Something else was there. I was finding that it was almost impossible to lie or misstate the truth during mind-speak. But I had a handle: the rest of the tool was buried somewhere, it just needed to be pulled out.

"Your explanation is too simple," I accused.

"I/we sense reservations within you, Robin. Do you wish the Prism of Truth?"

The soup closed in on us, seeking to compel me to follow the Hemn's direction, whatever that direction was. Shadow was fading from me, mentally, and we groped to strengthen our link. My physical perceptions became tenuous; smell, touch, and feel worked, but sight and hearing were failing. I felt a tremendous urge to comply with the Hemn's wishes. I found Shadow's spark and together we nursed the relinkage, and it grew. Our power was increasing. Eventually, I came to my senses and found myself clinging to Shadow. Swiftly, we built new and better barriers, striving to overcome the influence of the Hemn.

Presently, we were back to normal, or almost so, able to see about us and manage our own thinking in our own manner.

"Robin, they are trying to subvert our minds," said Shadow. Her voice was shaky.

"You have proved that you are capable of the Prism of Truth," said the collective voice. But I thought that there was more behind it than what they said. Perhaps they were surprised at our joint strength in withstanding them. Could the Prism of Truth be yet another attempt to control us? Was the first wave, that which we'd just experienced, a failure on their part?

I was becoming doubly wary of the Hemn's motives. During the confrontation I had been too busy trying to regain my senses to notice, but I recalled that I had wanted to believe everything they had said, a blind trust, as it were. Yet I'd been too involved to let that seed grow. What was next?

"If it isn't too much trouble, what is this Prism of Truth?" I asked.

"I/we find that your combined mental capacities are too complex for me/us to convince you of my/our intentions. The Prism of Truth allows you to look into my/our soul. What you see there will prove my/our claims." That's the way the ideas translated into words, but what I actually saw was a complex concept of mind-joining, where culture, alien life of two kinds, could inspect the other without fear of interference or misdirection.

"It is safe," said the Hemn, obviously reading my doubts. "It was developed for communicating with intelligent life forms inferior to me/us. Each party merely sees the mind of the other party. It was thus that your Professor used the monkeys to convey data to me/us."

Sure, I thought, and hastily buried these thoughts in Shadow and my fortress where they couldn't be touched, and why can't the Hemn use this process on the Others? Why then did the Hemn need me as a communicator-negotiator? The answer was simple. They were afraid of the consequences of direct communication. Either the Hemn or the Others, or both, were vulnerable. What they were implying about the Prism of Truth conflicted with their earlier statements, indicating inability to communicate with other races. Therefore, the Hemn must think that they had Shadow and me under at least partial control, causing us to ignore discrepancies in their statements.

We were submerged again, but this time we retained control of our minds and bodies. Shadow and I linked up, physically and mentally, and watched. I didn't believe it, but there was a simulacrum of a prism in the mind-environment around us.

We saw that what they said was true. The Hemn were showing us a world unlike anything I'd ever imagined. It was a water world, teeming with Hemn vying for room and sunlight. Underwater, there was a vast civilization; mineral harvesting was done on the ocean floors, and strange technology abounded. Their motives were pure; there was no conflict within the view we were afforded. Complacent thoughts assailed us.

While I was taking all this in, I felt Shadow leaning out of her position in our fortress, looking elsewhere. Her practicality pulled me in to her side. Inherent in a prism is bending of waves. She had found another facet of the Prism of Truth, and together we looked within. Scenes of the Hemn's home world faded, and we were back into abstract concepts once again. I felt the Hemn react in surprise at our unexpected strength.

Then we saw the Earth, polar ice caps melting, ocean level rising, hot and humid atmosphere almost the same as jungles I'd heard of on the southern continent; in front of us the Earth changed from three-quarters covered by water to all but a few points on the surface immersed. I saw hordes of Hemn, all seas a growing-ground for Hemn. The Hemn realized that we, in fact, were seeing them as they really were, and sought to withdraw from the prism. I could not prevent this premature conclusion of our information-gathering. It was if we'd been caught stealing, and the avenue closed to us.

This new slant on the truth showed that they weren't exactly benign.

In their terms, they wanted a Hemn ecologically balanced Earth for their own. This eco-balancing was well underway, with a target date so far in the future that I could not comprehend it. Further, they had in mind for me to lead an uprising, the purpose of which was to eliminate the Others and their parasite lackeys. Or was it? Additionally, I felt rather than saw an incipient fear of the new humanity they had described, a new humanity which the Hemn perhaps could not control.

A final question popped into my fortress-mind before all was shut out. Why did earth crabs live in their environmental "solution"?

This was the last thought I remembered before we fell into unconsciousness.

CHAPTER TWENTY-EIGHT

I had weird dreams, those of fighting a phantom enemy, until Shadow and I withdrew into our fortress and then I slept easily. I sensed the recovery processes of my body taking over, shutting out the conscious brain from active control. My physiological functions regenerated much the same as they had at the citadel when I was prisoner of Evan. The fortress-barriers we'd constructed and the body regeneration seemed to seclude me from this unknown domination. Another strange thing occurred. Shadow seemed to draw strength from me, which I subconsciously and willingly gave, for a similar regeneration of faculties.

I woke with Shadow shaking me.

I rubbed my jaw and found that I had an extra twenty-four hours of growth there.

"What are we going to do, Robin?" Shadow demanded.

Hell, I didn't know. I'd seen enough during the mental exchanges to know that everything the Hemn had told us hadn't been falsehood. What they said about the Others was totally correct. So we did have two alien races doing their best to conquer Earth and change it to meet their own specifications. Each was antagonistic to the other and eventually fatal to humans.

But the pressing matter was the imminent threat of the Others and their New Christian allies, or puppets. I judged that the Others were now more dangerous to us. And here were Shadow and I caught right in the middle of their war. I had been so confident! Simply get an army of autistics together and lick the world, I thought bitterly. With my eyes wide open, I'd walked us right in the middle of a shooting war, sort of allied us on the side of the guys without effective weapons who wanted to take over Earth themselves, and, in effect, enabled the Hemn to take us prisoner.

"You are not prisoners, Robin," interrupted the Hemn. "But it would be unwise to depart at this time, as the New Christians are immediately without. Their intention is to exterminate this nest and all who are within it."

That would include us, all right.

We, at least, still had our lasers.

"I suggest then," I said, "that you call in reinforcements from your orbiting ship."

"That ship has returned to the homeworld for supplies and new Hemn."

"Great. I don't suppose the Others are up there orbiting right now, waiting their chance to get at you."

"No. Else they would vaporize this section of the Earth. I/we were hidden here and elsewhere upon the departure of my/our ship. Carlsbad has been my/our secret base for centuries. The Others merely plant parasites in selected organisms and the parasite does the rest. They will return eventually to check on progress and introduce more parasites if necessary. However, doubtless that ship is now harvesting some other world."

"We certainly have an interesting future to look forward to," I said. It seemed that the more ridiculous things got, the more flippant I became.

"Your future is by no means assured, Robin. The parasite-controlled New Christians are currently assaulting the entrance above us."

I had a thought. "If the Others' ship has departed, then who were the New Christians communicating with while they interrogated me and the other autistics in the citadel?"

"I/we are familiar with their practices. The Others have obviously left a decision-capable computer behind to oversee their operations."

"Your defenses?" Back to the problem at hand.

"They have been destroyed or rendered ineffective by the weapons of the Others."

"Fireworms?"

A veil lifted in my mind, and Shadow joined. We saw the outside of the cavern entrance. Fireworms lay dead and smoldering all about. Mother fireworms were being cut down y some large weapon—"ion-beam cannon" leapt into my mind—and the scene was of utter destruction. Still, fireworms swarmed at the New Christians who slowly made their way into the entrance.

The fireworms had taken their toll by sheer strength of numbers. I estimated the NC force was cut in half.

"I/we need your help, Robin."

The picture, or view-scene, remained in a corner of my mind and I could monitor the progress of the fighting. But we were pulled back into the cavern.

"I have no interest in helping you," I said.

"Your lasers would assist much; my/our monkeys cannot handle weapons accurately if I/we had any such."

I snorted. But Shadow and I were to be on the receiving end of the NC advance. Two lasers wouldn't make any difference anyway.

"Robin, listen to me," said Shadow. "The Hemn and our own goals coincide for now. Logic dictates that we must aid them. Should we perish here, no one will know the facts we know, and either of the two aliens, whoever wins, will have an upper hand."

"That's true," I replied. "Besides, the New Christians are against the autistics and technology both. At least we can live with the Hemn for awhile until that problem is resolved." Although behind my barriers, I thought differently. It wouldn't do to have the Hemn suspect me of duplicity.

"Robin," said the Hemn, "should the New Christians prevail now, they would advance their timetable, have children with inbred parasites, and increase their numbers exponentially once they know the opposition is removed."

"That could be," I admitted.

Shadow was already striding off in the direction of the climbing walkway leading to the surface. I hurried to catch up with her.

"Maintain the scene-monitoring for us," I commanded the Hemn.

"It is done." The view-scene unfolded in our minds.

We followed the progress of the battle. The NCs had gained a foothold in the entrance. Most were still firing at the swarming fireworms, smoke from burning flesh partially obscuring our vision; other soldiers were constructing some device. We hurried through the caverns while this task was being accomplished.

Finally, a metal pyramid was erected in the center of the entrance. A black box was attached, a power source I somehow knew, and it began vibrating. The fireworms' attack slowed as if it were freezing and stopped. Then the fireworms turned and made away from the vibrating pyramid. They were successfully repulsed. Many did not depart in time to save themselves. These writhed and died.

The scene closed in on the New Christians, and I could see Lord Evan efficiently marshal his troops. The ion-beam cannon was set up, facing outward, guarding their rear.

Shadow and I were running now. We passed the Hemn sentinel position and the pool was empty. Not even monkeys were here.

What could we do with two lasers against an army of well-armed men?

"Shadow, you stay here or return below." I didn't want her involved in this suicide mission.

She didn't answer, she just kept running.

We were on the upward path now, and the scene in our minds showed the New Christians carefully descending a thousand feet above us.

We ran on, disturbing bats clinging to the roof of the cavern.

About halfway up, I stopped, choosing this location as the best defensive position we could find. We took cover and the New Christians approached, bolder than before, since they had met no resistance within the caverns.

There were perhaps three hundred New Christians left. A rear guard of twenty remained above with the ion cannon. The rest came down toward us, bunching up in groups. The first group approached, but we held our fire.

Then we could wait no longer and opened fire upon them. The narrow beams cut through them like a scythe through wheat. Many leapt from the path, but their great numbers hampered them and made them easy targets. Fifty or sixty had died before any organized resistance came.

We ducked as the air about us was lanced with laser beams.

The view within our minds showed the battle scene from above. Lord Evan was arranging his troops to counter our fire. He disposed them like a true general. I had hoped to get him in the initial ambush, but that hand was yet to be played.

I saw that if we did not retreat soon, there would be little chance that we'd live much longer.

Above us, the bats had been mightily disturbed by the fighting. Apparently they didn't like lasers any more than I did.

An idea sprang into my mind. I focused my attention on the bats and commanded them to fly at the New Christians. I don't know if my efforts worked, but the bats surely became more agitated, and soon the air of the cavern was full of the airborne rodents, buzzing like angry bees.

Shadow bent her mind to help and I shot a thought to the Hemn to aid also. Soon the bats were launching themselves at the New Christians relentlessly. Lasers fired into the air, slicing swaths of bats out of the air. Yet they came, thousands, perhaps millions, of them. Then the New Christians got smart and used wide beams, creating an umbrella effect over their heads.

At this point, I thought it wise to withdraw. We scrambled up and ran down the path to the room with the first pool in it. Here we established positions so that we might pick off the New Christians when they entered.

The view showed us that the New Christians had killed most of the bats. But it was costly. The NCs had lost more men. I guessed that they proceeded down toward us with no more than one hundred and fifty soldiers. With their firepower, we could not hope to hold them, much less eventually triumph over them.

"We are all doomed," I told the Hemn, "unless we can come up with a different plan of defense. Send the monkeys to us."

"No. I/we will be unable to function long without them."

"You'll all be dead soon, then." I wracked my brain for any idea. Shadow exuded confidence that I would come up with something. There had been no opportunity for negotiations or bargaining.

The New Christians came on, carefully this time to avoid recurrence of the ambush. When we nailed a few of them, their return fire was so concentrated that we had to take up our retreat again. Using the shadows, we flitted past the onyx-gabled doorway into the circular room filled with the age-old formations built by constant water-dripping action. Ensconcing ourselves on the far side, we waited.

The New Christians pushed on relentlessly. Apparently,

Evan thought he was close to victory, so the sacrifice of manpower was high. We killed our share. The delicate formations within the room were ruined in the fighting.

Again we ran ahead of them, down the corridor leading to the giant cavern which housed the Hemn. The New Christians were almost at our heels. We conducted a running firefight, snapping shots behind us, hurrying to get out of the corridor before we were killed.

Shadow stumbled and I helped her up. We ran on. Lasers chipped rocks and mineral deposits around us. The air was thick with the smell of vaporized water. Reaching the widening portion of the corridor that indicated we were in the main cavern, we found nooks to hide within and make our last stand. The New Christian advance had slowed so that they might consolidate their forces. Evan still had some one hundred men to rely upon. We had taken our share of life that day.

They came on and we fired. The power within the cavern faulted once, then regained its normal brilliance. I felt a surge of panic from the Hemn when the power faltered. Perhaps they were dependent on the light for survival, I didn't know.

The air was full of laser beams, most directed at Shadow and me. But we were well protected and kept our heads down. Occasionally we leaned out and fired and then quickly dodged back into shelter. The New Christians were pushing us closely. None of them wanted sure death, so they advanced by running from one protected area to another under cover of fire from their comrades. I caught one across the eyes with a shot and he screamed for a long time until his friends put him out of his misery.

Under this distraction, Shadow and I crawled back into the cavern to new positions. The rocks around us had been heating up from the barrage of laser fire. I dropped a few more who were prone to expose themselves, and the crackle of Shadow's laser showed that she was doing the same.

We slithered to new positions once more, this time behind the first of the manufactured pools. I sensed panic within, and agonized death screams came into my mind when lasers sought us out and vaporized the pool. The mental screaming abruptly ended and the Hemn adjusted their combined mind to the loss of some of their number.

I was busy building a farewell speech to Shadow when she interrupted.

"Look." She pointed.

Monkeys streamed from behind us, scampering over rocks and pools and crystalline projections alike. Some climbed along the walls of the cavern, like ants covering carrion. Most carried any weapons that came to hand: sticks, rocks, fragments of crystal, metal objects, and broken-off points of stalactites and stalagmites.

When the New Christians realized what was happening, they raised a howl as the monkeys bore down on them. I'd thought the laser fire was concentrated before, but now the very air smelled of burned oxygen. Monkeys were incinerated by the hundreds, yet they continued on. The Hemn had sacrificed their servitors.

Despite the deadly curtain of fire, some made it through and attacked the New Christians ferociously. Too, the monkeys had given Shadow and me respite. We could and did fire without hindrance. Lord Evan's forces were dealt with. A few remained alive only to throw themselves into the line of fire, trying to their last to get at the enemy.

We had a bare few minutes together while the New Christians mopped up the last of the monkeys. Shadow crawled over to me. She tossed her weapon aside.

"It's out of power."

That figured. She lay at my side while I fired and then my weapon was drained of its energy also. Evan gathered his forces about him, evidently assuming that they had finally killed us.

The view from above showed that he was giving instructions to his troops to spread out and advance.

Suddenly, that view was interrupted and faded into the scene at the top of the incline, showing Evan's rear guard and the ion-beam cannon.

Something was tugging at my mind, and I had to free another channel to figure out this new development. I was straining to my utmost, trying to do something totally unfamiliar to me. I wanted to talk to Shadow, but couldn't spare the effort. One part of my mind was on the command channel with the Hemn, another part was isolated on the view-scene they presented us, and yet a third part of my consciousness was being pulled away. My brain felt drawn and quartered. But with my growing mastery, I managed to control my mind and parcel out the appropriate channels.

The portion of my mind that was being pulled away exploded into familiar contact.

"Willy!" Shadow said aloud.

"Are you inside?" Willy demanded.

"Yes," we answered simultaneously.

"Watch out for the force at the entrance," Shadow shouted into my mind.

"We see 'em," said Willy. "Jesus, somebody sure croaked a lot of fireworms." A mental smile told us that Elana Garcia was in on the conference.

A myriad of thought waves scrambled our thoughts, like static on the New Christian radio we'd stolen.

"Stop," commanded Shadow. "Use the receive mode only. Willy and Elana will do the communicating for you." So there were more autistics out there.

"How many are you?" Shadow asked.

"Over a hundred," Willy said. "Elana and Diego didn't have time to wait for more."

"Do not approach the entrance," Shadow told them. "There are twenty men with weapons that killed all those fireworms."

"Do you need help?" Elana asked.

"Yes, but it would be death for you to come in," Shadow replied.

I was busy observing Evan and his troops deploy.

"Besides, you will be too late to do any good," Shadow told them. Quickly, she briefed them on the whole thing, the Hemn and the Others, so that if we did not escape, they could do whatever they wished, at least alert the rest of the world.

Again my thoughts were interrupted. The mental airways were becoming clogged with all the transmissions. I had to pull my attention back to the Hemn.

"Robin," they screamed into me, "those New Christians remaining are primarily parasite-infested men. Can you not attempt to control them?"

"Hell, I'll try anything once."

Cautiously, I felt out with my mind and made tentative contact. Their minds seemed like ordinary human minds, similar to those that I'd been involved with at the citadel. I didn't sense anything alien about them.

I tried to impress upon them, as a group, that they should lay down their arms. But it didn't work. Perhaps several of them faltered, but it did not halt their advance. The leaders were within a hundred yards of us now.

I switched back to the Hemn. "Can't you help me with your brains, give me a power boost or something?" I found that Shadow had hitched back into this channel and was funneling the entire scene to Willy and his army.

"No. I/we can only communicate with any success. Individually, perhaps I/we could attempt to control, but not one who is inhabited by a parasite. They are too alien for us to match."

Shadow was giving Willy and Elana instructions. The view-scene changed and I saw them all on a ridge overlooking the entrance to the caverns. They sat down and grasped arms with each other, forming a giant circle. Their thoughts became one and focused to us, lending their strength. Shadow joined me in my mind and together we searched out into the New Christians.

I felt the added power immediately. It surged through me, raising my hair, tingling my scalp. More than one hundred strong, we lanced into their minds. I sensed the Hemn vicariously watching through me. But I had no time or energy to waste on the Hemn, so I ignored them.

I selected the foremost New Christian soldier and concentrated on his mind. A small kernel appeared, perched at the base of his brain and wrapped in folds of matter.

The parasite!

I focused upon this alien rider and struck at it with my mind. It recoiled in horror and the soldier staggered. Surer of myself this time, I employed the entire mental shroud Shadow was funneling to me, and touched it again.

It shriveled upon itself and died. The soldier slumped to the ground. A hollow cheer rang within my head.

I searched out another opponent and sent a mental bolt into him as well. The alien presence was more pronounced within him, or maybe my perceptions had sharpened. He died instantly.

The other New Christians had by now guessed something was wrong, and the entire cavern lit up with randomly fired shots to eliminate whatever new threat had arisen. I curled around Shadow, protecting her and presenting as low a profile as I could. I closed my eyes and struck out again, this time seeking them out blindly. I found that I could identify the alien parasite without looking at the body which carried it.

Thereafter, I simply slew them. When the mental death screams threatened to tear me apart, Shadow extended herself and dampened them. After awhile, only a few remained.

I killed them one by one.

"No," shouted the Hemn within the core of my brain. "Keep some alive for questioning."

"Kill the bastards," Willy likewise shouted. "Don't leave one of them alive!"

Elana then counseled humanity, saying, "They are not their own masters, Robin. Have mercy."

Evan's mind comprehended—perhaps he was strongest among them—and pleaded for mercy.

My whole world was aswirl with demands, pleading, shouts, and unwanted advice. I was losing my concentration and the link with Willy's group.

But I knew what I had to do. "Silence," I commanded, "and lend me your power." To their credit, they complied.

I literally ripped the parasite from Evan's brain, burning it alive, without atmospheric oxygen to aid in the combustion. He died a most horrible death.

The few remaining New Christians died swiftly. I then moved back to the entrance of the caverns. The view-scene disappeared.

"You must leave some alive, Robin," the Hemn told me.

"Why? Do you not fear what I may learn?"

"Nay. Slay them, if you must, but I/we shall not help you."

The Hemn knew that I knew, and their enmity was obvious. Yet they were now defenseless, aside from their collective mind power. The Hemn wanted some New Christians left alive to kill me in a double cross.

"Better the devil you know," I said. They recoiled. And Shadow, ever-present Shadow, looked into my mind and agreed with me.

"Attend me," I told Willy and his group. They lined the ridge now, giving me a view of the cavern entrance. Shortly, all twenty New Christian defenders lay dead on the ground.

A ragged cheer rose from the crowd on the ridge.

"Stay with us now, stronger than ever," Shadow told them. They reformed their circle.

I stood and pulled Shadow up. The millions of cubic feet of air within the great cavern stank of death. Wearily, we walked forward and picked up a laser apiece from lifeless hands.

"Robin?" The Hemn tentatively spoke.

"So you studied me, did you?" I asked. "And what did you find? Something to fear worse than the Others and their parasites and the New Christians? Something terrible enough to use against your enemies and then double-cross?"

I sensed a question mark from Elana and Willy both, but Shadow shushed them. Too, I sensed a welling fear from the Hemn.

"Everything you said about the new phase of humanity was correct, wasn't it?" I asked. I didn't wait for the answer because the Hemn knew that I knew.

I continued relentlessly; they were at our complete mercy. "And what do you fear? Could it be that you cannot dominate this new human mind?" They were struck dumb.

"You controlled my mind enough so that I would gather all the autistics I could who were mind-capable and brought them here. But your timing was off and the New Christians and we did not battle. The parasites tricked you with false information. Do you see your dreams of a Hemn eco-changed Earth fading?" They shouldn't have left the scavenging Earth-born crabs in their pools where I could see them.

"My/our servitors, the monkeys, are all dead now. I/we cannot combat you. Leave me/us."

Shadow and I were walking along a tunnel now, toward the source of muted sound. We came into another cavern, smaller and lower than the one we had just quit. Great machines rumbled.

"Without the monkeys," I said, "your power may fail and not be repaired before your ship returns or other Hemn on Earth can come to your rescue. In that case, you will die. The light is your source of nourishment, as oxygen in the air is ours, is it not?"

"Robin, I/we saved your life many times."

"To enslave a world."

As if one, Shadow and I raised our weapons.

"I/we beg of you . . ."

We aimed and fired.

Small explosions rumbled throughout the cavern; smoke

rose and machinery screamed in protest. Fires began raging, and Shadow and I withdrew.

With the lighting flickering, we ran along the main cavern again. We felt screams from the Hemn, mental mind-wringing agony. The lights faded out completely. I reached out one last time for the Hemn.

There was no collective response, only incoherent individual torment. That, too, gradually died, as the Hemn died.

When we finally strode into the sunlight, stepping over the bodies of the New Christian rear guard, I thought of the "cursed ones," and other Hemn networks across the globe. Eventually ships of the Hcmn and the Others would return to Earth.

"We do have a lot of work facing us," Shadow said.

I saw Willy and the others of our autistic army running down the slope toward us. Maybe, just maybe, we'd be up to the task.

DAW sf
BOOKS